THE CROWNLESS KING

DRIA ANDERSEN

Edited by A.K edits linktr.ee/adotkedits

 Formatted with Vellum

This is for my husband and kids for every second of support they offered. To my Aunt Cathy who fed my love of reading from the beginning. To my older sister Catina who encouraged me even when I was winging this whole thing. To my friend Shirelle who was there affirming and validating. To Rayshawnda for always being there to listen. To every fan who picks up my books. And lastly, to me, for not letting doubt eat me alive. To future me, keep going, as Tia Love says, 'Slow motion is better than no motion.'

CONTENTS

AUTHOR'S NOTE

Well, y'all, welcome to the Southern United States. It's a whole new world, with new rules and new supernatural creatures that I hope you come to love. This story takes place a few months after One Night Until Forever leaves off. You don't have to have read it to understand this book, but it's a good precursor. This story is more fantastical than my others. It's still set in a contemporary world, but it's an alternate timeline than our own. I'm excited to explore this world, and all I ask is that you keep an open mind. It's not a dark story, but it's certainly a lil darker than you're used to getting with me.

Trigger Warnings:

Violence, cussing, blood, kidnapping, coercion, did I mention violence? These vampires sometimes get into some gangsta shit, so if you're sensitive to that, please prepare. In the story, Levi is going mad, being driven crazy by the power he's stolen. It can read a little rough and be triggering to some, just as a warning.

INTRODUCTION

In 1833, in the night and early morning of November 12th and 13th, the Leonid meteor shower blazed across the sky of what was the United States of America. 50,000 to 150,000 meteors fell each hour. Seen from as far north as New York, all the way down south, the meteors struck fear into the hearts of many. No one could ascertain the origin of the phenomenon, nor could science explain the sheer number of 'falling stars'.

Only a small group of shamans, gathered and bound on the last slave ship headed to the eastern coast of the United States, understood what happened. See, they had called on the Celestials, imploring them for intervention.

Their call was answered.

Nestled in between those meteors showering down on the Earth were powerful Akachi stones. These stones contained *chaos* magic, derived from the very power source that controlled the cosmos. The Akachi stones would land only in the South, giving rise and power to a people oppressed under the boot of the cruel capitalist system of slavery.

By the time dawn streaked across the sky of a new day, a unique power was granted to the enslaved. Supernatural magic imbued them, granting their fervent wish for freedom.

Four different powers emerged, each unique in its abilities. The Chawi were witches and warlocks, capable of wielding natural magic, direct descendants of the Shaman who'd called upon the Celestials. The Mujaji, *storm gods*, were able to wield the power of the four elements. The Mages, magicians of extensive power, able to control the very chaos magic granted from the Akachi stones, which were the source of their power. And lastly, the Bayi, powerful vampires who gained their power from the blood they ingested.

An uprising resulted from this newfound power, as civil war broke out across a country still in its infancy. Armed with power none had seen before, the supernaturals won the war. The resulting shaky truce called for the country to be split into two. The Northern USA, where humans fled, and the Southern USA, now filled with former humans, who held supernatural power.

To control and prevent misuse of these new powers, the Collective was born. One elder member of each of the newly formed powers, gaining a seat on the council and speaking for their respective group. The Archives were built to store and hide the Akachi stones that had fallen from the sky. Protecting the source of the South's power, their number one priority.

Despite the treaty, the North tried one last ditch effort to take over the South, wanting the power for their own. They recruited vampires from Europe, hoping to undermine the fledgling country. The Buru vampires descended on the South, and for years, small skirmishes disrupted the newly formed country. Magical borders were erected around the South, controlled and monitored by the mages. Not even erecting those barriers was able to prevent the descent of the creatures.

From the chaos rose a Bayi vampire determined to rid his city of the evil that was the Buru. Never had he imagined he would carry the entirety of the South on his back.

PROLOGUE

Fog surrounded her, the moist air clinging to her skin and slowly dampening the thin robe she wore. It didn't faze her or move her from her post. The gateway opened only once a century and she would not miss it. Many women in her family had stood in this exact spot and others like it for years before her, waiting on their chance. Even now, countless women were lined along the rivers that bisected the south, all hoping for the smallest window of time and magic. Bria was determined to be the last.

It was a risky gamble on soil not native to them, but according to all the elders before her, this spot along this river would work. She prayed they got the timing right.

She fingered the dagger on her belt and rolled her neck. From every story passed down to her, this opening gateway was the only way into the temple. A solitary entrance point, a single solitary moment in time to rush through its gates and demand the end to her family line. If Bria squinted her eyes just right, it was if she could almost make out the ghostly form of the temple.

Bria cocked her head as a sound intruded on the still morning. Her eyes never strayed from her prize, but her body tensed as her other senses reached out find the source. She inhaled slowly, pulling in the damp air and a smell she would recognize for as long as she lived...and according to new family legend, that could be centuries yet.

"You'll not sway me from my course, Caden." Her soft voice carried on the dawning morning.

He stepped from the fog, an apparition that could disappear at a moment's notice. His black pants clung to his muscular thighs, a woolen jacket opened to reveal the loose black t-shirt underneath. Caden had his dreads pulled up in bun atop his head leaving nothing to detract from the face God himself had chiseled. He watched her, his hazel eyes stark against the dark brown of his skin.

Bria shivered as those eyes traced her body, the possessive look one she knew all too well. His full lips turned up into a smile, his teeth straight and white except the two canines, sharp and growing longer as he stared at her. She scoffed and turned back to her watch, but her body warmed all the same. He knew what he was doing, the memories the sight of his teeth would provoke. She could almost feel the phantom rake of them down her back. Her body arched, and tingles traveled the length of her skin.

Damn him.

"Maybe I just came to keep you company while you wait." His voice was molasses sliding against her skin, warm and sticky.

Another trick of his.

She swallowed a sigh. "Go away, Caden."

"Have you thought this through, Bria?" He made no moves to close the distance between them.

"What is there to think about? If I can stop my father, how can that be anything but good?"

"At the risk of losing your life?" He hissed.

"To save millions of others?" She gave him an incredulous look, "Absolutely."

Caden growled and stomped closer. "I won't let you do this."

"Unless you plan on killing me, there is no way for you to stop me."

"Bria."

"Caden," she mocked.

"Ending your family's line—"

"Means that there won't be another like my father and his brothers. It means the one they prophesied will never exist. How do you have a problem with that?"

"You don't know the consequences." Caden gripped her shoulder and turned her to him. "We can defeat your father without you sacrificing your life, love."

"Don't do this. Don't make this harder than it is, Caden. You promised." She whispered, avoiding his eyes.

Caden nuzzled into her neck, his warm breath sending goosebumps down her arms. He scraped his teeth against her skin. Bria shuddered, her body coming alive under his touch.

"There has to be another way." He murmured.

Bria stepped back and hugged her arms around herself. Not that it did anything to still the heat igniting in her body. She cursed the thin temple garb she wore.

"In the years we have searched, this is the only way we've found. The Celestials are the only way to end this."

"They'll dead your whole line." His voice was tight with anger.

She shrugged. What could she say to that? Her only alternative was to allow her father to overrun the rest of the world, leaving swaths of death and destruction behind him. Nothing, in the years since he'd come into power had been able to stop Jeremiah and Bria was weary of fighting. Hell, every woman in her family was tired. They fought the vampires from the north, while still battling the last dissenters of the south.

Had Jeremiah only set his eyes on conquering their oppressors here in the South they likely would not have interfered, but that was not enough for her father. He wanted all of the newly formed country, to then set his eyes back at their homeland. His goal had started noble, but his execution smashed all beneath his boot, even those the Celestials had gifted. He wielded his control over the Bayi vampires like a cudgel, killing any and all in his path.

"They created us; only they can end him." She whispered.

He cupped her chin. "We always fight together, why should this be any different?"

Her eyes traced the face of her mate, the man tied to her soul. "Only a direct descendant of the original shaman is allowed through the gateway, you know that."

"According to smuggled-in records so old they're nearly indecipherable. Who's to say it can only be you, or that it would even work? This is not our land. Who's to say the Celestials will even answer the call here?" He growled and turned his back to her.

"They answered our call, sent their gifts. Our connection to them wasn't severed just because we were forced away from the land we knew." She snapped. "I won't risk you."

She'd left their house before dawn to avoid rehashing their argument and yet here he was. Bria scrubbed at her shorn hair in frustration. It was cut years ago by her former owner's vengeful wife. She refused to allow the length to grow back, reclaiming the haircut as her own.

Light shimmered between the naked branches of the tree she stood under. Bria whipped her attention back to the lake, gasping as a temple appeared, becoming clearer with every passing second. The haze surrounding it lifted slowly. Her throat closed with unshed tears.

She was here!

The gate was actually opening!

She would be the one to take down her father and save the world...at least from this. Humans would have to figure out the next apocalyptic event on their own.

"Bria, please." Caden begged.

The surface of the river rippled, solidifying and darkening as a bridge rose from the bubbling water. Bria pulled the staff from her back, pushing a button in the middle. The metallic ring of the blades sliding out rang out and she smiled. *She would be victorious.*

Caden stepped next to her, pulling a sword from his back.

"What are you doing?"

Bria's gaze barely flickered to him. She would not lose sight of the gateway.

He turned, facing the dead forest behind her. "Having your back."

"Fuck." Her breath left her mouth in an angry puff as the air around them slowly dropped in temperature.

She was dumb to think her father wouldn't send someone to stop her. Of all the women sent out tonight, he had a direct blood tie to her. Of course, he found her. Why did she imagine different? The air shimmered around them battling with the magic from her father's minions, crystalizing the fog surrounding them. Droplets of ice formed around the gateway slowly opening, falling in brittle pieces at her bare feet. She glanced back and saw shadows slithering through the trees. Her conscious pricked at her, her mind spinning. Caden was a formidable warrior, but to go alone against her father's horde?

"Go, Bri."

Duty and honor warred within her as she waited on the gateway to finish opening. "You shouldn't have come, Caden."

A whooshing sound preceded the horde's attacks. A rain of arrows thudded into the ground around them. Bria threw up a shield, cursing as one came through, slicing across her shoulder. Wind whipped around them as the gateway finally opened, and the bridge to the temple settled into place.

"This is the only chance you'll have Bria," Caden shouted over the noise.

Their eyes met, and decades of history, words never spoken danced between them. She glanced at the bridge, one that only her family could travel as they were direct descendants of the Celestials. The horde would never make it past the entrance to the gateway, the taint on their soul would bar them from the gods, their deaths instant and most important...permanent.

Would her love for Caden shield him from that same fate? The horde struck again, their magic beating against the shield Bria had built around them. There was a possibility that Caden would die if she took him with her, but if she left him, death was certain. Her father had sent out the big guns to stop her.

Did she trust herself to keep him safe?

Bria looked out into the amassing horde, and then back at the gate. What choice did she have?

She held out her hand.

Bria bent over, sucking in air as the echoing boom of the door closing sounded in the cavernous temple. She didn't know what she'd been expecting, but this cold tomb was not it. Before she could adjust to the darkness, a stone rolled and cool, sweet-smelling air blew in. She instinctively knew that she needed to go in that direction, but first...

"Are you okay?" Her eyes examined her mate, her magic adjusting her sight to see in the darkness.

Caden nodded. "Are you sure about this?"

"The choice was to lose you. That's not an option," Bria told him firmly. "Let's go."

Caden gripped her hand and they took a step towards the opening in the cave. The light wasn't any brighter as they entered a second section of the tomb. Water splashed underneath their feet, getting deeper with every step. They were knee deep when the air thickened and the once dim light brightened. It was as though the wall in front of them disappeared, replaced by an explosion of stars.

Bria's breath caught as a dark form moved from the stars and a face appeared. It wasn't just one face though. It moved from woman to man to an androgynous form in between the two. The hair stayed the same with each face, the kinky, coily curls fanning out amongst the stars. She didn't know what she was expecting, perhaps three separate bodies? Either way, awe and reverence filled her chest until tears stung her eyes. She lowered her head in respect.

"Why have you sought us out, daughter?"

A lump blocked her words for a moment. Instead of letting fear steal away this moment, she raised her head and squared her shoulders. For a moment the face changing made her dizzy.

"I've come to ask for help. The gifts you've blessed my people with..."

"The gifts they prayed so fervently for?" The male voice boomed throughout the cavern before the face softened into the androgynous being.

She nodded and took a shaky breath and lowered her gaze. "My father has used them to inflict the same oppression, if not worse. He...he's using the Bayi to poison those gifts."

There was silence, thick and oppressive, Bria dared to raise her eyes again, this time looking to her mate for guidance. He shrugged, his gaze raking her with concern.

"The Bayi raze the continent and yet you've brought one into this sacred place?" There was no malice in the question, simple curiosity.

"I meant no offense," she lowered her torso, bending at her waist.

Heat moved through her body, she felt it burning past the shields she'd spent years erecting to keep other magic users from her thoughts. The silence stretched as she felt power probe her mind, even her chest tingled as they searched her soul.

The Celestials hummed. "You are tied to this Bayi at the soul level. What you are asking will sever that possibility for many others."

Her mouth dropped open.

"Your father uses his mate's Chawi power to control the Bayi, and wield the gifts passed down through the witch's blood. In order to remove that, those ties must be severed. The nature of the Obayifo increases power throughout the entirety of the children born under the light of the Akachi. Their unity is what has made the whole of you strong. Without it, you will descend into smaller tribes, easily conquered. Are you willing to risk that outcome?"

Bria's chest hurt from how hard her heart was thumping. They'd barely survived the civil war. Her father was able to gain power because both halves of the country was still torn from that war. Could they keep the North from invading again without that power?

"He will destroy this world. It isn't a fear of mine, it's a proven fact, backed by his own words. My father wishes death to all conquerors, and he has no interest in a peaceful resolution."

"And why not?" The Celestials asked. "Death to those who would oppress others is a justice. You would ask that we have empathy for people who destroy with no thought to how it affects those with whom they share the planet?"

Bria looked to Caden. She had no answer to that.

"Is my father not simply another conqueror? I've nowhere near the power you possess, but our seers have divined the world as he would leave it. It is a world where there is no room for any other power. Including the ones who bestowed our gifts."

A buzzing sounded in the chamber and Bria winced as the sharp sound vibrated her ears.

"To stop the power of one, all will lose it." They reiterated, three voices sounding together.

"What does it mean for the rest of us?" Bria asked with her heart hammering.

Would she lose Caden?

"You worry for your soul tether to this one. It will remain intact, but the power from the current Obayifo will not. The power exchange ends. Is this something you would sacrifice?"

"To save the rest of the world, yes."

Another hum and silence.

She looked to Caden again and he gripped her hand and squeezed.

'Whatever the outcome,' he said to her mentally.

She nodded understanding that he would stand beside her through it.

"This pairing, the Chawi and the Bayi will always carry the danger of reigniting that power." The Celestials warned. "Do you understand what this means?"

Bria racked her mind to piece together what they were saying. "Another like my father can rise from the power?"

"Or perhaps one that will save you." Their tone said that either was a possibility and they didn't care either way. "You'll have to keep the two separate or else take the risk."

It would take work, but surely, they could keep the witches and Bayi from mating. They would be weakened, and it wasn't a decision she wanted to make alone, but there would be no other opportunity to call upon the Celestials. Just imagining the damage her father could wrought in the between time made her sick. All would die under her father. She had no choice.

"But we would separately have our powers?" She clarified. It would be useless to make them all weak to stop one.

The Celestials nodded. "Your individual powers will be halved as it has flourished under the Obayifo bond. But, each group will keep the gifts given. As we warned earlier, the soul tethers between witches and Bayi could eventually restore that power, but in order to delay the inevitable, any offspring of the match will be wholly Bayi."

Bria nodded in relief. She would be the last hybrid born, just as she'd expected.

"Your request is bold Bria Cauly, but we will grant it. It will be interesting to see the outcome. You are dismissed."

Before Bria could blink, a force pushed against her chest and wind moved past her body as she was thrust from the Celestials' plane. She and Caden both landed with a hard thud against the dirt. It took her a moment to gather air, her mouth opening and closing as she coaxed her body to breathe again.

"Caden?" she managed to choke out.

"Here, love." He tightened his grip on her hand, but neither of them could move.

Bria rolled over, her blurry vision raking over her mate. "Have we done the right thing?"

Caden cupped her cheek. "Only time will tell."

CHAPTER 1

PRESENT DAY

What would life look like without this sense of urgency that plagued her every waking moment?

It was a thought Amaya had often. Every bus ride to and from work she daydreamed about what her life could be if her circumstances were different. Adjusting her bag tighter against her, Amaya leaned her head against the window of bus and gazed out at the darkening night. She'd cut down the number of days she worked, so that meant longer hours. Which had her going home late in the evening.

This close to a full moon was just asking for trouble.

It wasn't as though she had a choice. She was the primary care-giver for her mother, and so she was in a delicate balance of making enough money to make sure they had a roof over their head, but not working too long because she couldn't afford to hire anyone to sit with her mother while she was there.

Amaya worked at the Archive, which was a library of sorts. It housed all the history of the supernaturals and most importantly, it contained the original and largest piece of the meteor responsible for the power inherited by all of the occupants of the southern USA. The Akachi, as they called it, was the source of the chaos magic that ran through the blood of every supernatural. Chaos magic was volatile and hard to control. Maintaining the balance of the Akachi and keeping that chaos magic contained to safe levels was Amaya's job.

She worked in the sacred garden at the Archive. It was her mother's job before her, and was responsible for Anita's current state. Amaya and her mother were chaos witches, and thus able to wield the raw, unfiltered magic that emitted from the Akachi. Their magic kept them from being as susceptible to the crude power as other supernaturals. But, working with chaos magic came with pitfalls. Eventually, the magic turned on its wielder, eating at their mind. It was the fate of any chaos witch, no matter the power level. All of the women in their family were chaos witches, and all met the same fate. But because Amaya and her mother worked with the Akachi in the sacred garden, they met their fates sooner.

Her mother, though barely over fifty was going mad. And there was nothing Amaya could do to stop it. It meant Anita required constant supervision, and that was the source of all the hoops Amaya jumped through with her work schedule. Her mother had her lucid days, but they were few and far between.

The bus pulled to a stop and Amaya sighed, steadying herself for the walk to the neighborhood where she and her mother were renting a house. They could've stayed at their family's compound, but since her mother had moved out at eighteen, Anita had been adamant that she would never go back. The way the women were treated once their magic turned on them...needless to say, going back home was never an option for her mother, and Amaya honored that request.

Their current neighborhood wasn't on the best side of town. And if she ignored the hustlers, criminals and drug addicts that inhabited some of the houses around them, Amaya could pretend she was doing well for herself. Shuffling off the bus with her head down, she made her way home.

Dodging the catcalls, and sinister looks, she hustled toward her house.

She lived in the part of Black Hollow that was inhabited by the supernaturals that were making the best of the hand life had dealt them. Not quite the misfits of society but certainly those who were alone in this world. There was a rough element as it was in any part of town. Here, lone shifters occupied most of the run-down homes that lined the street. It made moving around any time close to the full moon harrowing.

"You need help, little chawi? It'll only cost you a teensy bite," a shifter sitting on the front steps of his battered home taunted.

The moon was barely up and already the air was thick with magic and menace.

Moving faster, Amaya didn't breathe easier until she reached the entrance of her neighborhood. It wasn't a compound, but after years of chawis without covens settling there, the whole neighborhood had been warded against most dangers posed to the witches. Their landlord had even put up some extra warding on their house.

Amaya growled in aggravation when she got home and noticed that her uncle's car wasn't in the driveway. Hastily unlocking all four locks on the front door, she rushed inside.

"Mom," she called.

Their house was small, the entrance leading directly into the living room. From the front door, Amaya could see into their small kitchen and down a short hallway to the two bedrooms that flanked each other. There was a single bathroom down that hall as well. Her heart raced as she spotted her mother outside in the postage-stamp sized backyard. Anita stood at the back fence.

What was she doing?

Dropping her bag onto the sofa, she walked towards her mother. There were no smells other than the ones of the plug-ins she used to keep their neat space smelling good. Which meant that her uncle hadn't even cooked before he left. He was a terrible caretaker, but he was all she had at the moment. She took a deep breath to wipe all the stress from her face and opened door. Anita could read her well, and sometimes, she would react to Amaya's stress.

Those were long evenings.

"Mom," she called gently.

Anita turned and smiled. "Sweetheart."

"What are you doing?"

"Just talking." Anita wiped her hands on her clothes.

Amaya was her mother's twin. From their high cheekbones, and full lips to their almond shaped eyes and thick lashes. The only difference was that Amaya was full-figured, where Anita was tall and trim. Her willowy figure was currently swallowed in a comfortable off the shoulder cotton dress that her mother wore to lounge in. She was beautiful and despite her dementia, kept her appearance up.

Mostly because Amaya was sure Anita often forgot that she wasn't going anywhere.

Her mother still got up and dressed for work some days. The fact that Anita was dressed so casually meant that at least her Uncle Paul had not dragged her out of the house as he was wont to do. Amaya tried not to be so hard on her uncle, because if nothing else, he made sure his sister lived as normally as possible.

"How long ago did Uncle Paul leave?" It was a question that would test how lucid her mother was this evening.

"Not too long," Anita said absently walking up on her daughter. She cupped Amaya's cheek. Without promoting, her mother's magic soothed the stress tightening her daughter's shoulders. "You look tired. Have we had dinner?"

Amaya swallowed the lump in her throat and shook her head. "I was thinking of making soup. Fall is in the air."

Fall was finally pulling the temperature down sure, but mostly, Amaya didn't think they had groceries to make anything else.

Anita gave her a bright smile. "Soup it is then."

Amaya released the breath she was holding and returned her mother's smile. "We can put your vegetable garden to use."

"Great idea. My cabbages look amazing."

Guiding her mother inside, Amaya felt lighter. No matter the hardship she went through, seeing her mother happy was worth it. Anita sat at the two-seat dining table in their kitchen and watched her daughter with a wistful smile.

"How was work?"

"Same ol'," Amaya answered opening the fridge.

Her mouth dropped open in surprise. There was food in there! See, this was why she could never stay mad at her uncle. Yes, he was irresponsible, but when he came through, he came through in a major way. His contribution of groceries would let her check stretch just a few more days. A blessing, really. It wasn't as though the Archive paid her pennies, but with the fact that she couldn't work that many hours, her pay was lean. Smiling, some of the stress that had been riding her shoulders was shed. It was only a small reprieve, but she would take what she could get.

CHAPTER
ONE

Anger consumed him.

Some days it felt as though it ate away at his sanity, while other days it was a simple buzzing in the back of his brain that blocked out other, productive thoughts. Levi had quickly discovered that the unpredictable emotion was one of the side effects of the Akachi meteorite he'd acquired months ago.

It wasn't as though he hadn't been warned, but hubris was a motherfucker.

Levi had attained the Akachi to help his coven gain power. It had certainly done that and then some. There were days where he could fight through the chaotic power of the stone, but then there were other times when the beast that lived inside the Bayi vampires got the better of him.

That monster demanded blood. Greedy and insatiable, destruction and chaos were the only thing that could feed it.

Levi lifted his head as he realized the silence around him. His second in command and best friend was staring at him as though waiting on an answer. Levi didn't even realize they had been talking. How long had they been in conversation? He was almost afraid to ask because both Sebastian and Lucas were staring at him. The two males were his top enforcers and closest friends. Hell, only friends. Even before he was under the influence of the Akachi, Levi didn't trust anyone except this very limited circle.

Lucas' gaze flickered to Sebastian and it carried the worry of a friend unsure of what to say in an awkward conversation.

"What?" Levi growled tired of the silent judgement.

Both of his friends' eyes dropped to the ground in front of Levi. In deference? Certainly not, he never required it of them. Then why...

Levi stepped back and he looked down. His hands were covered in blood, his claws extended. The trek of his eyes from his hand to the floor was the longest ever and shock kept him still when he saw the body in front of him. He blinked, unsure how much time had passed. Or for that matter, who the body was in front of him.

He straightened and stepped back. Sebastian handed him a towel and Levi looked around to orient himself to his surroundings. He was in his office at his logistics warehouse. Which, he was thankful for. Had he been in his office downtown, getting the blood out of the carpet would've been a chore for the office staff.

Wait.

Why was he in the logistics office? Tugging on his ear, he debated how to ask the awkward question.

Lucas snapped his fingers and Levi's warehouse staff materialized, dragging the body from in front of him. Levi moved to the battered desk and sat on the edge.

"Your highness," Sebastian started, sharing another glance with Lucas.

"Just spit it out," Levi told his friend, suddenly tired as hell.

"Far be it for me to alarm you, but you're three bodies deep and we're no closer to the answers we've been seeking."

"Which are?" Fuck it, he didn't have the mental capacity to guess.

"Who stole from you," Lucas supplied.

That answer had a fresh cloud of red obscuring his vision. Levi breathed through it, gripping the towel in his hand tightly.

"We should call it a night. Tomorrow is a new day." Sebastian said.

Levi took another look around. "Have I been to the office this evening at all?"

Bas sighed and crossed his arms over his chest. "Briefly. We had a meeting with a couple of border mages."

"The Buru," Levi murmured. "Have we figured out which border they were infiltrating?"

Lucas nodded. "We narrowed it down to the north of us though we don't know the exact spot. The Lathams control the eastern border and their record is impeccable. If anything, or anyone gets through that border they don't make it far."

Levi tossed the towel down on the desk. "The north of us is Lucian's men."

The memories were trickling in, though they were spotty. The meeting he'd held in his downtown office was with a pair of border mages Lucas had...convinced...to talk with Levi. According to the males, their section of the border was suffering from increased breaches.

"And they didn't have answers?" He asked, standing straight.

"No. And barring torture, we couldn't compel them any further if we don't want to attract attention."

Levi nodded and walked towards the door. "I don't want Lucian or the Collective in my business, so we'll increase our patrols of the city and deal with it our way."

Sebastian and Lucas fell in behind him as they exited the office and the warehouse altogether. Levi owned the trucking company that occupied the space, using it to move both legal and illegal items across the southern USA. The warehouse was where he conducted activities that he couldn't at his downtown office.

Sliding into his armored SUV, Levi closed his eyes as Lucas pulled off. They were quiet the whole way back to their compound which was a relief really. His head was pounding, and the disordered thoughts swimming around his mind didn't help. Lucas was pulling through the gates of their compound sooner than he thought, but he was happy for it.

Stepping out, he lifted his head in a nod of greeting to the night guard standing at the front door. He frowned. Why was an extra guard at the door? Out of habit, Levi's steps took him to his throne room and the Akachi stone. The meteorite had a hold on him. He could hardly go a few hours without touching it.

By the time he'd reached his throne room, he'd managed to calm the buzzing in his head. Until the moment he'd set foot inside the room and found it in disarray.

"What the fuck happened here?" He turned and asked his friends.

Before either could answer Levi tilted his head as he realized something. The source of all that roiling power beneath his skin was missing.

The loss of it should've been a relief, and yet it was as though a void had opened within him. Anger, and indignation filled him, because who the fuck would dare steal from him?

"Who was last in here?" He asked Bas.

Sebastian frowned. "If you're asking who's responsible for the mess, it's you, boss."

"You don't feel the fucking vacuum of power?" Levi snapped. "Someone has stolen my Akachi, that's what I'm talking about."

Lucas stepped forward. "Yes. That's why you were at the warehouse. We questioned the workers that were at the big house today."

"There were strangers on this compound today?"

"We managed to track down three of them. There are two more." Sebastian told him.

Levi turned in a circle and shook his head at the damage. The throne room had come with the compound he and his men had taken over when they'd defeated the Buru who previously occupied it. The whole room was twice the size of a large dining room. Not quite ballroom size but close. He called it his throne because of the gaudy gold chair the previous owner had placed on a dais in the front of the room. A red carpet ran from the entrance all the way to the chair.

Levi didn't care enough to move it in the ten years they had occupied the mansion.

There had been piles of jewelry, weapons, and all the spoils of war in the corner of the room. Now, it was strewn across the floor. A too big chandelier hung in the middle of the place, a huge table was tucked into an alcove and was big enough to seat twenty. He supposed it used to hold the Buru's old team, but it was just another thing Levi had no use for. The chairs that were normally tucked under the heavy metal table were toppled to the floor, some broken.

The expensive paintings and tapestries that had previously been on the wall were ripped and on the floor. The whole room was gaudy and was near destroyed and Levi remembered none of it.

"The security footage?"

"That's how we found out who did. We'll find the other two," Bas promised.

Levi rubbed a hand down his face. "Why hasn't the staff come in and clean?"

Lucas chuckled. "Don't another motherfucker enter that room.' Your words to the staff."

Levi sighed. "Get this shit cleaned up," he ordered his friends. "I'm going to my room. Let me know when you find those thieves."

He was going to tear their limbs from their bodies. He only hoped he would be lucid enough to enjoy doing it.

CHAPTER
TWO

"Did I ever tell you about the time I got slutted out by a vampire?"

Amaya choked on the water she was sipping, her eyes watering. She tucked the phone into her shoulder, so she could talk and wipe her face. "Trace, please."

"Nah, I'm for real. By the time he was done, I was ready to sign up for a convent. I was finna give my life up to the Celestials."

She busted out laughing because her cousin was entirely too much. "Please be for real."

Thankful for the end of her shift, Amaya carefully stripped off the clean suit she wore on top of her street clothes. Working in the sacred garden, they had to be careful of outside contamination.

Tracy sighed on the other end of the phone. "I almost asked him to marry me, but you know how the Chawi are."

Amaya nodded though her cousin couldn't see. They were both Chawi, or witches as humans would call them. There were strict rules in place about the Chawi and Bayi marrying and mating. While not exactly illegal, it was strongly discouraged, the results a curse over the whole family that none wanted to risk. She shuddered thinking of the stories her mother and grandmother told to discourage such a pairing.

"Besides, if I were going to risk the wrath of my parents, let it be for one of those fine ass Bayi in the balaclavas." Tracy lamented.

Amaya snorted. "You don't even know what they look like under those masks. Not to mention every last one of them are killers. You'd marry a killer?"

"And would," Trace said quickly.

"How are we friends?" Amaya shook her head as she rolled her clean suit into a ball.

Tossing it over to the basket for laundry in the corner of the employee locker room, she shimmied her shoulders as it landed in the basket. Smoothing down the top of her hair, she tuned back into their conversation. Not that Tracey would stop talking even if Amaya wasn't listening. Her cousin was a yapper.

"Girl, you need me, or else your life would be boring. Speaking of, are you coming out tonight? You don't have work for the next couple days."

"I promised mom I would spend time with her tomorrow," she said.

"What that got to do with you coming out tonight? Besides, it's the full moon, you can stay with me after and avoid them wild ass shifters that live around there." Tracey asked.

God, that sounded tempting. Their neighborhood got wild on the full moon. There were four silver locks on their front door to ward them away from her and her mother. It didn't stop them from banging on the door trying to get inside. An unmated, and unchaperoned Chawi was a powerful temptation to most supernaturals. The witches' magic tended to combine with whomever they mated, making the match a powerful one. Their landlord didn't allow individual wards other than what they put on the house Amaya and her mother were renting, which was understandable, but put them in a precarious position during the full moon.

"The answer is still no." She told her cousin, leaving the locker room and tracking through the archive towards the exit.

Checking the time, she relaxed, knowing she had a good thirty minutes before the bus that took her home every night arrived.

"Want me to talk to you while you ride the bus? Your stalker is probably waiting patiently for you to get on."

Amaya snorted. "That man ain't worried about me."

At least she hoped not.

Her and her alleged stalker rode the same evening bus, and sometimes Amaya caught the stranger staring at her. Mentioning it to Tracy had garnered the man the title of stalker, and her cousin brought it up every time they talked.

"It's all that chaos energy. It brings out all the looney birds. Which brings me back to my point. You should come out with me, and stay the night on the compound."

"And leave my mama to the marauding shifters? Girl."

Tracy cackled. "Not marauding. Spell it."

Amaya joined her in laughter, her smile dropping when she stepped outside and spotted her uncle pacing the stairs that led to the archive where she worked.

"Trace, let me call you back. Uncle Paul is standing out here looking mad suspicious."

"Stay on the line, girl. He could be worse than the stalker." Tracy joked.

"Bye."

She disconnected the call and eyed her uncle before stepping closer. He was her mother's youngest sibling, and the only one who was consistently in their lives. As the baby of the family, he was spoiled and, in his fifties, that hadn't changed. Her Uncle Paul had a desire for riches, but lacked the funds and common sense to get there. Knock of labels, fake accessories and strong, cheap cologne was his daily uniform as he went from one hustle to the next in search of easy money.

Paul looked up and relief flooded his face. "Maya," he breathed out, closing the distance between them.

"What's happened?" She eyed him.

He looked around paranoid and her gaze swept the entrance to try and discern his worry.

"I need your help."

Her heart started thumping. "Who's with mom? Is she alright? Did you leave her alone to come here?"

Amaya was starting to get pissed the more questions that popped into her head. Her uncle was the only person she could count on to watch her mother while she worked. There were some days when Anita didn't need it, but then, there were days when the magic ate away at her mother's mind and she was delirious and needed minding. Fear was swirled within her anger. Amaya couldn't afford a nurse to sit with her mother, and she'd already cut her working days down to three a week. Anything less than that and she and her mother would be out on the street.

"Uncle Paul!" She called to gain his attention when he didn't answer.

He ignored all her questions. "Listen to me, Amaya. I need your help. I need you to shield me."

"From what?" Her eyebrows bunched, but then her magic gave her the answer to the question a moment later.

All around him, residue of chaos magic encircled him. Out of place because her mother's brother didn't have access to it like Amaya and Anita. The jagged edge of the power was familiar to her and there was only one source that left behind that type of magical signature. She grabbed her uncle's arm and led him from the entrance to the archive.

"Where did you get a piece of the Akachi?" She hissed, careful to keep her voice down.

He snatched his arm away. "Come with me and I'll explain."

Reluctantly, she walked with him to the beat-up car he'd had for as long as she could remember. Carefully sliding into the passenger

28

seat, Amaya sighed at all the old candy and food wrappers strewn everywhere. She buckled in and he sped off.

He didn't speak until they were well away from the Archive.

"I got the piece from the Bayi."

"Oh, fuck no," she said, unbuckling her seatbelt. "Stop the car."

She reached for the door, ready to hop out the moving vehicle. They hadn't quite reached the highway that would take her to the small house she shared with her mother. She could probably survive if she jumped at this speed.

"Would you just calm down," he snapped.

She growled, balling her hands into fists in her lap. "What do you mean you stole an akachi piece from the Bayi? What Bayi?"

She wracked her mind. The Akachi pieces were heavily monitored when they were found. The power in the stones were unpredictable and dangerous and most times when a piece was found it was voluntarily turned into the Archive. So, how would her uncle even come across a piece to steal?

"I was doing work at Levi's compound."

"King Levi! You done lost your damn mind."

She did open the door this time and her uncle swerved to brake on the side of the road. She was out before it stopped moving.

"Amaya," he yelled, jumping out his seat and standing at the door. "I just need you to shield me for a couple of hours and I will make enough money to move you and my sister out of that dumpy—"

She cut him off, not bothering to slow her steps. "Fuck you... respectfully. You don't just steal from the King of the Bayi. He's going to send his enforcers to kill you and I would like to be on the other side of the city from you when that happens."

Her Uncle Paul was her mother's youngest brother and Amaya had lost track of the numerous schemes he cooked up to earn 'easy' money. Every chance he had to hit a lick, he took and as usual, the family was left to pick up the pieces.

Not no more.

She was excluding herself from this foolishness. She valued her life way too much for that.

"Amaya, please. I left the piece at your house."

She stopped walking, and her heart beat stopped with her feet. She whipped around. "Surely you...tell me you're lying."

"I'm sorry. It was the only thing I could think to do. Your mother's power..."

He didn't need to finish the sentence. Her vision dimmed along the edges, her breathing choppy as anger filled her. Her magic flared out and the metal street signs near them bent towards her, sand swirling and kicking up at her feet.

"You know the consequences of your sister using her magic and you still... I will never forgive you for this."

Paul blanched, his caramel skin going ashen, "I'm sorry, and I understand, but I'm doing this for Anita."

"Fuck, fuck fuck!" Amaya chanted on her way back to her uncle's car, tucking in her magic before any real damage could happen.

She slammed the door as she got inside. They took off, the silence thick in his junky car. Her leg was shaking as she sat forward, willing his car to go faster. If the Bayi beat them home before she could fully shield her house. A shiver went down her spine and tears filled her eyes. She didn't want to lose her mother. For a moment she breathed easier when she got to their house. Dusk had fallen and night was beginning to cool down the air. The Bayi could move around during the day, but they mostly kept their hours to full night. If she could just...she shook her head and pulled out her house keys with shaking hands.

The first tear crested her eye when she found the door unlocked. In her heart she already knew what that meant. The door was pulled opened and she came face to face with a balaclava clad giant. He was way taller than her and his presence more so. The vampire grabbed her arm and snatched her inside while his counterpart did the same as her uncle tried to run. The front door fed right into the living room, so there was no time to prepare herself. Two steps in and she came face to face with the King of the Bayi.

Levi Longford.

The tall brown-skinned vampire wore all black. A simple t-shirt tucked into cargo pants and combat boots, yet even that didn't diminish the power of his demeanor. The gold chain that laid against his shirt sparkled in the darkened room, matching the diamond studs at his ears. His narrow face had high cheekbones, a stately nose and full pink lips. The beard framing his elegant and angular visage was cut low. By the time she made it up to his dark, menacing eyes, Amaya understood that there was no getting out of this situation. She could only hope that this night would not be her last. The smile he gave her was sinister, the gold of his bottom grill glinting in the dim light.

It was the last thing she saw before a bag was tossed over her head.

CHAPTER
THREE

From the moment the black bag was ripped from her head, Levi knew he was in trouble. Her rounded heart shaped face and high cheekbones were covered with deep mahogany melanin. Her eyes were large, almond shaped and dark. From the thick lashes down to her full pouty lips, everything about the beauty was a work of art. Levi had seen beauties, but none had ever captivated him the way she did.

A demon knew his days were numbered when a woman could look them straight in the eyes. The dark beauty before him didn't lower her gaze. No, she lifted her chin, the anger on her face daring him to break her. Despite the dried tears on her cheeks, she didn't cower and that intrigued him more than anything he'd ever encountered.

She was exquisite.

And he had to have her.

Levi Longford was a lot of things, depending on who was asked. A demon, evil, benefactor, savior, king... He'd been them all in one form or another. For her...he was willing to be more. It was interesting.

He turned to the male who was in direct contrast. The pussy had his head lowered, his body trembling. The male had twice the muscle of the beauty and yet he cowered under Levi's infuriated gaze. Even the sickly woman that he had secured in one of the bedrooms upstairs had been quiet as she awaited their fate. He leaned back in the throne that he'd unironically come to love. When he and his Bayi had taken over this particular compound, he'd found the whole thing hilarious. It was where the moniker of king had come from. Two years later and it was stuck, along with the gaudy décor that decorated the mansion.

His fingers drummed along the golden arms as he stared at the two before him. Once he tired of the male's whimpers he spoke.

"You stole from me."

A simple sentence, and yet both flinched. *Interesting.*

The male lifted his head, but kept his eyes down. "It was a mistake. My niece can attest to that."

The woman shot him a deathly glare that would've amused Levi under any other circumstance. But in this he was not amused.

"And can you, beauty? Attest to the truth of that statement?" Levi knew the male was lying but he'd already lost interest in him. His attention was wholly on the female.

Her gaze swung back to him and he could admit to being mesmerized. Her magic crackled around her, the chaos that ran through all their power concentrated in her curvy, voluptuous body. The creator didn't play fair when he shaped this beauty. From the thick thighs encased in jeans, to the ample breasts she had hidden underneath the hoodie she wore.

Hunger rumbled his chest.

"Leave. All but her," he told the room.

'Levi?' His best friend and captain of his guard questioned gently.

'I'm under control.' He reassured his friend, though that may or may not have been the truth.

He didn't know what the feelings rioting through his chest meant. From the first moment he'd touched the akachi piece, his thoughts and emotions had been out of his control. His men moved to do as he ordered, dragging the uncle with them. Until there was just him and beauty.

"Your name, baby doll." He demanded.

She didn't speak. It pulled a smile from him. He left his throne and stepped down until he was close to her. The pulse at her neck thundered, but the female wasn't scared. Interesting indeed. He pulled her scent into his lungs, deciphering the layers of her recent surroundings from just the smells that covered her lovely body. He took it all in, from the smell of her shampoo, the scent of the dark night she'd moved through, even down to the odor of cedar and old books that told him she spent a lot of time in a library. Likely the Archive.

Did that mean she was a librarian or a simple student who studied there?

Her face gave nothing away of her age, so either statement could be true. The cool scent of her magic confirmed her as Chawi, even without that, the press of her power against his skin marked her as such. What kind of magic did she hold? It was something he could discern in the time he'd spend with her.

He decided in that moment that he would be spending a lot of time with her to find out.

"Do you have nothing to say of your situation?" He said softly, his breath brushing against her ear.

Her body shuddered. "Just do what you need to do."

Levi closed his eyes as the hoarse timbre of her voice dug deep within him and awoke the beast he spent most of his time suppressing. It was never a good idea to catch the attention of the blood-thirsty creature that inhabited his body.

Especially lately.

Ever since he'd been brought a piece of the Akachi stone, that monster had roamed wild within him. Uncontrollable and damn near insatiable. In the months since he'd had it, his baser instincts had been trying to take over and by sheer grace had he been able to control himself.

He circled her, slightly irritated that she was in the company of some piece of shit who would easily throw her to the wolves. She should be protected...cherished. He'd had every intention on killing the thief, but she...he leaned over her shoulder and inhaled her scent at her neck. He wanted her for himself. His gums ached, the desire to taste her throbbing through his body.

"He doesn't deserve your help, beauty."

She scoffed. "I'm well aware of that."

He reached his hand out and trailed it down her arm. She shivered, and the scent that drifted from her was most decidedly not fear.

"Why then would you not fight to clear your name in this?"

"Would it matter?" she whispered and the sadness that wafted from her made his decision for him. She sighed. "It's done. You or the Buru, the outcome would've been the same. Paul was always gonna be the one who got our family into some shit."

He hummed, and rubbed his cheek against the back of her hair. He didn't like being compared to the Buru, but he would let it go for now. She had no way of knowing him outside of his reputation and he took great care to make sure his brutality was well documented and known. The city knew not to fuck with him, and he was on his way to make sure all of the South knew the same.

"It matters to me."

For her at least. For others, nothing would've been able to sway him from killing them. Stealing from him was a crime that he never forgave. This one would be the first exception to that rule.

"What would you do to save the lives of your family, baby doll? Would you give your life to me?"

Her curious gaze rose to meet his as he circled to the front of her body. Anger flashed in her gaze, and her magic thrummed against his skin. Fucking delicious. He licked his lips, the need to taste her sending his senses reeling.

"A strong woman like you shouldn't even be mixed up with a bitch ass like him."

"Do you plan to taunt me? Just do whatever it is you need to do."

He smiled at her bravado. "Answer the question, baby doll. Would you give yourself to me to save your family?"

Her breath hitched and the heat of her magic filled the space between them. Tense silence had him on the edge as he awaited her answer. A few moments later, her shoulders slumped and her head lowered for the first time since he'd had the bag removed from her head.

"Yes."

He wanted to shout out in victory, but he restrained himself. Bas would be pissed, but there was no help for it. He would take her anyway that he could have her. For a moment, sanity tried to take over and tell him that this was not the way to get what he wanted, but that insatiable beast in him wanted her and that part of him didn't care that she would have to be coerced to be on board.

He smiled. "Let's have witnesses to that statement then, shall we?" He told her, stepping back and walking over to his throne.

He used his connection to call back Sebastian. The doors opened and his team entered, dragging her uncle behind them. He waited patiently as Bas kicked Paul in the back of the knees, sending him down to the ground.

"You got your family in some shit, Paul. How does that make you feel?" Levi asked out of curiosity.

"King Levi, if you'll allow me—"

"I've allowed you to live a lot longer than I should've. You have your niece to thank for that." Levi cut him off, irritated that the bitch was finna start begging.

"You have your stone back. We can call it even and I will never bother you again." Paul begged.

Levi snorted and his niece let out a disgusted sound.

"You triflin than a motherfucker, but luckily for you, I got something even rarer than the Akachi out of this."

Paul and the beauty next to him looked up at him in curiosity.

"Your niece has exchanged her life for yours," he informed the jackass.

Paul gasped. "Amaya, no."

Amaya. Her name at last.

In her gaze, he saw her waffling, regretting her decision and that pissed Levi all the way off. He wanted her and he would have her. He refused to give her uncle time to talk her out of what she'd promised him. Moving from his throne lightning quick, he snatched back the male's head and struck, driving his teeth in deep to feed from him. Levi didn't bother with pheromones, wanting her uncle to feel every second of the pain. He stared at Amaya as he leaned over Paul's neck and drank.

"No, please. I agreed to what you wanted," she objected.

Levi closed his eyes to block out her horror and plundered through Paul's memories. Finding out what he wanted, he tossed him down. From the whimpers, he was just shy of death. Levi licked his lips. The monster in him was barely satisfied.

Knowing blood dripped from his chin, he studied his beauty. Ah, and there was the fear finally. But she kept his gaze, ever defiant. It made his dick hard.

"If he's dying, then release me. You have no reason to keep me." Her voice was shaky as she tried to negotiate with a beast that held no human morals to speak of.

He smiled, his fangs still extended. "Oh, but I want you, baby doll. And you've made the mistake of agreeing already. How fortunate for me."

"Send him to a healer," he ordered his men as he wiped his face. "Bas, please find suitable accommodations for our guest."

His request shook her from her stupor. "What will happen to my mother?"

He sauntered to her and she flinched as he gripped her chin. He hated the fear that now filled her eyes and infused her scent but there was no help for it. From Paul's memories, he understood the precariousness of her mother's situation. That the bastard would risk his dying sister's life made Levi want to retract his agreement and kill the man.

"Our agreement keeps her safe and under my protection." He licked his fangs, and battled down his excitement. "You only have to seal the agreement."

The fire in her eyes quickly replaced the fear. "Do what you gotta do."

He nuzzled the side of her face. "Are you so eager to taste me, baby doll?"

"Fuck you," she hissed.

He chuckled. "In due time, Amaya."

Her heart was racing, her pulse thumping against her throat. He didn't know when but someday soon, he planned to leave his mark in that spot. Darkness crept into his vision, the out of control monster that he'd been battling for months rearing its head despite the fact that she had momentarily calmed him. He licked his lips and gave her time to digest what he'd told her. Her eyes widened and she gasped when she finally realized what he had said. He shook in hunger. It wouldn't be a mating bond, but the blood bond would be the next best thing. It would allow him to get into the thoughts she was hiding behind her enigmatic gaze.

She sucked in a breath when he leaned over her neck. When he took a blood bond, he normally did so at the wrist. But for her, he needed to taste her pulse point. He inhaled her skin, humming in anticipation.

"Just get it over with," she whimpered.

That helpless sound ratcheted up the tension between them. Feeding the monster right below his skin.

"This moment can't be rushed, baby doll." He put his lips at her ear. "Later, when I'm stroking my dick and thinking about your taste, I want to remember every exquisite detail."

A mewl was her answer to that. Levi chuckled and licked her

pulse point. This time the noise she made was a moan that hardened his dick even more. He would wait on his mate for sure, but nothing said he couldn't enjoy the small taste of her in the meantime. Taking a deep breath, he scraped his teeth down her skin and prayed for control.

Closing his eyes, he pumped up his pheromones and bit down gently. The first taste of her blood buckled his knees and Levi damn near moaned. The chaos power she held within filled his body and shut down the monster that had wholly taken over his life. For the first time in months, his thoughts were clear. He drank and peace suffused him.

'*Your majesty,*' Sebastain mentally called out to him.

His best friend's voice brought him back and he reluctantly pulled from her, licking his bite closed. Amaya shuddered in his arms, a small whimper escaping her.

Fuck.

Levi took a shuddering breath and stepped back. Hands shaking, he used his nail to slice through his wrist, holding it up to Amaya's mouth. He held his breath in anticipation. Fear and trepidation covered her countenance, but she lifted his wrist and placed her lips on his skin.

"God damned, baby doll," he whispered in yearning.

His pulse beat heavy, his dick hardening as she sucked on his skin. It took every ounce of his control to keep from taking her in front of his men.

"Enough," he said hoarsely, extracting his arm from her.

Amaya looked up at him, his blood on her chin, and a dazed look in her eyes and control be damned. Levi grabbed the back of her neck and pulled her closer to him. He licked her lips before plunging his tongue into her mouth. The kiss he took was rough, desperate. He tasted the combination of their blood and knew instinctively that they would be magnificent together.

'*Levi.*' Bas's tone was firm.

40

He stepped back and nodded to the maid he'd summoned. The humans had come with the mansion, enslaved to the Buru who had originally owned the compound. Levi had freed them all, but because of the spell the vampires had over them, they stayed. Their loyalty seemingly came with the compound no matter its occupants. It had taken him years to get used to having domestic help and no matter what he'd tried, they'd remained under some kind of thrall.

The maid grabbed Amaya's arm gently. Amaya snatched it from her and the woman looked to him for guidance.

"Amaya, don't take your anger at me out on my staff. It would change my assessment of you."

She stared him down before nodding. She followed the woman from the room, her head held high.

Absolutely exquisite.

His best friend sighed as he approached, handing him a towel. "The hell are you doing, Levi?"

"She's stunning, Bas." He wiped his face of the blood trying to dry on his chin.

"Fine as hell, but that doesn't answer the question. Why are you keeping them here?"

He sighed, the problem with having friends for decades is that they didn't let you get away with shit.

"She's mine," he said matter of factly.

Bas snicker. "You can't keep the girl because you feel like it, Levi."

"Says who?"

The chuckles of his men filled the room. Bas just shook his head.

"You wouldn't have had to buy a whole separate condo for your mate if you had just kidnapped her." He reminded his best friend.

Lucas busted out laughing. "Raven would've burned all this shit down around us if Bas had kidnapped her."

His men agreed, joining Lucas in laughter and Levi waved them off.

"She'll get over it." At least he hoped so.

Bas crossed his arms over his chest and stared his friend down. "How long you keeping her?"

He didn't answer because he didn't know. How long did it take a woman to get over a kidnapping and willingly come into his arms? Until she agreed to be his?

Sebastian snorted. "You don't think that will complicate matters? Last thing we need is the Collective searching around for them."

Levi grunted. "Weren't you just complaining about being bored?"

"That was you and Lucas." Sebastian growled.

He snickered, because yeah, that had been them. He spent his days running his empires, both illegal and legal and the shit was becoming monotonous. And yet, as Bas so kindly reminded him, the Collective had been on their heads, watching them, fearing that Levi would use his Bayi to overrun the South. He'd already ridded the city and state of the Buru and it was his intention to do that with the rest of the south, but running shit had never been his intention, despite his moniker. He kept the Bayi under his rule loyal and well fed and that was all anyone could really ask of him.

Being King of the Bayi was title enough for him.

Being King of the South held no appeal to him.

He'd taken the piece of Akachi to aid him in ridding the rest of the Southern USA of the Buru, but the stone had proved harder to control than he'd anticipated. Raven, Sebastian's mate, had warned him that the pure chaos magic would be too much. He'd taken her words into consideration and still thought the risk was worth it. He was paying for his arrogance. Madness was creeping in and though he hid it from his friends, he was starting to get worried.

For a moment, with Amaya in his arms, all that had gone away. Could that be why he was drawn to her? As he inhaled, her scent lingered in the air and gave him his answer. It wasn't the Akachi stone controlling his reaction to her. He wanted her.

Everything in him was telling him that Amaya was what he'd subconsciously been searching for. Holding her here against her will wasn't necessarily a good start to that. His gaze went back to the door she'd exited. Her taste lingered on his tongue and if he closed his eyes, he could see her beautiful, defiant face.

Fuck it.

There were worse ways to start a mating.

CHAPTER
FOUR

Amaya paced the luxurious bedroom, her heart thumping through her chest. But, it was still hers, inside of her chest and functioning. That was a victory in and of itself. Even with her limited knowledge of the king, she knew that not many escaped his wrath.

How was she getting out of her predicament? One would think that fear was what was hindering her thoughts but...no. Her magic was flaring wildly around her as her body battled arousal and need. For once, not a single thought in her head was helpful. Her mind was crowded with the king of the vampires. His chiseled face left no room for anything else.

She flashed back to an hour ago when she'd taken his blood. Amaya had looked into his dark eyes and saw the flames swirling within. She could almost feel the monster he was clawing to come out and devour her. But what choice had she had?

Amaya's body shuddered as she remembered the way his teeth had pierced her throat. The pain had been instantaneous, but quickly swept away by pleasure that had swamped her body. Even the memory of it heated her skin until the air around her left prickles of sensation. Not to mention her magic reacted to him. The greedy chaos of her power wanted to attach itself to him and lavish in his dark aura. It called to her magic in way she'd never experienced before. She took a deep shuddering breath and headed to the window in her prison.

Escape was a ridiculous notion, especially since he held her mother somewhere in this compound. While her power was useful for the archive, it would be futile against a mansion full of vampires. She turned from the window and paced. Had she made the right decision? Would he allow her to change her mind? She bit her lip, because she couldn't in good conscious let him kill her uncle.

Looking around the lavish bedroom she sighed. This...prison was a lot better than the bedroom of the small house she and her mother were renting. She shook her head, what was she thinking? Not even in hour alone and she was already rationalizing the situation.

"Get it together, Amaya," she muttered in disgust.

She rushed to her bag the maid had left on the bench in front of her bed. Eyebrows lifting, she was shocked to find her phone. Rolling it around in her hand, she debated her actions. She could call her cousin, and then what?

The rest of her family is involved. To what end?

She stared at it as a text came in.

> Trace: What did Paul want? Did you make it home?

Her hands shook as she typed out the lie that would keep the rest of her family safe.

> Amaya: Girl. Same shit different day.

An eyeroll gif was her cousin's response, but she didn't question it further. Amaya was thankful that Tracy left it at that. She lifted her head at the knock at the door. She ignored it, not ready to deal with what was on the other side. Holding her breath, she waited on another knock, when it didn't come, she released the air in her lungs and flopped down on the bed.

Closing her eyes and fighting to center herself, Amaya fought through the panic waiting in the wings to take over. Her hand went to her neck, her fingers trailing the spot where King Levi had bitten her. The skin still tingled in that spot, but closing her eyes, the image of his blood-soaked mouth filled her vision.

She had to get out of here.

Her stomach grumbled as she sat up. Dinner had been long forgotten, and now all she could think about was her mother. Was she alright? Amaya rushed to the door, regretting ignoring the knock the first time. She turned the knob, shocked to find that it turned. She wasn't locked inside.

As she opened, her breath stalled and she took a shaky step back. King Levi stood at her door, a tray of food in his hand. With every step he took inside her room, she fell back.

"What are you doing here?"

"You refused the tray from the maid I sent earlier," he told her.

She shook her head because she hadn't realized how deep in her thoughts she'd been. How long ago had that knock been? Levi set down the tray and turned his full attention to her. All the air in the room was sucked out. His presence left no room for anyone else. Amaya knew power, she worked around it all the time, but this was raw, untamed and it took her breath away. Her body sought to tune itself with his.

The pulse that was once racing, slowed to match the hard thump of his. She could tell that he hadn't fed in a while, but how she knew that was a mystery. Surely it had something to do with the blood bond. Amaya examined her mind, there was a tether to him, though it was light. It was enough for some of his feelings to come through. She sensed his wariness and that...she didn't know what to do with that. Why should he be wary? He was holding her hostage.

"Not hostage, baby doll."

He answered lowly and she shook away her scattered thoughts, immediately slamming a shield up over her mind. Him having access to her thoughts would be dangerous. Her brows lowered and she pinched her lips to keep in all the vile things she wanted to hurl at him. Her mother's safety was contingent on how she acted. And from the way he clenched and unclenched his hands, patience was not something he had in stores. Relaxing her shoulders she took a deep calming breath. With it came his scent, and her body warmed. Damn this man. Why was her body betraying her like this?

"King Levi," she started, working to put as much respect in her tone as she could. His smirk did not help. She smoothed out the expression on her face. "Is my mother safe?"

"I don't hurt innocent people."

"Now how I'm supposed to know that?" she snapped. She took a deep breath and corralled the magic that wanted to flare out at this man. "Can I see her, talk to her?"

"You and I need to get some shit straight first."

She swallowed down a growl. *It's for my mother*, she told herself.

"You've kidnapped me. What could we possibly have to discuss? Hell, you got the Akachi back and we've exchanged blood, you don't even need to keep me here. You can call me to you at any point."

That was probably what offended her the most about this agreement she'd bound herself in.

Anita had never liked living on the Chawi compound, and thus Amaya had grown up free of their restricting rules. From the moment she'd turned eighteen and her mother's magic started to eat away at Anita's mind, there had been no one for Amaya to answer to. To make it to her late twenties to turn around and be...beholden to another...

The vampire could call to her and Amaya would be forced to answer. Bitterness and anger stewed within her.

Levi smiled, madness swirling in his gaze. "Oh, but I want you, babydoll."

Faster than she could process, the king was in her face and space.

He leaned over nudging her head to get access to her throat. She stopped breathing, her heart rate accelerating.

"I decided the moment I saw you that I would have you."

"I'm not an object for you to collect."

He chuckled and rubbed his nose down the side of her neck. "Fuck, you smell amazing, babydoll. I know your pussy is fire."

Amaya gasped and stepped back from him. "You need to let us go so I can properly care for my mother." She couldn't help the tremble in her voice.

Just his presence this close to her was rattling her senses. The small amount of blood they'd exchanged was doing its job. She craved him. It was the blood...right?

"Need? No. I *need* to taste you," he licked her neck, "Need to feel the way you'll grip my dick, feel your curves against me. Those are needs, babydoll. You *want* to be released, and I don't think I will. I think I'll make you keep your word to me."

Mad at the way her body melted for him, her temper rose. So badly she wanted to lash out with her power, but besides the fact that she didn't know how he'd respond to the aggression, her magic was a passive thing. As offense it was nothing. Dampening power and magic, what was that to a vampire when his strength was three times her own? She was sure he wasn't interested enough in her to ignore an outright attack.

"You and your gold fanged gang can't just go around kidnapping people." She breathed out.

"I haven't kidnapped people. I've taken a thief into my custody. I can't imagine the Collective would care about that."

"Not that you would care either way."

He shrugged his eyes spearing her, seeing places within her that she kept hidden to the world. "Look at you already knowing your man."

Those words momentarily struck her mute. They stared at each other, a maniacal light shining in his gaze as it raked over her body.

"I have no intention in being food for you unless you plan to take my blood without my consent."

His growl stopped her words and rose the hair on the back of her neck. "I don't have to take shit from no one. Ain't never had to. You'll come to me of your own free will and you'll love it over here."

Though his words held a hint of teasing, Levi's eyes were hard, a flicker of a flame on the inside. He was mad as hell and she needed to tread carefully.

"Can I please see my mother?"

He grit his teeth, battling with urges Amaya prayed he beat, before his face cleared. "Your mother is safe and comfortable."

"I don't believe you."

Stepping from her, Levi held his hand out towards the door. Wary, Amaya took a deep breath and she walked past him, closing her eyes as his scent wrapped around her. When she reached the hallway, one of his enforcers was there standing at a door a few feet away. Instinctively, she knew that was where they were keeping her mother. Taking shaky steps, she closed the distance between her and the wooden door the enforcer stood in front of.

A shuddering breath shook her body as she turned the knob. Her mother was sitting in a chair at the window, her visage peaceful, no hint of distress. Tears crested Amaya's eyes and while fear was still with her, having her mother safe was her top priority.

Anita turned to her and smiled softly. "There you are."

She rushed to her mother's side, kneeling. "Are you okay, mama?"

Her mother nodded, "better than I've felt in a while. The Bayi have treated me kindly." Her mother cupped her cheek. "Are we in trouble, Amaya?"

She closed her eyes and swallowed down the sob. "Uncle Paul did put us in a bit of a predicament, but I'll get us out of this." She promised.

Her mother hummed. "I tried to keep my brother on the straight and narrow, but you know your uncle." She sighed. "I trust you to work out something. In the meantime, this situation doesn't feel dangerous."

Reassured by that, Amaya lowered her head. With the riotous thoughts in her mind, she wasn't sure she'd be able to trust her own instincts. While having her mother lucid comforted her, she wasn't sure how long that would last. And would it make it better having Anita aware of what was happening to them?

"How long will we be here?" Anita asked. Her eyes were clear of the madness Amaya was so used to seeing her in gaze.

"I don't know yet."

As though a switch flipped, Anita's eyes clouded over and a sort of blankness overtook her mother. Amaya noticed that it happened most in high stress situation and she cursed her uncle all over again. It was the reason she took great pains to keep her mother home safe and resting.

"Mom," she whispered. Anita didn't answer, and her hand fell from Amaya's cheek. Sighing she sucked up her pride and stood. "Can you help me, please?"

She was reluctant to ask, but she didn't want to risk carrying her mother and causing her injury. She expected the enforcer to come up, but Levi was next to her, gently moving her aside. He lifted her mother and carried her over to the bed. Silent at her side, he waited as Amaya moved the blanket back. Her gaze strayed to the king's face as he placed Anita on the bed gently and stepped back. There was empathy in his gaze, an understanding that told her he was suffering similarly as her mother.

Well, with the Akachi in his possession she wasn't surprised. Still, her own empathy was stoked for him. Furiously smashing the emotion down, Amaya tucked Anita in, her heart pinching at the vacant look on her mother's face.

"Can you..." she swallowed and paused her words.

With every favor she asked, she understood that she would be further in his debt.

His hand landed on her shoulder. "I will have someone with her twenty-four hours."

She nodded. "Will I be able to see her?"

"You are not a prisoner here, Amaya."

"That's funny because it certainly feels like it," she said, shaking off his hand. "Thank you," she whispered.

She leaned down and kissed her mother's forehead.

"You can leave," she told him going towards the chair in the corner and dragging it to the bed.

His presence still took up the room, until it didn't. Moments later, the soft click of the door closing made her flinch. She settled in the chair beside her mother's bed and laid her head down, releasing the sobs trapped in her chest.

How in the hell would she get them out of this?

CHAPTER
FIVE

Amaya winced as she slid the jeans up her leg. They had been her only wardrobe for the last three days and she would throw them in the trash the moment she got home.

She scoffed, who was she kidding?

She couldn't afford to be throwing clothes away. Still, it would be a while before she wore them again. She had a feeling that every time she wore them she would be reminded of being held hostage by the king of the Bayi.

Shaking off the thought, she slid her arms into the hoodie and braced herself.

Tonight, she was going to escape.

Amaya had walked the perimeter yesterday and scoped out the best chance she had to escape. There was shielding over the whole of the compound, but because the vampires within were arrogant, they hadn't given her any thought as she hung out along the southern wall. It had taken some finessing to keep her power under wraps, but she'd managed to open a small spot for her mother and her to escape. She had already called Tracey and sent her the location where she could meet them.

She could possibly be sealing her and her mother's death warrant, but sitting around and not trying didn't sit well with Amaya. Her whole life had been her and her mother surviving the best way they knew how. There were lean days, and there were days they feasted, but through it all, it had been the two of them together. This would be no different. Luckily for her, Anita was having a lucid night and if she could time it correctly, they should be off the compound before that changed. In the few days that they'd been here, her mother's lucid states lasted longer than when they were at home.

When she'd approached her mother earlier in the day about the plan, Anita had agreed, though somewhat reluctantly. Anita had been having a grand old time in the King's compound. True to Levi's words, her mother had twenty-four seven care, the servants catering to her mother every need and whim. Amaya imagined it was what it would feel like if she could afford a nursing staff to care for her mother.

Anita was probably going along with the plan moreso in solidarity with her daughter, than a want to escape the mad king.

For the week that they'd been here, Amaya had been creeping around the mansion and nightly she heard the proof of what the Akachi did to one's mind as the king paced the floors of his compound, his anger and confusion blanketing the atmosphere. How did his men live here with him? Though, in their defense, Amaya's tie to chaos magic was what made her so sensitive to Levi's moods and aura.

She outright avoided him, refusing to eat dinner with them and keeping him locked out of her room.

It was risky pissing off someone with Levi's power, but...she had a feeling it wasn't just her life she would be risking being anywhere alone with that man. The taste of his power she'd experienced when he'd forced her to feed from him was still in her mind. It was imprinted on her body, and just the thought of it brought a flush of heat.

She needed to get the fuck out of here.

So, last night while her mother was in a healty place, they carefully tweaked the escape plan Amaya had come up with. She could only pray that they would pull it off and her mother was still on board with the plan.

Levi and his main goons were gone for the evening, so Amaya didn't anticipate any one caring enough to stop her. Originally, she'd thought to escape during the day when the vampires in residence were sleeping. But Anita, who seemingly knew every-damn-body in this house, had informed her daughter that shifters roamed the property during the day. So evening was their better option.

Knocking on her mother's door softly, she crept in. Anita was sitting at the chair at the small table in front of the window.

"Mama," she whispered.

Anita turned. "Is tonight the night?"

"I think so," she told her softly, creeping closer to the window in the dark. "Are you sure this part will work?"

Anita sighed. "Amaya, I've taught you how to create objects using your power, you just have to trust yourself. Or you can just let me do it and it will be done faster."

Amaya shook her head. "We can't afford for you to keep using your chaos magic, you know that."

Anita smiled sadly. "Let's get to it then."

Amaya went to the window and prodded it with her magic. Not finding any spells to keep them in, she released a breath of relief. Lifting the glass, she bit her bottom lip as she determined how to make the stairs.

Anita placed her hand on her back. "You can do this, May."

Nodding, Amaya focused her magic, building the stairs one at a time, keeping them translucent in case someone walked by. The second story wasn't as high as some mansions, so it didn't take too much effort.

"I'll go first just in case," Amaya told her mother.

Anita nodded and Amaya lifted the window fully, stepping her leg out. Standing, she found the stairs sturdy. Giddy excitement filled her, both at her accomplishment and the fact that her plan could work. Her and Anita crept softly down the stairs and Amaya dissipated the magic when both of their feet touched the ground. Leading her mother towards the east side of the property, they slipped through the shadows of the small cabins scattered around. A vampire stepped out of the darkness and her heart knocked against her chest.

"Why are you skulking?" he asked with a curious tilt of his head.

Before she could answer, he slumped down. She turned and looked at her mother for an explanation.

"We don't have all night," Anita whispered in explanation.

They reached the south wall of the property and Amaya was relieved that no guard manned it. She just prayed that she could duplicate the stairs. First, she needed to get through the shielding. Waving her hands, she used magic to make the spell visible. She started work on it yesterday, leaving just a small bit of the power intact to allay suspicions. Painstakingly, she took apart the last of the magic, keeping it confined to one section so as not to raise an alarm.

It took her five minutes longer than she'd planned and she hoped no one noticed that she and her mother weren't in their rooms. Another vampire came out and like before Anita put him to sleep.

"Mom, you can't keep using your magic," she admonished.

"Why would I use my magic?" Anita said and Amaya's heart dropped.

She turned and her mother's face showed her confusion. The fugue state had taken over. Tears gathered at the corner of her eyes, but she could still make the plan work. Quickly, she built the stairs and guided her mother onto them. When she reached the top, on the other side, her stomach dropped to her toes.

Levi and Sebastian stood on the other side, legs parted and arms crossed over their chests.

"Will I need to reinforce all the shielding around my property?" Levi's voice was bored.

Cursing, Amaya tried to think of anything she could use to fight the Bayi king. She descended the stairs on the other side of the fence and faced off with the vampire. He looked sane now, but there was no telling if that would change. Fuck it, using chaos magic, Amaya created a staff, swinging it at Levi as he tried to step closer to her and Anita.

Levi stepped back and held up his hands, anger flashing in his gaze. "You plan to defeat us both with a stick?"

His taunting pissed her off, so she sharpened the end of the wooden stake with her magic and jabbed it towards him. "I could stab you in your heart."

He laughed. Laughed, damn him.

"Could you?" He stepped closer and she swung again.

"Maybe not now," she said, her chest tight with frustration, "but you have to sleep sometime."

"Threatening me, baby doll?" He asked, his voice silky menace. All traces of amusement was gone from his gaze.

"Just let us go," she whispered.

Headlights cut through the dark night, illuminating Sebastian who had not moved in an inch during any of the confrontation. Amaya's heartrate sped, thudding hard against her chest. Her cousin had such unfortunate timing. Levi turned to her car and hissed. Before she could even yell out a warning to her cousin, Levi jumped in front of the car. Tracy slammed on her brakes, her scream escaping the confines of the car. Levi leaned on the hood of the car, his fangs lowered.

"Don't kill her! I'll go back!" Amaya yelled out.

Levi gave her a sinister smile before turning back to Tracy. A lump formed in her throat and helpless tears escaped her eyes. Tracy stiffened in her car and Amaya couldn't tell what was happening, but without saying a word to her, Tracy completed a three-point turn and drove away.

Amaya released a shaky breath. "What did you do to her?" Amaya whispered.

"I ain't lay a single finger on her, baby doll. She'll be home in bed soon, with no memory of this happening. You should thank me for that grace."

"Fuck you," she hissed.

Now that Tracy was out of danger, the need to curtail her words was gone.

Sebastian sighed and shook his head. The smile dropped from Levi's face.

"Inside. Now." The king snapped.

"I hate you." She told the vampire and he flinched.

"Maybe today, but not forever," he whispered.

Amaya guided her mother back into the house, defeat lowering her shoulders.

She had been so close.

CHAPTER
SIX

How many days had she been under his roof?

Two?

Three?

The way the Akachi had his mind, it was hard for Levi to keep track of the days, but he knew the moment he opened his eyes and his mind was semi-clear, it was because she was here one floor beneath him. It still amazed him how much peace the spiteful stubborn witch brought him. Sebastian had hypothesized that it had to do with the fact that she could control chaos magic. Having no other theory to combat it, Levi had taken his friend's theory as law. Though, in the end, the why didn't matter to him.

All that mattered was that being within a few feet of shawty allowed him to think and that was priceless in his current state.

The shutters in his room rose, the clicking sound shaking him from his lucid thoughts. Just that quickly, his mind clouded and the irritation that had been his new companion filled him. Through the cold shower, his wake-up hygienic routine, all through him getting dressed there wasn't a single thought Levi could chase down to conclusion. As a result, impotent anger filled him.

Growling, Levi stepped onto the balcony that flanked his bedroom, flopping down into the chair he kept outside. He quickly lit the pre-rolled he kept outside on the table and inhaled deeply, the weed clearing some of his thoughts. An artificial calm filled him and the fact that it wouldn't last tightened his shoulders. The drug would only do so much. He turned his head at the knock on his door, probing the thoughts of the person on the other end. He bade Lucas to enter.

His friend joined him on the balcony, leaning against the wooden railing.

"She's demanding to leave again. This time she says she has to work." Lucas announced.

Levi growled. Through his blood bond with her, he could feel her frustration, though her thoughts were hidden from him. It was puzzling how she was able to keep the shield over her mind. It shouldn't have been possible.

"What you wanna do?" Lucas interrupted his train of thought.

He gave Lucas a droll look before changing the subject. He wasn't ready to allow her to leave. "The men at her house report back?"

"The Buru came just like you predicted." Lucas crossed his arms over his chest.

"Did they get rid of them?"

Lucas returned the look Levi had given him earlier. The question was rhetorical. Of course, his men got rid of them. Any Buru that stepped into Black Hollow met with the same fate.

"You want them to hang around?"

He shook his head. The Buru could well send reinforcements, despite the fact that they shouldn't even be getting past the border into the south.

"How would her uncle have even been in contact with the Buru?"

Levi waved away that question. He frankly didn't care about any of the stupid moves the mage had been making. "I want to know how they keep getting through our borders."

Lucas shrugged. "We can meet with the border mages, but likely it'll piss off the Collective."

Levi used the tip of his fingers to put out his blunt. "You know I don't give a fuck about that."

Lucas snorted. "And the girl?"

"Is mine." The answer came of pure instinct. He wasn't giving her up. "Her staying here will keep her safe, in case the Buru came back."

Surely that sounded sane?

"That safety excuse will only go so far. If she works for the archive like she says, Ms. Fine-ass-Sophia is going to come looking for her." Lucas warned him.

Levi grunted already knowing that Sebastian wouldn't buy his excuse either. Keeping her had been impulsive but damn if he could feel any regret for it. It wasn't a great idea but the way he felt around her made him less inclined to give her up. He walked back into his room and started pacing. He sighed as he felt Sebastian's energy coming closer. His best friend, was always able to read Levi's moods so he should've known he would come to his room sooner or later. It was a down side of their tight bond.

"What are you doing, Levi?" Was Bas' first question as he entered the room.

He didn't address him by his title which meant his friend was worried and coming to him as a brother and not a soldier. Lucas gave him an 'I told you so' look before leaving the two alone.

"She's mine," he snapped.

Bas hummed. "And this is the course you wanna set with your mate?"

"What other choice do I have, Bas? I let her leave here and what else will her fucking uncle get her into? Buru were circling her house just last night. What if they send more after her and her mother?"

"Perhaps explain that to her." Bas's tone was reasonable and yet...

Anger, raw and scathing burned through Levi. In the back of his mind, he understood that the Akachi piece was causing the emotion, but he couldn't seem to stop it from spilling out of him.

"Shawty's mine and I can do what the fuck I want with her. I dare a muthafucka to come in here and take her from me!"

Bas sighed, used to his emotional outbursts. They were coming more frequently. Levi could feel his control slipping through his fingers like sand.

"I got your back whether or not I agree with your actions, Levi. You know that." Bas assured him and Levi tried to breathe through the volatile emotion.

"Leave me, Bas," he whispered and his friend did as he asked.

He lifted the lamp at his bedside and tossed it at the wall, satisfied at the crash that sounded. Taking pleasure in the sound, he lifted something else. When he came back to himself minutes later, all around him lay destruction, proof that he was losing control again. He didn't even know how long he was out this time. Before he could consider it, the door opened and servants entered, immediately cleaning, like automatons, quietly and efficiently cleaning up the mess he'd made.

Sighing, Levi stepped from the room and onto the balcony. Taking in the cool damp air of the evening, he lowered his head. He couldn't lead his men this way. Raven's warnings sounded in his head and he understood that his arrogance had gotten him into this position. Sebastian's mate had warned him in a respectful way that the power of the Akachi stone would eventually be too much for him to take.

He thought he'd weighed the pros and cons, deciding that the power that surged through him was worth whatever the consequences. He needed that power to secure the Bayi's position in this world. He would no longer allow the Collective to overlook his vampires. The Bayi were done paying for the crimes of a long dead ancestor.

Deciding to go see the woman who plagued his thoughts, he headed downstairs. He found a maid coming down the hallway with the tray he knew was for her. Amaya was still refusing to eat her meals with him. He grit his teeth as he tried to determine how much longer he would allow that.

"I'll take it to her," he told the maid, grabbing the tray.

A docile bob of her head was her answer as she stepped aside

Taking a deep breath, he knocked at the door before turning the knob. He growled when it refused to give way. Using his power, he attempted to push through the lock. Frowning, he tried again and still the door didn't open. Using his magic, he probed at the opening, realizing that not only had she locked the physical door, it was shielded, keeping his magic from inside the room.

"Amaya."

"Go away, King."

"Open the door, Amaya before you piss me off." He stated it as calmly as he could.

The door opened, and Amaya stood on the other side, ever defiant. In between them, a shimmer of her magic kept them separated. Despite the opening, Levi knew he still couldn't enter her space. Her magic was preventing it.

"I'm ready to go home." She stated, her eyes full of fire.

"So, you've told my men. Over and over. Why are you refusing dinner with me?"

Why had he asked her that? He shouldn't care.

"Because you kidnapped me. This ain't no resort, *King*."

The mocking nickname was finna send him spiraling, Levi could feel it. "Amaya, you 'bout to piss me off."

She faked a gasp. "Oh no. The king is mad. Is the dungeon the next level after this?"

"Why do you insist on thinking the worst about me?" He snapped.

"You have me locked in this room!"

Her power flared, dampening the sound around the estate, almost wrapping the two of them in a cocoon. The beast inside of him wanted to consume that magic. It made him frantic and edgy,

"Because your aggravating ass keeps trying to leave this estate. You think I don't feel you poking at my damn shields? What did you expect when I caught you climbing the fucking fence?"

"It's been almost two weeks. I can't just miss work. I've told your men that."

Two weeks.

Gods, he'd lost track of time that badly? A sliver of fear sliced through him and for a moment Levi was speechless...helpless, which fed into the anger and confusion. He was losing his grip on reality more by the day. He tried to reconcile the conversation he'd just had with Lucas and Sebastian with her revelation. Surely that conversation had taken place this morning? So, then...wait.

No.

That's not right. He looked down and saw that he was dressed for work, so that means the conversation happened...

When?

Something like panic tried to take over his mind, but he squashed it.

"Hello!" Amaya snapped her fingers in his face. "When can I go to work?"

Shaking away the tumultuous thoughts, Levi gave her his attention. "What part of danger aren't you understanding, shawty?"

"There is only one danger I see here and it's a selfish vampire going mad from playing with power he can't handle."

Incandescent rage filled him and the tray he held flew from his hand, slamming into the wall down the hallway. Amaya flinched but she stood her ground. Lowering his head, Levi breathed through his nose and tried to control himself. She raised her hand, but it lowered before she could touch him. Instead, small probes of her magic cautiously moved through his mind and the fog of anger dissipated. The weight on his chest preventing easy breaths was lifted.

Still...

She'd pissed him off.

"Fine. Then if you can't eat with me, you'll starve." He turned and left her door way.

She sucked her teeth and leaned out of the doorway. "We weren't even talking about that...Keep up, King."

"Kiss my ass, Amaya," he said.

She slammed the door and he blew out an impatient breath. Instead of heading back downstairs to eat, he instead turned back around to Ms. Anita's room. He usually had someone escort her down to dinner when she was up to it. Unlike her sickening ass daughter, the older woman had a reason for missing dinner with the rest of the house. He knocked gently and waited on her. Her soft voice told him to enter.

There was a maid in there, braiding the woman's long hair. A simple maxi dress covered her thin frame, the jade color beautiful against her skin. Amaya looked exactly like her mother and it told Levi how beautifully she would age. Anita turned at his entrance, and gave him a chiding look that told him tonight was a lucid one. The high cheekbones that were softer on her daughter's more rounded face gave Anita a regal look that made her expression more piercing as her dark eyes assessed him. There was more of a... knowing in her gaze than the last time he'd visited her.

When had that been?

As though she knew the direction of his thoughts, empathy filled Ms. Anita's gaze and if anyone understood what he was going through it was her. It was the reason he found himself in the older woman's room some evenings before he went to work.

Their shared battle had forged a bond that hadn't taken blood. The urge to apologize to her for her and her daughter's current circumstance hit him and he bit his bottom lip to quell it. Levi dismissed the maid and the female ducked out quickly.

"How are you doing?"

Anita cocked her head before answering. "Ah," she said after a moment.

He frowned because he didn't know what that meant.

"My daughter is something of a rebel," she said finally.

"She is stubborn," he conceded.

"I guess it depends on what you're trying to get her to do. She's been caring for me for the past years. That kind of pressure can make one hard."

He nodded in understanding.

"Are you here to escort me to dinner?"

He held out his arm and the woman grabbed it and got out of her seat, the smile she gave him was so reminiscent of her daughter that it made him mad at Amaya all over again. Before the feeling could overtake him, her mother pressed a cool hand against his forehead and the cloud of anger dissipated. He gave her a startled look.

"If no one understands the way the Akachi leaves you, I do."

He nodded, a lump in his throat.

The woman sighed, "I wish I could help you, but there are days that I am not myself. I'm useless to my daughter, I can't even get her out of this."

He wiped the tear from her face. "I would never hurt Amaya."

She hummed. "There are many ways to hurt a person. Amaya has had to fend for herself for years. Pushing her will get you nowhere. Taking her away from her work will hurt her as surely as you raising your hand to her."

"You heard our argument?" He sighed.

"It's not as though the two of you censor your volume or tone," she scolded him.

He nodded, properly chastised by this tiny woman that was so important to his mate. It had been at least sixty years since he'd allowed anyone to take him to task. His mother had been the last and surprisingly, he was allowing Ms. Anita to fill a spot so long abandoned.

She looked up at him and smiled. "Are you here to escort me to dinner?"

His heart clutched. Was this his future?

"I am, if you're up to it," he forced out around the lump in his throat.

"Of course. Dinner with vampires. Not something I get to do every day." She said excitedly.

He walked her downstairs. He groaned when he saw Raven in her spot at the dinner table. She worked nights now that she and Sebastian were mated, so most times, she missed dinner. She only came to the 'big house' as she called it when she didn't feel like cooking. If he thought Sebastian gave him shit, his firefly would cuss him up and down. She stood when she spotted him and Amaya's mother.

"Ms. Anita," she rushed forward. "What are you doing here?"

"Raven? My goodness, do you live here too? What are you doing in a house full of Bayi vampires?"

Raven helped the woman into a chair before turning her gaze to him. "Your highness?"

The questions swirled in her eyes and Sebastian stood, unsure how Levi would react. It hurt him that his best friend could no longer trust him, though he understood. Shame filled him and Bas' face morphed into empathy.

"Red," Bas said softly, calling his mate back to his side.

"What's going on?" Raven asked again ignoring her mate's call.

"Amaya is staying here." Levi answered, his nails digging into his hands as he clenched his fists.

"Here, why?" Raven straightened and narrowed her eyes, her gaze sweeping the table.

"Her uncle stole the Akachi piece from Levi." Sebastian told her. She gasped.

"He was going to sell it to Buru." Anita provided and Levi gave her a surprised look. She had known what her brother was up to?

"They've been circling their house for the past week and a half," Lucas added.

Despite the conversation around him, his shoulders slumped in relief. It hadn't been two weeks as Amaya had claimed. The days were still foggy, but he took comfort in the fact that he hadn't lost that much time. He could add gaslighting on top of the shit his little witch was doing to him. He sighed. It was well what he deserved, but he would rather go completely mad than release her.

He tuned back into the present conversation, his feet a little firmer beneath him.

Raven frowned. "Then why haven't I seen her around here? Or at work?"

"The archive needs janitors that bad?" Lucas scoffed.

Raven flinched. "Did she tell you she was a janitor?"

"She told me she cleaned," Lucas said with a shrug.

"Magic. She cleans the magic around the Akachi meteor pieces. Sophia will lose her shit if she doesn't show up for work."

"You want to fight both the Collective and the Archive?" Sebastian asked him telepathically.

Levi growled. *"Fine. Allow her to go to work tomorrow but send a team with her."*

Bas and Lucas both nodded.

"I'm done talking about it," Levi said louder and he watched Raven swallow her words.

Likely her mate requested it. Whatever the reason, Levi was satisfied. Arguing with his friends would trigger him and one episode tonight was enough to scare him.

CHAPTER
SEVEN

When a knock rattled the wood of her bedroom door, Amaya didn't flinch. She'd been awake for hours going over the argument she'd had with Levi. He deserved her ire, but her words to him...she sighed. Her mouth was reckless, always had been, but she did regret taunting him about losing his mind. It wasn't fair. Especially in light of the struggle her mother was going through. Glancing at the time on her phone she rolled her eyes and stood. It was barely six am.

"If you're not coming to tell me I can go to work, you're wasting your time," Amaya said as she opened the door.

She gasped and stepped back, surprised to see a bulky shifter at her door. The darkskin male was handsome, locks pulled back into a low ponytail, his yellow gaze telling her that he was a wolf. He held out a bag and she grabbed it in confusion.

"King Levi says that you can work today," he told her gruffly, holding out a shopping bag.

She eyed the bag suspiciously before grabbing it. "And you're my guard?"

"Guard, driver, whatever you need. I'll be downstairs at the door." He left without waiting on her response.

She slammed the door in irritation. Not even work would allow her to escape Levi's tightening grip. Damn him! It's wasn't like she would attempt to escape, he had her mother. In the past few days of her prison sentence, she'd been discussing it with her cousin and Tracey had pointed out how much safer she was at Levi's place. It had pained her to agree, but her cousin had been right. To add to that, her mother had so many more lucid days here. Stress and using their power played a big part on how the sickness progressed. Did Anita do well here because she was less stressed and used her power less?

Their neighborhood hadn't been the safest, but with her uncle watching Anita, her mother shouldn't have had to expend that much magic to keep them safe. Had her uncle been leaving his sister alone more than he'd let on?

Anger filled her chest and her decision to save the jackass pissed her off.

Amaya finally opened the bag that the wolf had dropped off, surprised to find clothes. Despite her irritation, she was happy to be going to work. She knew that her boss would only take the excuse of caring for her mother but for so long. At one point, she'd been tempted to ask Ms. Sophia for help, but pitting her boss against Levi was selfish. She'd gotten herself into this and she alone would get them out. It was the same thing she'd told Tracey when her cousin had suggested telling the heads of their family.

Going against the king of the Bayi was a death wish. One she would not wish on anyone she cared about.

She went through her morning routine, throwing on the wide legged jeans, with the white button-down shirt that had been in the bag. The designer label on the clothes was something she would've never been able to afford. Her shifter escort was waiting at the front door as he'd promised. He helped her into a high sitting black SUV without a word and Amaya wondered if she could perhaps coax him to her side.

"Remember what's at stake, Amaya." Levi's voice filled her head. *"Have a great day at work."*

She growled at the intrusion and his mocking tone. She hadn't needed the reminder. The ride to the Archive was quiet and security at the door took twice as long because of her new shadow. The front desk security had greeted her warmly, asking after her mother, but they'd eyed the shifter warily. They had confiscated the shifter's various weapons, promising to return them when he left the Archive.

Rolling her eyes, she motioned for her guard to follow her. As they entered the atrium of the archive, Amaya took a deep breath. The ceiling was three stories high, wooden slats going from one end to the other. In the middle was a huge skylight, giving a peek of the fourth floor where all the offices were and the glass of the archive roof.

Greenery filled the area, from the trees that scattered the atrium, to the ivy draped against the wall nestled among more wooden slats. Light filled the atrium from the floor to ceiling windows at the front, and where the sunlight entered the skylight.

"Wow," the shifter next to her said.

Amaya smiled. "You've never been to the Archive?"

"Not this one. Never had a reason to." He answered.

She nodded. Shifters got their power directly from the moon, they never had a need to come into the archive. It was reserved for scholars and elders mostly. Sometimes they had the littles come through with a field trip. Because this was the main Archive, there was still a lot of traffic, but people walking in off the street was rare.

Speaking of littles. In the middle of the atrium, at her favorite part of the Archive, a full class fieldtrip stood in front of a six feet black stone. Etched into the marble was a rendering of the Leonid meteor shower that was responsible for the awakening of the Southern USA. Amaya passed it every day on the way to the sacred garden, and she always paused.

"Records of the meteor shower responsible for our powers was reported in human newspapers. There were hundreds of meteorites that fell that evening. So many that a lot of the plantation owners released their slaves in fear that the end of the world had arrived. The Leonid lit the sky as far north as New York, but the Celestials hid the Akachi stones inside of that meteor shower, directing straight to us in the south."

Amaya smiled wistfully and continued on to work. She'd been equally fascinated by the story of their awakening. The Celestials had blessed the populace that had come over on the ships with power to defeat their oppressors and with that power they'd claimed the entire bottom half of what was supposed to be the United States of America. After the war between the states, the country had been permanently divided, with the Northern USA full of humans who had not been gifted by the Celestials and the Southern USA completely taken over with supernaturals. They shared the land with the indigenous humans who had chosen to stay in their ancestral lands coming to a treaty that had held for centuries.

That's not to say there were no supernatural beings in the North. The Buru vampires who regularly plagued the south came from Europe, but the northerners had tried to use them to overpower the south's inhabitants. The vampires had at one point worked to undermine the leadership here, but the rise of the Bayi and Levi, king of the vampires, had put a stop to that. She rolled her neck, immediately tense at the thought of Levi.

They reached the interior of the archive where Amaya worked and she prepared to explain again why she was accompanied by a shifter. It wasn't as if he could enter the sacred garden, but the security mages here had worked with her so long, that they knew her and would ask more questions than the ones at the door.

"You'll have to wait for me up there," Amaya pointed to a set of stairs that led a viewing room of the sacred garden. "You'll be able to see me from there as I work. No one is allowed inside. This is the only entrance and exit. No funny business, I promise."

The shifter inhaled deeply, she guessed checking her for lies. After a long moment he nodded and walked towards the stairs. Releasing a breath, Amaya used her badge to enter the front room of the sacred garden. Magic filled the small, dark room. The only light came from narrow windows at the top of the wall, which were from the skylight in the garden. At night, muted light would come in the form of the recessed lights built into the ceiling.

Power from the Akachi meteorite behind the iron door of the garden leaked into the space. The small piece that Levi had had nothing on the pieces stored here at the archive. She took a deep breath closing her eyes, enjoying the feel of it on her skin. A Mujaji guard stood at the door. Malik was one of the regular guards, his magic being able to withstand the energy from the garden. The guards rotated throughout the day, none of them in the room for more than an hour at a time.

"You in trouble, Maya?" He asked with a smirk.

She rolled her eyes. "What have you heard?"

He held up his walkie talkie. "Heard you came in with a shifter?"

"Uncle Paul," was her answer.

Malik shook his head. The two of them had worked together long enough for the male to hear stories about the trouble her uncle often got them in to.

"If you need help…"

She waved off his offer. "I got it."

The locker room where she stored her stuff was even smaller than the front room of the garden. There were four lockers and a bench that went the length of them. Going to her locker, Amaya stared at the four clean suits that hung within. The staff there cleaned and replaced them once a week. Though she called it hers, it was highly impersonal. There was nothing of Amaya inside of it. Except for the size of the suits, her locker was no different than the others. No pictures, no trinkets, jut a place to store her purse until she was done working.

Despite that, it was home and she'd missed it. She loved her job.

Sliding on the white Tyvek jumpsuit and tucking her hair beneath the hood, Amaya closed her locker, and headed back out to the front room. She took a deep breath at the iron door that kept most of the power confined to the garden. She nodded that she was ready and Malik pressed the button. The iron door slowly slid open and the power hit her full force. The chaos feeding her magic. If her hair wasn't covered, she knew the strands would be glittering in response. The meteorite was maybe three feet around and yet the punch it packed was indescribable.

The black mass was nothing spectacular but at certain angle you could see the magic shimmering around it. The piece that Raven had brought in months ago flanked the other side of the main stone. There were small stones scattered around the garden, feeding the magic that most of the mages in the south used as a power source. She stood and tilted her head and probed at the meteorite. The legend surrounding it made her proud. She was standing in front of an important piece of history for the southern USA.

She started cleaning.

Using her magic to change the direction of the sand to visually confirm that she was finished. The gray sand that surrounded the meteorite was now black with saturated power. Her job was to cleanse the darkness from it and funnel it back to the stone in a purer form. The sand held minerals that kept the rock stabilized, and her work would aid in that. As she worked, the sand slowly leached of its color. She used her power to agitate the sand, sweeping it into a circular pattern.

There was a total of ten stones scattered across the sacred garden and this was the biggest. She always started here so that she could take a breather after. No one other than Chawi witches and mages were allowed in the sacred garden. Chaos Chawi were rare, Amaya was one of six who worked in the garden on a rotating shift. The other six were all her family. All women, with the eventual same fate. She swallowed and shook the negative thoughts from her head.

"Okay class, Careful on the glass. Each archive was built on the site where the Akachi landed. There are over a dozen smaller archives but only five major ones. If you notice, the chawi below. She's carefully cleaning and shoring up the energy that the meteorite gives off. Who can tell me which of our friends use the chaos magic from the Leonid?"

Amaya didn't need to look up to know the hands would be lifted.

"The Chawi, Aziza and Mujaji," they all yelled out.

She remembered her first trip to the archive as a kid. Her mother had worked in the archive her whole life and she thought she knew everything there was to know. She was so smug. She smiled wistfully. Amaya looked up and waved at the kids, smiling at their happy faces as they returned the greeting. She loved when field trips came through her otherwise quiet shift. She gave them a show, using her hands to sweep the sand in the other direction, making the stone shimmer. The oohs and aahs made her chuckle.

By the time she was done for the day, she was wiped out. Harnessing chaos was no small magic. Dampening the residual energy from the meteorite took a lot out of her. She went through steps to decontaminate herself signaling for the door to open. Taking off her clean suit and chucking it into the basket, Amaya looked forward to collapsing on her bed. Just two weeks off and the endurance she'd built for the job was wiped out.

"See you tomorrow, Maya. A new class of mages will be in tomorrow." Malik told her.

"Really? It's that time of year already?"

The mages annually came to renew their power. It was a big to-do and the sacred garden would be crawling with Chawi and their respective mentors and elders. The shifter met her at the door as she exited.

"Even at the viewing station I could feel the power. I can't imagine how you sit in there all day." He said to her.

"Are you going to be my guard every day?"

He cocked his head at the change in subject, but nodded.

"What's your name?"

"Bronx."

She nodded. "I'm starving, Bronx. Do you have to take me straight back?"

Though Levi didn't keep his promise to make her starve, he still made her wait until he left for the night before he allowed the maid to bring up a tray. They were at an impasse. She refused to break bread with him and he made her wait to eat. It was petty, but she was going to win at least one of their arguments, damn it.

"'Fraid so."

She sighed and followed him from the Archive. The ride home was just as silent as their earlier one. Bronx pulled up to the front of the house. He didn't get out. As she opened the door, his question stopped her.

"My wolf is calm around you. You naturally dampen magic?"

"Yeah."

He nodded. "You want coffee tomorrow morning?"

She smiled. "I don't drink coffee, but I wouldn't mind a tea."

"See you tomorrow, then."

Satisfied that she and her guard would be on some kind of even footing, Amaya trudged back inside of her prison. To her surprise, her bed was full of boxes and bags. Peeking in, her mouth dropped at the clothes and luxury skin products. Her eyes widened and reluctant excitement filled her. She couldn't wait to try some of the stuff. Despite her tired body, she hummed in the shower, enjoying the gifts left for her. Wrapping a towel around her body, she prayed Levi left for work early so she wouldn't have to wait forever to eat.

She squealed when she entered her bedroom to find the object of her thoughts sitting on the edge of her bed. Amaya sighed. She'd been too tired after work to put up the spell over her door.

"What do you want."

"You're refusing dinner with me again?"

"You may have me here, but you don't have me under your control. You're a king with no crown, and no power over me."

Levi closed the space between them quicker than she could blink.

Her breath got stuck in her throat. His power probed at her thoughts, his magic and glamour raining over her. Her body heated. Levi scraped his teeth down the skin of her neck and her stomach tumbled low, liquid sliding from her sex down her leg. She couldn't help her body's reaction to him. She whimpered as need flooded her body.

"And yet, here you are, baby doll, in my grasp...under my power." His hands cupped her throat, his claws touching her skin, the sharp points lightly digging into her skin.

Her heart thundered, filling her ears with its staccato.

"You live because I will it, because I desire it. The minute that changes is the moment you take your last breath. You might wanna be nice to a brother." He hissed and let her go.

She dropped to the ground, her legs unable to support her. He watched her, a flame in his eyes.

"I ain't got but so much patience, shawty. Remember that shit next time you trying to pop off. Lock it," he told the guard at her door and she rushed to the door right before it slammed shut on her.

She slapped the door.

Why couldn't she keep her mouth shut!

CHAPTER
EIGHT

That fucking woman!

Levi stomped down the hallway, the tenuous grip on his temper getting thinner with every step he took away from her room. He hadn't intended to get into an argument with her stubborn ass. Swear he went in there to come to some kind of compromise with Amaya, but every lucid thought in his head had scattered the moment she'd slipped out of her bathroom. The towel had barely covered her curvy body, and how the fuck was he not supposed to react to her soft dewy skin?

Even now his hands trembled with his need to touch her. Why did he think having her under his roof would be easy? Levi prided himself on his calmness and every day with that stone in his possession, he was losing that. A year ago, a woman with a mouth like Amaya would have turned him off. But with her, all he could think about was fucking the back of her throat until her attitude sweetened.

"God damnit," he cursed.

Both Sebastian and Lucas were waiting there to see what he wanted to do for the evening. His life was now split into two time periods. Before the Akachi and after. Before the Akachi, Levi's schedule had been written in stone. Dinner, work and then back home. Sometimes a stop at the club to feed, but for the most part, he was predictable.

After the Akachi, Levi would be lucky to remember what he did the day prior. His friends had taken to checking in at the beginning of the night to gauge his moods. That would determine their schedule for the evening.

"You need to be nicer," Lucas chided when he met him at the bottom of the stairs.

"Nah, because shawty tap dancing on my last fucking nerve," Levi grumbled.

"You did kidnap the girl," Bas reminded him dryly.

The two of them snickered at his expression.

"When did both of you turn into captain save-a-ho?" Levi snapped.

Bas sighed and shook his head. "Luc, you got him?"

Lucas chuckled. "Yeah, I got his angry ass."

Bas walked away to go pick up Raven from work and Levi envied his friend the easy relationship he had with his mate. But like Lucas reminded him, he did kidnap Amaya. Instead of heading to the dining room to eat, he headed for the front door.

"Office tonight," he informed Lucas.

Lucas snorted but informed the rest of the enforcers. By the time Levi reached the high rise where he conducted his more legal affairs, he'd managed to calm himself marginally. Lucas exited the SUV first, his balaclava pulled down. Once his friend deemed it safe, Levi left the confines of the truck and entered the building with three other Bayi at his back. He ignored the stares of his staff as he headed for the elevator. Once he reached the top floor, Lucas locked the elevator so that no one could enter his floor without their permission.

Entering his executive office at one time had been a source of pride. He'd worked himself and his childhood friends up from the projects of Black Hollow, to an office that overlooked the whole city.

The continuous war with the Buru had cost him, Sebastian and Lucas their families, but the tragedy had brought the three of them closer together. They'd gone from fourteen-year-olds robbing for scraps, to money they couldn't spend in two lifetimes. And he was proud of that.

His office was a testament to that. The size of a small apartment, his office was the essence of luxury. From the leather furniture in the sitting area, to the mahogany desk he sat behind, all of it screamed money. Just how he liked it. It was a place where none from the Collective could look down their nose at him or the Bayi in his coven.

Lucas pulled off his balaclava and plopped down on the sofa, kicking his feet up.

"I know you got shit to do," Levi grumbled.

"I do." But his friend made no move.

"So go do that shit in your office, Mr. COO." Levi narrowed his eyes when Lucas didn't move. "Bas told you to watch me?"

Lucas shrugged. "I don't know what it is about Amaya, man, but you're a little more hostile than usual."

Levi closed his eyes and took a deep breath. Getting mad at his friend for giving him the truth would just prove Sebastian's point. Instead of saying anything else, he went behind his desk and booted his computer. Whether or not he'd be able to concentrate enough to get work done still remained to be seen. On paper, Levi ran a successful import and export business. A trucking company and freighter line were a part of that business and the logistics needed his full concentration. He had Bayi who took care of the more mundane tasks, but still a lot fell onto his plate. He blocked out his friend's presence and forced his mind to concentrate. He lost track of time, but Lucas standing in front of his desk caught his attention.

"What?"

"Governor's here."

Levi frowned. "The fuck does he want?"

He went through the million and one balls in the air to determine which ones would get the attention of the Georgia's governor but was drawing a blank. Wiping a hand down his face he leaned back in his chair.

"Fuck it. Let him in."

From the moment the older male walked in in the double-breasted suit, and a haughty expression, Levi was reminded of what business they had together. The governor of the fair state of Georgia liked to gamble, and as Levi controlled most of the illegal spots in the city to do so, the governor owed him a lot of money.

Lucas shook his head. *"He finna piss you off,"* his friend warned.

"I'm already knowing," Levi said, leaning back in his chair. "I assume you came all the way here from the capital building to pay me my money." He said aloud.

"I need more time." Kelvin explained.

There was not enough fear in the male's face for Levi's liking. Which mean the man thought he had something on Levi. Big mistake. He didn't invite the governor to sit, instead making Kelvin stand in front of his desk.

"Time, huh?"

"I could have your whole operation shut down, you know."

The false bravado pissed him off and since he couldn't take his anger out of Amaya, the governor was the next best thing. Levi left his chair and walked around his desk, sitting on the edge.

"That's the route you wanna go with this?"

"I'm...I'm just saying this relationship is mutually beneficial. I allow you to run your businesses with no obstruction from law enforcement."

Levi caught the governor's gaze and pushed his power into the male, taking satisfaction when Kelvin's gaze went slack. Levi beckoned him closer, the governor's steps choppy since his movement was all involuntary. Through the male's panicked gaze, Levi felt him fighting through his power which...

Foolish.

He brought the male closer, making him fall to his knees in front him. Growing out a claw, Levi gripped the governor's throat tighter, releasing Kelvin from his thrall. Fear had the man's breathing rapid, and his pulse elevated. Levi took pleasure in his terror.

"You run this state because I allow it, not the other way around. Don't ever forget that shit." Levi pressed his nail into the male's skin, hunger rising at the blood sliding slowly down Kelvin's neck.

"I don't have the money," the governor whispered.

Levi growled in irritation. It wasn't like he needed the money. And truthfully, the governor owing him was worth more. But, the very fact that Kelvin swaggered his trifling ass into his office made Levi want to prove a point.

"You can't kill the governor in the office." Was Lucas's bored warning.

Levi smirked with his fangs extended, making Kelvin pale. *"I can do what the fuck I want."* He reminded his friend.

Lucas snorted. *"Fine, but I don't want to hear shit when they send the police to harass you for months about it."*

Levi sighed because Lucas was right. They wouldn't arrest him, but the ensuing trouble wouldn't be worth it. He had bigger plans either way. He released the male and stepped back around his desk.

"You have two days."

"And then?"

"And then I take it from your life insurance policy." Sitting down, Levi studied the trembling male. "Or..."

"Just name it," Kelvin said quickly.

"For now, I have two freighters stuck in customs at the dock in Monterrey. I want my shit able to be unloaded, without inspection in the next couple of hours."

Even through his many attempts, Levi hadn't found a way to get through the border mage family that ran the docks. They gave him hell every chance they could and short of outright killing their elder, Lucian, Levi was stuck bending to their whims.

Kelvin stood and nodded. "I'll get it done."

Satisfied that at least one of the problems on his desk was done, Levi dismissed the male.

"Think it will work?" Lucas asked.

Levi shrugged. "Even if it doesn't it keeps me from having to deal with Lucian. I have my hands full with the witch at our house."

"Speaking of..." Lucas trailed off.

"We were not speaking of her," Levi shut that conversation down.

He wasn't ready to discuss Amaya. Until he knew what the fuck he could do to get his mate to give him the time of day, there was nothing to talk about.

CHAPTER
NINE

In the weeks that Amaya had been trapped in Levi's mansion, she never missed her evening walks with her mother. Despite the hard time she gave his men, they never stopped the strolls. She was thankful, because the last thing she wanted was her mother restless and agitated. Sliding into a light pair of linen pants and a t-shirt, Amaya left her room. She spotted Raven coming up the stairs.

"Amaya. Just the person I was coming to see."

She waited on the woman, curious. "I assume I have you to thank for the toiletries and such?"

Raven nodded. "I just found out that you were being held here. I also told them that Ms. Sophia would show up knocking all this shit over if he didn't allow you to go to work."

"Thank you for both. I was going to go crazy if they kept me locked in that room."

Raven frowned. "He locked you in?"

"My mouth may have had something to do with it." She admitted.

"Before the stone, maybe Levi could be reasoned with, but under the power of the Akachi there isn't anything I can do to help you. Where are you headed?"

"My mom likes to walk after dinner."

"Can I join you? That way you can explain how you got yourself into this situation."

Amaya nodded. Having company was a good thing. She'd only had her mother and the wall to talk to in the evenings. She gathered Anita and the three of them traipsed downstairs out a side door to the back yard. The night was humid and she was glad that she'd already wrapped her hair for the night.

Walking around the Bayi compound was way safer than in their old neighborhood. Even though her Uncle Paul took his sister out some days, Amaya had still used their evening walks to allow her mother to get out of their small house. Anita walked ahead of them, humming to herself and she and Raven hung back a bit to talk with some privacy.

"So, explain," Raven demanded.

Amaya laid out everything from the moment her uncle met her outside of her job until she found herself locked in a posh bedroom.

"I should've just let him kill Uncle Paul," she muttered as she finished.

Raven gasped. "Girl."

Her mother turned around and gave her a chastising look. Amaya held up her hands. "I didn't mean it."

At least she hadn't mean to say it out loud.

"Lucas said Buru have been at your house."

Her heart rate picked up. "Seriously?"

"Despite the fact that I don't like the way this went down, I think, in his way, Levi is trying to keep you safe."

Amaya rolled her eyes. "Is this your way of keeping me from asking to go home."

Raven shook her head. "I'm not fixin' to stop you from trying to get out of here, but I will give you something to think about. Do you think Ms. Anita will be safe at your house when you're not there?"

Her heart clutched. Her mother had so many good days in this mansion that it was making Amaya more reluctant to leave, so Raven's words were unnecessary. Still, she pondered them. Trusting her Uncle Paul to watch his sister was no longer a viable option and if she cut her hours anymore, she and her mother would be eating ramen noodles for the rest of their lives.

Going home to an empty house with no one there for her mom during her work days would be troublesome.

"Did your mate send you to convince me the king a chance?"

"Guilty." Raven admitted with an impish smile. "And not really to give Levi a chance. Bas was hoping you would stop...poking at him. His temper these days..."

Amaya sighed. "Fine."

"I've never seen him this...obsessive," Raven told her. "Mind you, I've only known him for a couple of years, but still. He's single minded when it comes to you. If it weren't for the curse, I would almost think..." she trailed off.

"What?" Amaya's stomach rolled in nervousness.

Raven shook her head. "Nothing, it's silly. We both know what would happen if a Bayi and Chawi mated, so I'm sure it's not that."

Amaya bit her lip to keep from asking more questions. She didn't want to mate Levi, so the point was moot, but...did he think she was his mate?

"Ms. Anita, would you like to have tea at my place?" Raven changed the subject and walked to catch up with her mother.

Amaya was perfectly fine talking about something else so she didn't object.

"You have a house here?" Her mother asked.

Raven nodded. "My mate built it. Some of the enforcers live in the cabins that are scattered around the grounds instead of the big house."

Raven walked with them, pointing out the other parts of the compound and explaining how Levi and his coven had expelled the Buru vampires who had set up the place. She even explained how the staff had come with the house, seemingly under some kind of spell that tied them to the place. No one had been able to break that spell.

"How is it being back on a compound?" Amaya remembered that Raven had vowed never to go back to her family's compound. They had bonded over it.

"I thought it would feel suffocating, but Bas is good about taking me out. It keeps me from feeling trapped."

"Tell me about it," Amaya muttered.

Raven gave her a sympathetic nod. "I can't believe you were impulsive enough to make a deal with a Bayi vampire," her friend gently chided.

"Trust me, Raven, I'm understanding my foolish decision."

"Are you getting along any better with Levi?"

She gave her friend a droll look and Raven chuckled.

"The only person I know more stubborn than you, is him," she told her. "He's a sweet man under all that power."

"He should rid himself of the Akachi before it's too late," her mother spoke.

"I've warned him," Raven said.

"How long has he had it?" She couldn't help but to ask.

"It's going on eight months."

Amaya frowned, that was long.

"Is your room comfortable Ms. Anita?"

Her mother nodded. "Comfortable, and you know, I never thought I would feel so safe in a house full of vampires. This is the safest I've ever felt since I left my family's compound."

Raven rubbed her mother's arm.

"It's a beautiful night. There's not a lot of people watching to do here, though," her mother said offhand.

Amaya chuckled. "That's for sure. You were liable to see all kinds of things in our old neighborhood."

"I can feel him on the edges of the compound, but now that we're not at the house he doesn't come close." Anita said sighing.

Amaya frowned and looked at her mother. "Who are you talking about, mom?"

"It's a beautiful night," her mother said instead. "Perhaps he'll come see me."

Her heart pounded. "Mom."

Anita turned to her and her eyes were clouded. "Amaya, what are you doing here? Shouldn't you be at work?"

Her shoulders slumped and Amaya gave Raven a regretful look. "I should take her back inside."

"Can we sit out here?" her mother asked, surprising her. "Maybe in the front," Anita said softly.

"Okay, mom. Rain check on tea?" Amaya asked.

"Of course. Good night Ms. Anita." Raven wrapped her mother in a gentle hug.

Her mother smiled with no recognition in her gaze. Amaya turned and walked her back around the house to the front. She was surprised to see a hanging swing on the front porch. Had it been there before? Guiding her mother gently into it, Amaya sat beside her. They sat in silence until her mother sighed.

"There. I can feel him better, now."

Amaya didn't know what to say to that. Instead of speaking, she rocked the swing softly.

"Mating with a Bayi could be so dangerous," Anita said out of the blue.

"Why would you say that, mom?" Her heartrate sped its rhythm.

"I see the way he looks at you, Maymay."

Her mother hadn't called her that in years and a lump formed in her throat.

"The longing that male has for you...it won't be long before one of you gives in. I worry for the consequences."

Amaya snorted. "I have no intention of falling for the vampire who kidnapped us."

Especially not when he kept locking her in her room.

The asshole.

She and her mother sat outside for an hour, before she called it a night. Her mother gave a little resistance but, she followed Amaya in. There was a maid waiting at the door of Anita's room. Amaya wanted to question the woman, but no matter how much she'd spoken to the young female who brought her food to her, the woman would never speak back. Amaya entered her room and rolled her shoulders. It had been a long day. She should take a shower and call it a night, except...

A restless buzz skimmed over her skin and had her headed to the French doors that separated her room from the outside. She opened them and stepped out onto the small balcony, spying Levi walking through the woods towards the mansion. As though he could feel the pull of her gaze he looked up. Her breath caught and surely, she was imagining the hunger she could sense from him. He was too far to see her face clearly and yet his eyes met hers and burned with need.

"Come to me."

His word echoed through her mind, strong and deep. Her body took an involuntary step forward to answer his call. Was it true? Did Levi keep her in some bizarre way to claim her? The blood bond that she'd willingly entered to save her family was betraying her. Even with the distance between them, her body was tuning itself to him. She wrapped her hands around the balcony to stop their trembling.

"Come, baby doll," he coaxed again.

She wanted to deny him, ignore the yearning in his voice, but it was impossible. She could blame it on the bond but...that didn't feel like the answer. The power in his voice rippled across her mind, reinforcing his order and nothing seemed to matter to her but answering it. Before she could fully register what she was doing, Amaya was halfway down the stairs to answer his call.

Impulsive.

Foolish.

It was both those things, and yet, she continued her way to the exit of the mansion. In the time it took to make it outside, she'd had plenty of time to change her mind, to consider her impulsive actions, but his magic pushed through all of that. At the door Amaya took a deep breath and reentered the humid night again, this time walking towards a male who had already disrupted her life.

"What are you doing, Amaya?" she whispered to herself as she closed the distance between them.

Before she could answer herself, her feet brought her a few feet away from where the king was waiting. The fire in his eyes sent answering heat through her body. This was a horrible idea, but even that thought didn't stop her steps.

By the time she reached Levi, his expression was greedy...reverent. She flushed under his scrutiny and her power flared in answer to his nearness. The chaos magic that surrounded him was heady, and called to her magic like nothing she'd ever experienced.

"Your escape attempts have tapered off."

"I gave you my word." That was sounding less like that the real reason. "Besides, my mother's life is worth more to me than my freedom and I couldn't risk you making good on your threats."

She studied his face for any type of insight into his thinking. There was a small tic of a grimace at her words, but it lasted barely a millisecond. Had she not been watching she would've missed it.

"I would not have let you go if that is the answer you're searching my face for."

She shivered; he was telling the truth. She should be up in the safety of her room. Playing with this man could be dangerous. With no idea how to break the tense silence that had descended over them, Amaya clamped her mouth shut.

Levi hummed. "Let's walk, baby doll."

She didn't answer, but her hand was passive as he grabbed it within his own.

"Levi," she started after a moment, "what are you planning to do with me?"

He was so quiet that she didn't think he would answer.

"All my instincts tell me that you're mine. The man in me wishes I had done things the right way, but the monster doesn't give a fuck. I'm still trying to sort it all out in my mind, but you're mine, under my roof and I have no plans on letting you go."

CHAPTER
TEN

Amaya's palm was soft against his, and Levi reveled in the feeling of her hand in his. It was the first touch from his mate that he hadn't had to coerce from her. *'Be nicer to her'* were Lucas's words to him. He could start there, but he was at a loss of how to bridge the tension between them. He'd said...and done some things that he wasn't sure she would forgive him for. Her very freedom was at his whim. That's wasn't something he imagined she'd just get over.

Honestly, he was surprised that she'd answered his call. She'd resisted their blood bond every other instance before, he hadn't expected this time to be any different.

"How was work?" He finally broke the silence.

She scoffed. "Is this what we gon' do? Just pretend like you aren't holding me hostage?"

"Maya," he warned her.

She sighed. "I just promised Raven that I would watch my mouth around you. I don't know what it is about you that irritates me so."

He couldn't help the smile that tilted his lips. "Have you tried filtering?"

"I know you ain't talking."

He shook his head. "You right. It's been a long time since I've had to censor the way I talk to people."

"My mom seems to think you're nice, so clearly you can do it with her. Although, I don't know why I expect different since you did kidnap me."

"Woman, god damnit, if you say 'kidnap' one mo' fucking time I'ma lose my shit!" He snapped and stopped walking.

"Oh, so now I can't even speak the truth. News flash, you kidnapped me, ass—"

He cut off her words and gripped her chin in his hands, slamming his lips against hers. The kiss he took from her was hard, impatient, and it didn't take long for her to return it. Her mouth opened and his tongue swept inside, his second taste of her clenching his stomach with lust and hunger. Gentling his touch on her chin, he used his other hand to cup her face, tilting his head to get a better angle. She followed his lead, her body going pliant, softening. He finally pulled back and laid his forehead against hers.

"I'll give you more that whatever you could dream to ask for if you just give me a chance, Maya."

He was close to begging and instead of getting mad at the thought of that, his mind settled. It could be the result of him being so close to her, perhaps her magic. Either way, a calmness he'd not felt in months overtook his body.

"But you can't give me my freedom?"

"I can't give you that. The beast that lives inside me now won't allow it." He slid his cheek against hers, inhaling her scent. "I'll burn all this shit down behind you, baby doll. But living without you is not an option. If I have to lock you up for your own safety, then that's what it is."

She stepped back. Her eyes were in turmoil, the battle between her heart and mind fully exposed.

"This can't happen," she said softly.

"Says who?" He closed the distance between them, needing the touch of her magic.

"Says every text ever written about supernaturals. Bayi and Chawi are not allowed to mate, most especially chaos witches. We would be hunted down and killed or worse, cursed. Do you know how much danger that would put my mother in."

That was part of her appeal to him. Even in the midst of danger, his baby doll's worry was for her mother. He understood the selflessness that went into being responsible for others. They were kindred in that way.

Still, Levi scoffed at her worry. "It's been decades since I've followed someone else's rules."

Amaya sighed. "This isn't a good idea, Levi. And since you..."

He growled, "if you say that word..."

She gave him a shaky smile. "I can admit that put myself in my current predicament, if you can admit that this would be a bad idea."

He sucked his teeth. He would never let those words leave the confines of his mouth. Instead of answering, he grabbed her hand again and tugged. She had to work in the morning and needed sleep, but he wanted time with her where they weren't arguing. Amaya sighed, but didn't take her hand back. He would count it as progress.

"Levi," she started.

"No, baby doll. I don't want to hear it."

"You kind of make it impossible to be nice to you."

He snorted but didn't say anything. The night air clung to his skin, and hunger beat at him, but he didn't want to ruin the peaceful quiet between them. So, he walked, deep into the compound where trees surrounded them and the cabins of his men were long behind him. Where not even the light from the houses reached.

He frowned and shuddered as she pulled her magic back, withdrawing it into herself. It left him bereft of the peace her presence brought to him and all at once, her mind was shut off from him. Around the edges of his thoughts, confusion and frustration churned, waiting on the smallest show of weakness from him to take over.

It was exhausting.

It made him regret that he'd tried tussling with the power of the Akachi piece. He, who prided himself on control, was now utterly helpless in face of chaos magic that came from the stone.

"Have you finally decided to kill me, King?" Her voice broke into those morose thoughts.

"Damn it, Amaya," he breathed out impatiently.

"Relax, I'm joking," she told him.

"How are you managing to shield me from your thoughts?"

A teasing light entered her eyes. "Is that rare?"

They came to a clearing where a natural pond demarked the end of their property. The path around it was worn from where he'd spent nights pacing and planning. It was a spot where his men knew to leave him alone with his thoughts. He settled onto a bench that had appeared one day, likely left by Sebastian or Lucas. Even when he didn't want their help, his friends were always looking out for him. These days, with the chaos from the Akachi piece riding him, Levi didn't pace. He sat on this bench and fought the intrusive thoughts that waylaid him when he was awake.

Amaya sat next to him, tucking a leg underneath her. "This place is peaceful. How far are we from the house?"

"Had I approached you differently, how do you think this would've gone?" He turned to study her face, ignoring her other question.

She looked surprised and intrigued, her bottom lip tucking into her mouth as she thought about his question. He wished he could peer into her mind, to get even the smallest hint of the way it worked.

"I honestly don't know," she finally answered. "We've been told to be wary of vampires our whole life. Even though my mom and I didn't live on a compound, the rules she grew up with still applied. No clubs, no after hour spots where an innocent Chawi could possibly run into a vampire. I don't relish the thought of the Chawi elders hunting me down because I've ignored their decree."

"You didn't grow up on a compound?"

"Answer my question first," she demanded.

"Which?" he played dumb.

"Not being able to access my mind seems to offend you. Is it rare that you can't?"

He shuffled uncomfortably. How did he tell his mate that with his power, he regularly— with or without consent— probed the thoughts of the people around him. He considered it defense and normally had no remorse for it. But with her...he feared her judgement, so instead of telling her all that, he answered her question simply.

"Once I take blood from a person, I usually have unrestricted access to them."

She shivered and looked away from him. "My mom...the chaos magic inside of her is eating away at her mind and eventually her body. She taught me early to shield myself from my power when I'm not using it."

He hummed. "So, you shield to protect yourself and not necessarily to keep me from your mind?"

"It's both," she admitted with a shrug. "I already gave in to you, but it doesn't mean you get to have all of me."

And didn't that exasperate him, because he wanted all of her. He wanted to own every aspect of Amaya, from her luscious body, to every corner of her mind.

"Where do we go from here?"

She turned to face him. "What do you want from me, King?"

He shook his head. "You can't help yourself."

She chuckled. "You can talk to people any type of way, but you can't take it when I do the same to you?"

"Only you can make the title sound so mocking."

She shoved him gently. "You gave me a nickname, I did the same. Now answer my question and quit stalling."

Levi lifted her from the bench and into his lap, refusing to admit to her that the name had grown on him. He loved to hear it from her lips. The feel of her soft curves on his legs was nearly his undoing. The hungry growl he released was entirely involuntary. He lifted her chin to stare into her eyes. He wanted to tell her that he just wanted her. That his spirit craved her and sought her out as the balance between monster and man.

Watching Amaya's face let him know that she wouldn't take well to that answer. So, he tamped down on the truth and gave her a simple answer.

"For now, I want us on good terms. Can we at least call a truce?"

Her eyebrows bunched. "What does that entail?"

He shrugged. "I'll take you not cussing me out every time you see me to start."

The smile on her face made his dick hard, but that was neither here nor there. Her body relaxed in his arms.

"I can do a truce. But, I want more freedom. I'm done being trapped in your mansion under your thumb."

He scoffed. "At which point were you under my thumb? You won't even have dinner with me."

"I want to be able to move freely. See my cousins, hell, make stops in between here and work, small shit I took for granted."

"Fine."

She narrowed her eyes in suspicion. "Are you setting me up?"

"God, almighty, girl," he grumbled.

She laughed. "Okay, small truce."

"The guard stays because letting your uncle go means he could get you into some more shit. Which, by the way, I never do. If it gets out that I'm getting soft..."

"Relax, King. I can't imagine anyone calling you soft and living to tell the tale."

Tucking his face into her neck, he shuddered as her scent filled his body with comfort. He would take any concession from her that he could get, if only to be able to access this slice of peace she gave him.

CHAPTER
ELEVEN

It had been three days since she'd made her truce with King Levi, and he'd kept up his end of the bargain. He allowed her more freedoms...she grimaced at that thought.

Allowed.

Gods, how far she'd fallen. A male *allowing* her to do anything. She shook her head. *Going out sad, girl.*

"So...fine ass shifter is your shadow?"

Her cousin Tracy's words broke into her thoughts. They were having lunch at the Archive café and she'd been catching her cousin up on the bizarreness that her life had become. A month in Levi's mansion and honestly, Amaya couldn't complain. His house was better than the one she and her mom rented, and despite the way the relationship started, she felt safe. Which...

Amaya hadn't realized how bad it their life had gotten. The very fact that being kidnapped and kept prisoner felt safer than her old life was a damning testament. The whole time, if asked, she would've sworn that she and Anita were fine, but their time with Levi showed her different. Yes, she was stressed about how to get out from under Levi's control, but the first words out of Tracy's mouth when she saw her had been how Amaya was glowing.

Eating regularly and not stressing about her mother's health had done that.

"Tracy, why didn't you tell me I was fucking up?"

Tracy paused with her sandwich halfway to her mouth. She sighed and put it back on the plate. "Amaya."

A lump formed in her throat. "I was, wasn't I? Living on the edge of poverty, starving myself and neglecting my mother's care just to prove I could do it alone."

"You did what you thought was right." Tracy gripped her hand. "No one can fault the way you care for Aunt Anita. Your focus was on taking care of your mom and this job. When was the last time you took time for yourself? How many times did you decline my help? The family's help?"

Tears crested her eyes. "She would've wilted away on the compound."

Tracy nodded. "Fair. That didn't mean you couldn't have taken any help. Girl, I had to sneak groceries into your house while you were working. That's ridiculous."

Her heart stuttered. "I thought Uncle Paul..."

Tracy scoffed. "Bitch, please. Your uncle is a bum."

"*Our* uncle," Amaya corrected with a watery laugh. She put her head down on the table. "I thought I was doing a good job of keeping it together."

She was realizing that even before the shit Paul had pulled, she'd been days away from burnout. Had that contributed to her giving her life over to Levi? It probably had something to do with it. She'd been exhausted and at her wit's end.

"Listen, Maya. I've kept your little situation with King Dingaling of the Bayi quiet, but say the word and I'll alert the Elders."

The laugh that escaped was cathartic. If Tracy did nothing else, she was going to make Amaya laugh.

"King Dingaling. I'm gonna call him that," she joked.

"Chile. Your mouth too damn reckless for me." Tracy stole another glance at Bronx. "So, besides living in a mansion, being followed by a sexy shifter, and eating room service for the past few weeks, how has it been?"

"Why you said it like that?"

"Because that's how it sounds," Tracy pointed out.

"I was kidnapped," she whispered.

"Technically, you're a hostage at best. Recalling all facts, you willingly gave yourself over to King Levi to save Uncle Paul, so no kidnapping involved."

"Ain't nobody ask you for technicalities," she snapped.

"All the same, cousin." Tracy waved off her irritation. "How long does this play out?"

Amaya shrugged, a petulant frown tilting down her lips. Tracy hummed, but said nothing else. They ate in silence until she couldn't take it anymore.

"Let's say I managed to get away from King Levi. Do I just wait around for the next thing uncle Paul does to get us in trouble? Do I give up entirely and show up to the compound bags and pride in hand?"

Tracy gave her an empathetic look. "Okay, but let's say you leave the king and return home. What's left there for you? Work? The constant care for Aunt Anita? What time does that leave you for yourself? When do you get to live your life?"

"I could just make the best of the situation," she slid in, avoiding Tracy's eyes.

Her cousin snorted. "You like that man. I don't know why you trying to pretend you don't. Shit, the next vampire that bites me finna get the ride of their lives."

Bronx coughed and choked, proof that he'd been listening to their conversation. Amaya groaned, praying that he didn't report it all back to King Levi. She changed the subject.

"Have you seen Uncle Paul around?"

"He's been hanging at the compound more, looking like a

whipped puppy. My mom and Uncle Dean are taking bets on how long it lasts. The food here is banging by the way. We should do this more often."

Clearly her cousin was done talking about her situation and Amaya was happy for it. She needed to really evaluate her life and the decisions she'd been making lately, and she wanted to do that at home...sulking. Taking a deep breath, she looked around the airy cafe tucked into the back of the archive. The place was busy, the quiet murmur of voices soothing. Normally, she brought her own lunch and ate it outside. But, with Bronx swiping Levi's card, she'd been hitting them up since she'd started back at work.

By day three of Bronx watching her and realizing she had been skipping lunch, he was on her ass. After that first awkward day, they had relaxed around each other, and the shifter had no problem fussing at her for not taking care of herself. According to him, Levi refused to allow her to go all day without eating, which was rich. But she wouldn't argue.

After bidding her cousin goodbye and promising more lunch dates, Amaya went back to work. She pushed the thoughts of her current situation to the back of her mind. It took all of her concentration when she was in the sacred garden. But the moment she shucked herself out of her clean suit, all of them rushed back to the forefront.

Fighting to leave her current situation had been her mission and every morning she woke up trapped in that mansion had made her feel like a failure. But, confronting the way her life had been outside of the Bayi compound brought everything into a new light. Defeat lowered her shoulders and Amaya was reevaluating her whole life. Levi claimed that he had no plans on letting her go. A week ago, that would've felt threatening, but now...

How did she feel?

That would take more than a cursory examination, that was for sure. On the ride back to the compound, Amaya asked Bronx to drive through her old neighborhood. Seeing the unkempt yards and ramshackle houses that dotted the streets had a shudder going through her body. Every where she looked was proof that had not been doing as well as she'd thought.

The rest of the drive back to the compound was quiet, with Amaya stuck in her head. What Levi proposed was so dangerous. Even more so than being held hostage by a vampire. A Bayi and Chawi mating would bring the whole of the collective down on them. That was more trouble than her uncle could've ever gotten them into. There would be no saving her mother from that.

Amaya trudged upstairs, no closer to a conclusion. Her steps slowed when she got to her room and saw Sebastian, Levi's second posted up at her door.

"Whatever it is that Levi is asking for, the answer is no." She opened the door to her room and pushed inside.

Bas followed behind her without saying anything. Curious, she turned to face him. He was studying her, his dark eyes focused on figuring her out.

"You really don't know what all this is about, huh?" Sebastian said finally.

Dropping her bag on the desk in the corner of her room, Amaya sighed. "What do you mean?"

"Let me ask you a question; what purpose would you serve Levi in your current capacity?"

"I don't understand what you mean."

"As a prisoner to the king of Bayi. Why do you think he's keeping you here and not in the basement for instance?"

Her brows furrowed, her heart racing. There really was a basement? "I asked. He won't let me go."

He scoffed.

"I..." she paused. Because she didn't know what he wanted her to say. "He kidnapped me."

"You gave yourself to Levi," he reminded her.

She got frustrated. "I won't sleep with him just because he's not making me stay in a dank basement."

Bas shook his head. "Shawty, if he was just trying to fuck, his glamour is capable of bypassing your inhibitions."

She sucked in a surprised breath. "Does he do that regularly?"

"Hell no. That's not the point I'm making. He could've come in here leading with charm but that's not him. He's coming to you his authentic self so that you accept him. Why do you think he would do that?"

She clenched her jaw because she understood what he was trying to say. "He's holding me hostage."

Falling back on that flimsy excuse were her only defense to the emotions threatening to swamp her. Sebastian had caught her at a vulnerable time. She was already reevaluating everything she thought about her current situation.

He nodded. "Some missteps have been made."

She sucked her teeth at that bit of understatement. "You and your boss got a weird relationship with the truth."

"And another thing shawty. Your mouth reckless than a motherfucker."

"Let me go and it won't be a problem." She was absolutely bluffing at this point, because where the fuck would she go?

"I feel like you be goading that man, and it's aggravating as fuck."

Amaya shrugged, because she couldn't deny it.

Sebastian sighed. "Look. For the sake of all of us who have to live on the compound with the two of you, can you please tone that shit down?"

She opened her mouth to argue, but Sebastian lifted his hand to shut her up.

"Shawty, you see how Levi is fighting with the madness. I'm just asking you to be considerate of that."

Their eyes locked in a battle of wills before she nodded. "Fine."

"Thank you. Now, go shower and shit. We got somewhere to be."

Before she could argue, there was a knock on the door. She frowned when Bas stepped away and opened it.

"What's going on?"

"You're going out," was all he said.

What did that mean? The women came in with makeup and wardrobe. She looked at Bas, who was watching her from the door.

"Amaya, I'm asking you to go into this shit with an open mind." He paused to consider his next words. "The Levi you get in this house is different than how he has to be outside. How he reacts to disrespect once he leaves here..." He left with that parting warning.

Amaya closed her eyes and took a deep breath. She understood the threat beneath his words. When she opened them, the women were there, waiting patiently.

"Let me shower first, please," she told them.

She was going out with the king of vampires. She prayed that she could control her mouth, because she imagined Levi's reputation was well earned and the last thing she wanted was to get back on his bad side.

CHAPTER
TWELVE

He was nervous.

It was a revelation and a nuisance. Amaya vexed him! Her very presence drove him mad, and yet he took every opportunity to be in her presence. He adjusted the chains around his neck in the mirror in his office and clenched his jaw. Would she show up? The women he'd sent to get her ready had left half an hour ago, and nothing about their demeanor revealed anything to him. Had Amaya given them a hard time?

'*Your highness,*' Lucas cut into his thoughts. '*She's headed down.*'

Rolling his shoulders, Levi left his home office and joined his men in the foyer. They were all in black, from the henleys down to the thick combat boots on their feet. It was their standard uniform when they left the house with him. He'd joined them tonight, his combat boots laced tight, but he'd exchanged the cargo pants for slacks and a short sleeve button-down shirt. He was second guessing taking Amaya with him to this meeting, but everyday his emotions and thoughts were growing more erratic. It seemed the only time he had relief was when he was around her.

Hopefully, that would work tonight.

Amaya descended the stairs and he damn near had to force himself to stay in place. The clothes he'd sent up looked innocent enough on the hanger. A pair of black leather shorts and a button-down shirt. He wanted her to match him and his men, so he'd kept it simple. Why then, did she look like sin, personified? She had the shirt unbuttoned to right under her ample breasts, the lace of her bra peeking through. His mouth watered as he took in the expanse of thick thighs the shorts exposed. Her makeup was done to perfection, making her dark eyes stand out more, the dark red of her lips beckoning him. Her hair was down around her shoulders in soft waves and Levi clenched his hands tight.

'Aye, man, ain't no way I'm finna deal with a possessive Levi tonight. You gotta send shawty back upstairs to put on a sack,' Lucas grumbled.

Bas snickered. *'He picked that shit out himself. He must've forgot shawty thicker than cold grits.'*

'Both of you shut the fuck up!' Levi snapped, his eyes never leaving Amaya's form.

They were both right, unfortunately. Instead of heeding their warning, he waited with bated breath as Amaya walked towards him, sashaying in heels that were sky high. He swallowed, praying he wouldn't drool and embarrass himself.

"Where are we going?" she asked as soon as she got to his side.

"A business meeting," he managed.

"Interesting," she murmured, following Bas out the door.

"Fuck me," he whispered when he saw all that ass from the back. This definitely wasn't a great idea.

He helped her into the back seat, taking a deep calming breath before he entered in behind her. With her perfume clogging his senses, Levi was damn near drugged sitting next to her.

"You look amazing," he told her softly.

A head tilt and small smile was her answer to that. Could they get through this evening without fighting? The wall around her mind slowly dropped as they rode in companiable silence. It filled Levi with relief.

"Your shield is down." He probed at her mind slowly, bracing for her rejection.

"Since I don't know where we're going, I need all my senses," she told him wryly.

He sensed that she was hiding the full truth from him, but with his first touch of her mind in days, he would take what he could. Carefully, so as to not make her defensive, he filtered through her thoughts. There was no fear in her, just a quiet curiosity that gave him hope.

Amaya turned a surprised look to him when she took in their location.

"Business meeting?"

"I conduct business all over this city, baby doll," he told her as he exited the car.

He reached in to help her, his thumb caressing the skin of her wrist. She was so goddamned beautiful. Sebastian, Lucas and two of his other enforcers surrounded them as they turned towards the club entrance. There was a line wrapped around the building, and the murmurs started the moment he'd stepped from the car. He ignored them, playing the part that he'd willingly signed up for.

Levi stood out so that his men could stay in the shadows. While all the attention was on him, king of the Bayi his men could do the work of making sure his vampires were always at the top of the food chain. There were times when it aggravated him. Like now, when he had to make appearance for the sake of being seen. With his hand on Amaya's back, he guided them into the club. Levi would've skipped this shit altogether, but the young vampire had been requesting to meet with him for months. He hoped having Amaya at his side would keep him calm.

But, with the way his mate's mouth was set up he prayed he made it through the whole meeting without they themselves fight-ing. At his side, she looked and smelled like a million bucks and it was taking everything within him to keep his hands up at her waist. He had a feeling that Amaya would cuss him clean the fuck out if he touched her in the way he wanted to. Still, he couldn't resist sliding a possessive hand down her ass. There were entirely too many motherfuckers looking at her. She gave him a warning look.

"Sorry, baby doll, but you look downright edible in this shit."

A small hum was her answer to that. Sebastian led them through the building, and Levi actively blocked out the lust that was floating in the air. The club Bas owned was a popular place for vampires to find feeders. He, himself had been a regular. For the most part, he preferred to feed in privacy, but there were times where the thrill of being in public appealed to him. They skirted the dancing couples on the way to the back room. He noted the way Amaya's eyes darted around the place, taking in everything.

"If you'd like, we can stay after our meeting."

She shook her head and shuddered. "No sense in tempting fate," she said under her breath, though he'd heard her.

He suppressed his smile. That was a good sign. Was she becoming more amenable to the thought of them together? Time would tell. As they reached the back, a waitress from VIP came over to greet them.

"King Levi. Will you be at your usual booth?"

"Nah, love. We got business to handle," Levi returned her smile.

"If you change your mind, I can make sure I serve you tonight." The female's smile was wide, her eyes filled with lust.

Amaya's irritation was instant and traveled down their tentative bond. *"Send that skinny bitch on before you piss me off. She looks like she wants to follow us home."*

"Home, babydoll? I like the sound of that." He taunted his little witch.

She growled and gave him a glare that did the opposite of what she thought it would. He wanted to cancel this whole meeting and find out what else her mouth could do. That must have slipped down their link because her look darkened.

"Not even in your dreams."

The rough sound of his laugh escaped him as he dismissed the hostess. Was it bad that he loved sparring with his witch?

He wiped his face clear as Bas and Lucas entered the meeting room before him. The meeting was with a young coven leader and he and Sebastian had debated for a few hours whether or not it was safe to meet with them. Not that either of them had fear about the meeting. Levi didn't want it to seem as though he was accessible to just any fucking body. In the end, after checking into the youngblood's background, curiosity had won out. It only took minutes before Lucas waved him in.

"On your toes, baby doll," Levi murmured to Amaya.

She nodded and gripped his hand as they entered. The male stood at their entrance.

It was the same young Bayi that Levi had seen earlier in his rise to power. The male nodded at him in greeting. Bas and Lucas spread the men out and gave the okay for Levi and Amaya to sit.

"Your highness," the male started and Levi hid his surprise.

The last time he'd seen this male, the kid had threatened to kill him because Levi had killed his father. He'd found out that the older vampire was selling out his fellow Bayi to the Buru in the area and that shit wouldn't fly with him. Levi had been methodical in his takeover of Georgia and the small town had been hours away from Black Hollow, really no consequence to Levi, but allowing the Buru even the smallest foothold would be detrimental to them all.

Levi had refused to fight the young vampire and instead had instructed the kid to come find him when he was old enough and still wanted revenge.

"Deonte, right? Why have you requested a meeting with me?" Levi didn't bother with small talk.

The kid studied him. "When you came through our town ten years ago, I promised to kill you."

Levi smirked and that lurking beast within him sat up. "Have you come to make good on your promise?"

"I came to make a deal with you." Deonte said.

The vampire next to the kid scoffed, he looked even younger than Deonte. That was when Levi had remembered that he'd damn near wiped their coven out, rooting out the disloyalty from the top down.

"We have a problem?" Levi released Amaya's hands, wanting the freedom to move as needed.

"We shouldn't be trying to eat with someone who killed our last coven master." The young vampire snapped.

"Hale, man..." Deonte tried defusing the situation.

"You feeling some type of way about that, huh?"

"Aye fuck you, man."

That set Levi off and before the kid could say another word Levi rounded the table between them and slit his throat. The vampire fell back in his chair, hitting the ground with a hard thud as he held a hand to his throat. Bas and Lucas both pulled their weapons, aiming it at Deonte while his other guards aimed theirs at the others in the room. The tension in the room skyrocketed, power and magic suffocating the occupants.

Levi spit at the kid's feet, licking the blood from his fingers. The smallest spark would set fire to the room and he could give less than a shit. His thoughts were clouded with bloodlust, daring the male to stand up so he could really beat his ass. Before shit could really get jumping Amaya cleared her throat and a breeze went through the room.

All at once the tension dissipated and the males on both sides lowered their weapons. A shudder went through Levi as his murderous thoughts folded in on themselves, leaving him clear-headed. Not that he regretted what he'd done. Levi gave her a startled look. She had calmed the whole room and hadn't so much as moved in the chair. Bas gave him a look and Levi already knew what his best friend would say. He walked back around to his side of the table and took a deep breath as Deonte helped his friend up. The skin of Hale's neck was actively knitting back together, and the earlier angry look on his face was tempered with fear.

Exactly as it should be.

The kid would need blood, but that didn't have shit to do with Levi. He would be lucky if Levi didn't kick him out of the club so that he couldn't feed right away.

"What is that you've come for?" Levi directed his attention back to Deonte.

"I was left to pick up the pieces of our coven when you left town," he held up his hand, "this is not criticizing you. Once the dust settled, I understood that the shit my father was doing was not best for us. Now, I'm in a place where I'm responsible for a coven and I'm trying to make sure we prosper."

Levi nodded for him to continue.

"Your trucks move through our city undetected, and I want to add our weapons to them."

"I talk in numbers, youngblood."

Now that the room was calmer, Levi focused on the conversation though that blood lust was still churning within him. He grabbed Amaya's hand under the table and she gave him a curious side-eye but didn't remove her hand from his. With her touch, he was able to get through the rest of the meeting with no incident.

"You sure you don't want to stay and dance?" Levi asked Amaya as they were headed back to the truck.

She glanced at the dance floor and bit her bottom lip. Her eyes widened and she whipped her gaze back forward. "That's not a good idea," she said softly.

That's what her mouth said, but he clocked the way her eyes scanned the club in interest. He reached out to Bas.

"We're staying for a few," he warned his friend.

Bas shot him a surprised look, but nodded, leading their party upstairs to the VIP area. *"You sure this is a good idea?"*

"Nope."

Bas chuckled but left him and Amaya in the area to guard the front.

"Levi," Amaya sighed.

"Quit stressing, baby doll. Consider it a chance to get out and get some air."

She eyed him suspiciously, but then nodded, conceding to his point. Levi hid his smile. This was the perfect setting to see how far he could push his mate.

CHAPTER
THIRTEEN

Maybe I'm the problem.

That thought circled Amaya's brain as she stood at the balcony of one of the most exclusive clubs in Black Hollow. Although she'd never been inside, she'd heard about it, and from the stories her cousin told her, being here with Levi was a terrible idea. If she were smart she would demand the king take her back to his compound where she could pretend that he was holding her hostage and continue being mad at him.

She was still mad at him...right?

"A drink, baby doll." Levi slid behind her, handing her a glass of wine over her shoulder.

The press of his body on her back, and his firm, possessive touch on her waist sent a shiver down her spine. His cologne wrapped around her and seeped into her senses. Even taking a shower would not rid her of the smokey tempting scent. He was too close, and too... too...everything!

Fuck, this was a really bad idea.

"Levi," she tried to move, but his hand tightened on her waist.

He leaned into her neck and her nipples tightened in the most torturous way.

"Stay still, love."

The rough command stiffened her body. She clutched the stem of the glass in her hand and worked to regulate her breathing. She could do nothing about the pulse drumming beneath his lips. He didn't even kiss her, simply laid his soft lips against her neck, the warm air from his breath bathing her skin. As much as she wanted to fight him, her body was betraying her.

"I need to feed, Amaya," he said softly.

She scoffed. "I knew you brought me here for a reason."

He released her and stepped back. She hated the loss of his weight on her back, but she was glad for the space. It allowed her to come back to her senses.

"I would never force you to do something you didn't want." There was a smirk on his face that told her the king thought he could talk her into it.

Amaya shook her head and turned from him. "Get someone else to do."

Irritation spiked through her at even the thought of him feeding from someone else, but she would stand her ground about that. If she allowed Levi to feed from her, then every wall between them would crumble and the shifting sand of her fight against him would give way. He would win, and while a part of her was starting to become resigned to that, she would not give him the satisfaction.

If she thought her words would offend the vampire she was sorely mistaken. He chuckled and pulled her back into his chest.

"What do you need from me, baby doll? I thought we had a truce?"

She shrugged. "You need to apologize for kidnapping me. But even then, I'm still not feeding you. I don't belong to you."

That.

Those words seemed to piss him off. He stepped from her and Amaya couldn't resist peeking over her shoulder. What she saw in his gaze had her pulse racing. With a little fear, yes, but the fierceness of his gaze, and the chaos magic lighting his eyes drew her closer. Her magic responded reaching out for a taste of that madness.

This was not like what she'd felt during his meeting. There, she'd wanted to calm the turbulence, but now...her power wanted to ride it. To egg it on and bask in the ensuing turmoil. Amaya took a shuddering breath, scared for the way the king called to her body and magic. It felt wild and unruly. She placed her free hand over her beating heart, as though she could stop its hard thumping with her palm.

They stared at each other, a battle of wills that both were determined to win. The king's pupils were red, pulsing with power he couldn't get a grip on. For most, they would struggle with that chaos magic, and while the king did fight to keep it at bay, through their blood bond she saw the way he embraced it in this moment.

Motion in the corner of her eyes caught her attention and Amaya swallowed a growl as the hostess from earlier sauntered her thirsty ass into their section.

"You called for me, your highness," the woman cooed.

Amaya wanted to scratch her eyes out.

Levi smirked and walked backwards to the sofa in their section, his eyes never leaving Amaya's. the madness was still there in his gaze, the peek of the beast inside of him warned her that she'd pushed him, perhaps too far. Instead of cowering, she notched her chin higher.

Levi sat, and waved his hand for the hostess to come closer. "On your knees, pet."

His tone was cajoling, yet the unrelenting power beneath the words almost made Amaya obey his order. The hostess rushed to do his bidding, dropping into position beside him on the sofa. She didn't want to watch, didn't want to see him feed from another woman and yet, losing this battle between them seemed more important to her.

Levi lengthened his fangs, and lifted the woman's arms. The

sounds around her dimmed, her vision tunneling to focus on the king and his prey. He finally dropped his eyes to focus on the hostess and Amaya took what felt like her first breath in hours.

"How do you want it, shawty?" Levi's voice had deepened, its hypnotic tone lulling the woman at his feet.

"I want pleasure," was her breathless reply.

Amaya's magic roiled around her body, her anger feeding it.

"Should I allow her pleasure, baby doll?" Levi slipped into her mind, his tone taunting, menacing.

Instead of answering, she slammed up a wall between them. His eyes hardened even more, the fire within them glowing brighter as his anger fed the monster inside of him. His gaze pierced Amaya, as he raised the woman's arm to his face. The hostess sighed in pleasure as the king bit down. He closed his mouth over her wrist, his jaw moving as he fed from her.

Seething jealousy burned through her.

As he fed, Levi's gaze captured Amaya's eyes, and the walls she'd built around her mind was destroyed with his power.

"You are mine, Amaya. No matter how you fight me, shawty, I will win this war between us."

"I'm nothing to you."

"You are everything *to me."*

She tried to turn her body, to look away from the spectacle of him feeding but Levi's magic had full control of her mind. This was what Sebastian had warned her about. The king's power was immense, and she realized that up until this point Levi had been allowing her defiance. Because clearly, he could take what he wanted and there would've been nothing she could do about it.

It was a humbling feeling.

The sounds of the woman at his feet's pleasure tore through Amaya and she wanted to shut out the image, to look away. But, Levi held her in thrall, showing her that all along, he had been playing nice with her.

"You've proved your point," she whispered aloud.

Levi released her and Amaya quickly turned her body away from the scene in front of her. Her hands trembled as she lifted the wine glass to her mouth. She guzzled the whole thing to relieve her dry throat. The king's show of power shook her, she could admit that. She'd clearly been operating under false delusions. The vampire was everything they said he was, and Amaya had allowed his concessions to her to lull her into a false sense of security.

She needed to get away from him. To get her and her mother out of this current situation, but more than ever, his little display had reinforced to her how hopeless it was. She would never be free of Levi unless he allowed it and from his words to her, that would not happen.

"I'm not a bad guy, Amaya." Levi's voice at her ear startled her.

She looked back as he crowded her body against the railing. So lost in her thoughts, she'd missed when he finished with the hostess.

"I would be a fool to believe that."

Levi nuzzled into her neck and Amaya couldn't help the shudder that shook her body. "I'm trying to play nice, baby doll."

She heard the warning in his voice. He wrapped his arms around her waist, his hand splaying against her stomach. He kissed her neck softly and she reached back and mushed his forehead.

"Don't put your lips on me." She snapped.

He chuckled and pushed his hips into her where she could feel his erection on her ass. His cheek caressed her skin. "You so mean to me, little witch, and it makes my dick hard."

"You obviously have women more willing to help you with that." She couldn't help the jealous bite of her voice.

"But I don't want other women. I want you." His other hand cuffed the bottom of her throat and her knees went weak.

The king's power wrapped around her, none of the anger and madness from before infused within it. The feeding had calmed him and that sharpened the envy filling her chest.

"Say the word, love and won't another bitch touch me, or provide for me." The taunting was back in his voice, laced with the darkest, richest lust. *"It could be you who feeds me. You who gets the pleasure and pain of my bite."*

His voice filled her mind; his magic laced within it. It poured over her like thick syrup and once again, it was brought home just how much Levi had been sparing her from his power. She'd known that vampires could use their voice to mesmerize, but up until now, she hadn't been on the receiving end of it. Her body loosened and moisture slipped down her thighs in response.

He swayed behind her, dragging her into the motion. They moved in synch with the music blaring from the speakers below and Amaya closed her eyes. Levi used that opportunity to push his thoughts into her mind, showing her all the things, he wanted to do to her. It was so vivid she could almost feel the way the cool sheets would cling to their sweaty bodies. It was easy to be swept into the fantasy he spun.

"It could be so simple, baby doll." One hand tightened at the base of her throat while the other lightly skimmed up her thighs.

The king growled, and the carnal thoughts spinning through her mind became darker. Flashes of her blood on his chin, her back arched in ecstasy as he fucked her raised her body's temperature. A whimper escaped her, and Levi nipped her skin lightly.

"You need me to beg, my love?"

Amaya shuddered, seconds from giving in to him. He stiffened at her back, his head raising. It took her a moment to shake away the sensual fog from her brain. Levi released her abruptly, his hands going to the banister to cage her in. She blinked and turned to look at him. His eyes weren't on her though, they were on the dance floor below. She followed his gaze and gasped. Her uncle was there, with one of the elders of her family. Both were in a conversation much too serious for the current setting.

Would they be able to see her up here?

Her stomach dropped and anxiety made her hands shake. What would her family do if they caught her in Levi's arms? She needed to get out of here.

"We need to go," she told Levi.

He nodded, but his gaze was still on the scene below.

"Now. Please, Levi. I can't let an elder see me here."

His gaze hardened and the look he gave her held none of the warmth from before. She thought he would argue with her, but he simply nodded and pulled her away from the railing towards the exit. Sebastian and Lucas met them at the bottom of the stairs.

"You spotted him?" Bas asked.

Levi nodded sharply. "I will deal with him later."

Amaya wanted to ask him what he meant, but more importantly than that, she wanted to get out of this club before she was spotted.

CHAPTER
FOURTEEN

What am I doing?

It was a question Amaya asked herself every night when she crawled into the comfortable bed Levi had provided for her. Thoughts of escape had long faded as she got used to the luxury surrounding her and her mother. Had that always been a part of his plan? To make her complacent in the gilded prison in which she was trapped?

It had been a week since they'd gone out and the king had made no moves on her. He'd barely acknowledged her as a matter of fact. There were no more invitations to dine with him and he'd stopped dropping by her room.

Sad to say...she missed it.

That night in the club he'd taken off his mask and shown her the monster underneath and still, she missed him.

His show of power should've scared her straight, but these past few days of his silence had left her with nothing but time to think. And instead of fear for the awesome breadth of his power, Amaya felt emboldened. At any point he could've pushed past all her objections, ignored her lack of consent and taken what he wanted from her.

But Levi didn't do that.

He was moving at her pace. It made her feel secure when everything and everyone around her would probably tell her that she had no right to feel that way.

Restless, Amaya kicked the blanket from her body and sat on the edge of the bed. She looked at the clock and cursed. It was barely four am. She had to be to work in a few hours, and yet, tonight, sleep had eluded her.

Giving up the pretense altogether, she left the bed and her room. The compound was quiet around her, the stillness making her feel as though she were alone in the house. As she neared the bottom of the stairs, the noise picked up and the enforcers that made Levi's personal army moved around downstairs. She followed the noise to the dining room she'd been avoiding since she'd been kidnapped.

Her eyes widened with surprised as she observed the men eating dinner? Breakfast? It was the end of their day, either could apply. They stood as they noticed her and she waved them back into their seats.

"I don't mean to intrude," she told them softly.

Her nerves fluttered under their curious gaze. Sweeping a look around the table, she tried to convince herself that it wasn't disappointment deflating her chest. Of course, he wasn't there. She would've felt his energy had he been. The male she recognized as Lucas stared at her, a small smirk on his lips.

"He's not here."

She nodded, her cheeks burning, and hastened her steps to the kitchen and her original destination. Tea was her plan. Not that she thought it would help her sleep. But, she was up, and it would give her something to do other than brood in her room. Amaya's heart thumped as Sebastain entered the kitchen from the patio door.

"I didn't mean to startle you," he said softly.

"That's okay. I was just going to make tea."

Why did she feel the need to explain her presence? Sucking her teeth in irritation at herself, she headed for the cabinets to see what they had. Sebastian said nothing, but he moved around her and silently showed her where everything she would need was. She nodded her thanks, avoiding his gaze.

Gods, she was jittery.

His presence still loomed close, pausing her movements. She looked up and found him studying her, much the way Lucas had.

"Yes?"

"Levi is in a...mood. It would be best if you avoid him." His deep voice filled the kitchen with its quiet rumble.

She dropped the kettle onto the stovetop and sighed. "You act like I want to be in this mess."

Even as she said the words, guilt niggled at her. Amaya could admit that she needled at Levi, but what else was she supposed to do? Sit quietly while he controlled her life? Irritation made her skin hot.

Prodded by his silence, she closed her eyes and gathered her temper under control. "Fine, Sebastian."

He said nothing else, but she didn't breathe easy until his presence left the kitchen. She went through the motion of making her tea, her mind a jumbled mess. As though drawn by an invisible thread, her gaze strayed to the patio beyond the doors. The king lazed in one of the pool loungers, his body tightly coiled despite his pose. She hadn't even realized they had a pool. She shook her head. Staying in her room was just silly at this point. If she was going to be a prisoner the least she could do was enjoy the amenities.

Chuckling to herself at the silly thought, Amaya poured a generous portion of honey into her tea, her gaze unerringly straying to Levi. Through the panes of the glass, she could see the contemplative look on his face. He was still dressed for work, except the dark burgundy shirt he wore was opened at the throat, the tie loosened down to his chest. His suit jacket was strung over the back of the lounger where he lay. She should take Sebastian's advice and leave him be, and yet, as she bit her lip, her thoughts were reckless, impulsive.

"What am I thinking?" she muttered as she headed outside.

From the moment the door opened, Levi's eyes tracked her. With every step she took towards him, his predatory gaze scraped across her nerve endings, igniting both wariness and heat. The wild feverish look in his eyes gave her an idea of what was happening. Battling the Akachi was overtaking the king of vampires. Instinctively, her magic reached out to him, soothing the jagged edges of his power as she settled in the chair beside him.

"You should leave me, baby doll." His voice was barely a whisper. "I'm not fit for company."

Despite the desperate plea, Levi's power and presence did not diminish. If anything, the vulnerability stripped the ego that usually concealed the man beneath that power. It left him bare, exposed... and that made her feel...safer? Her eyes raked over his form. He was so gorgeous, it was unfair really. His dark copper skin gleamed under the recessed lights of the pool. She wanted to run her touch over his smooth, chiseled face. Her hands flinched as though she could feel the roughness of his close-cut beard.

Memories of the other night invaded her thoughts and her breath hitched. A part of her so desperately wanted to recreate the images he'd thrusted in her mind.

Damn it, she was getting side tracked.

"What are you sulking about?" She gripped her mug tightly to hide her trembling hands.

Common sense told her to go back inside, but somehow, she couldn't override her instinct to stay. Prodding him in his current state was not smart, but the other alternative was to reach out and pull him into her arms in an effort to soothe him and that was infinitely more dangerous to Amaya.

He narrowed his eyes at her question. "I figured after the other night you would be too smart to taunt me," he said in answer.

She shrugged with a nonchalance she didn't feel. "Bad night at work?"

"And if I said it was?"

What did she say to that? She fell back on flippant, much more comfortable there with him.

"What do you do anyway?"

"Kill people."

Her stomach dropped along with her jaw.

Levi scoffed. "Isn't that what you think of me?"

She rolled her eyes and released the breath making her chest hurt. She turned to face him full on and he didn't have so much as a smirk on his face. Amaya sipped her tea and debated what she wanted to say to him. He shifted on the lounger in clear agitation before sighing. Her magic reached out to him without any input from her, soothing him and long moments later his shoulders relaxed. He closed his eyes and laid his head back on the lounger. She thought he wouldn't say anything else to her and she debated whether or not she should leave him, but his eyes opened and he pinned her with a look.

"Did you sleep well?"

She tucked her leg underneath her. "Well enough. My mother is settling here and I don't know how to feel about that."

Where had that come from?

"She's more lucid here," she continued, the words tumbling out.

He nodded. "I enjoy our dinner talks."

She frowned. "You talk to my mother?"

"If you would leave your room more, you would know that I'm an exceptional host."

She scoffed, fighting a smile. She refused to find him charming.

"What do you talk about?"

"You nosy ain't it?"

She gasped affronted. "Excuse me for trying to make conversation with your grumpy ass."

"You're the reason I'm grumpy."

"What the fuck did I do to you?" She asked sitting straighter.

"Your very presence pisses me off!"

141

That hurt her feelings more than she was willing to let on. "You could let me go. I didn't ask you to keep me here."

He sat forward, his face inches from hers. "Don't you think if I could let you go I would?!" Rage and something like helpless desperation covered his face. "I can't sleep, or feed or fucking concentrate with you under my roof, but to let you go would destroy me."

She didn't...how...gods, did he truly mean that?

The silence between was weighted and pressed down on her until it felt as though she was trying to breathe under water.

"Levi," she finally managed.

"Go, Amaya."

Just him saying her name and not the nickname she'd been accustomed to shook her out of the stupor and had her darting inside the house because...what did she say to him? To that? She didn't take a full breath until she reached her room. She closed the door and leaned against it, her heart rate thumping. So much information to process, she didn't even know where to start.

CHAPTER
FIFTEEN

Levi waited until he was sure Amaya had made it upstairs before he stormed into the house. He skirted the dining room. To run into anyone else would set off the temper he was barely holding on. He needed...fuck!

What did he need?

He needed her.

Just her being next to him outside had calmed the beast that had rode him all evening while he'd tried to work. Her presence had soothed him and from the moment she stepped outside her magic had reached inside of him, balancing the conflicting drives between he and the monster the akachi had made him. And instead of basking in that he went and opened his mouth. Sitting next to her was both calming and stirring.

His night hadn't been particularly bad, but he'd spent the majority of it missing her. Frustration had his temper frayed. He'd thought giving her space after their night out would lower the tension rising between them, but if anything, it made it worse. Backing away from her had been hard, and he'd braced himself for her renewed requests for freedom. But no escape attempts or pleas came from his mate.

That confusing fucking woman.

He'd let his mask slip at the club and showed Amaya some of the power he hid from. Slipping into her mind past her shields had been easy, the warning in the action clear to them both. The thought that she would fear him had crossed his mind at the time, but it mattered more to him that he showed his mate just how much restraint he'd had when it came to her. It had worked, but it had also backfired.

The same images he'd projected into Amaya's mind played in an endless loop in his. Sleeping was out of the question, and most days, all he could do was sit in his office and watch her sleep. Did he feel bad for the camera he had in her room? Hell no. Did it make him a bit of a creep? Absolutely.

Something between them had to give, or it wouldn't only be the Akachi driving him to madness.

The moment they'd gotten back from the club, his stubborn witch had fortified the shielding over her mind, keeping him from any hint of her thoughts. All of the progress he'd made with her had been wiped out, but at least now he could lower the façade he kept over his emotions.

Let her feel how she affected him.

Except...Levi didn't know how she was feeling and that was starting to make him doubt himself. Was he doing the right thing holding her here? Yes, it would keep her safe, but that had nothing to do with his reasoning. Had he been less impulsive, he could've found a better way to get her to stay. For once in his long life, Levi found himself unsure...

He'd been ruler over his small coven for close to thirty years. Small shit in vampire years, but in that time, every step he'd taken had been determined, solid. His impulsive decision to secure the Akachi had been the source of his missteps and he was finally at a place where he needed to admit that.

He couldn't rule his people this way.

What then was the alternative? Run to the archive, hat in hand, and give back the stone? Pride wouldn't let him do that, and it had nothing to do with the Akachi. He paced his room and fought with his fractured thoughts to gauge a solution to that. Bas's touch through is mind, caught his attention.

"Your highness, a messenger from the collective has requested a last-minute meeting."

Levi checked the time on his watch... there was maybe an hour before dawn. He growled at the disrespect. Even though the Bayi were not beholden to the sun, but it was still presumptuous for the Collective to send a lackey to him at this hour. They'd caught him in just the right mood too. This messenger would be lucky if he left this compound alive.

"I'll be down in a moment." He told Bas.

His steps were unrushed as he headed downstairs. As he entered his throne room, Bas and Lucas were posted up next to his throne, their balaclavas in place. Settling into his chair, he eyed the Collective's messenger. The male cleared his throat.

"What can I help the Collective with?"

"The Collective is requesting a meeting with you," the male announced.

"That could've been an email," Levi said dryly.

"There are rumors that you are holding a Chawi captive. I've been sent ahead to see if there were any truth to that."

"Rumors? As in more than one person speaking on the business that happens behind my compound walls? Does the council have spies among me?"

There was a small flinch from the male betrayed the truth. Levi kept his face neutral even while anger bubbled in his chest.

"Bas."

"I'll get to the bottom of it." Bas reassured him, already knowing what he needed.

If there was a spy among his people, he wanted to know who it was immediately. He focused his attention on their guest. Using the power he'd received when Sebastian mated with Raven, he raised the temperature in the room. It could be the remnants of Amaya's power curtailing his temper, but instead of lashing out as he wanted to do, he regarded the messenger and allowed his anger to show on his face. Sweat beads gathered on the male's temple, and he tugged on the collar of his shirt. Levi let the male sit in the heat and uncomfortable silence for a long moment before he finally spoke.

"If you think I'll allow the collective to further disrespect my coven by allowing them to search my compound, you must be dumber than you look."

"Either that or he's ready to meet the final and lasting death," Sebastian spoke next to him.

The messenger lowered his head. "There was no disrespect meant. I've only come to deliver the message and—"

"—And put eyes on the unruly vampires." Levi growled, his patience snapping. "You have three minutes to get the fuck off my property or I'll send you back to your masters in pieces."

The messenger flinched, bowed and rushed from the room. He shared a look with Bas that needed no words to translate. Sebastian nodded and he and Lucas both left the throne room on the hunt for the source of the rumors leaving his compound. He knew part of those rumors came from Amaya's uncle. Trusting the male to keep his mouth closed had been a fool's errand, but he'd promised Amaya that he wouldn't kill him.

Sucking his teeth in aggravation, Levi leaned back on his throne, his gaze staring but unseeing. Putting aside the notion of a traitor, his thoughts immediately went to Amaya. The Collective could send as many messengers as they wanted, request however many meetings, and he still would not give her up. The insatiable need she aroused within him was all consuming and though it frustrated him, he would take whatever small part of her he could get.

As though just the thought of her had summoned her attention, Amaya entered his throne room. She hadn't knocked or asked permission, simply strolled in, her shoulders back a confident sway to her walk. She was exquisite. Amaya was dressed for work, a two-piece linen pants set that fit her wide hips, flaring towards the floor. The shirt was sleeveless the whole thing an emerald green color that made her brown skin glow. Levi licked his lips and shook his head. The way the woman filled out clothes was ridiculous. It made his chest rumble with hunger.

"I wanted to talk to you," she said softly.

Though she tried to appear docile, Amaya's strength was hard to hide. He motioned for her to come closer. She stared at him and he waited her out. Finally, after a few seconds of contemplation, she rolled her shoulders and closed the distance between them. Still, she stopped a foot away from where he sat on his throne.

"Before the other night, we were getting along better, right?"

He scoffed but said nothing. The mischievous smile she gave him had his dick stirring. Amaya stepped closer, until only inches separated them. His heart thundered. Levi breathed in slowly, drawing in her scent.

"Have you come to ask a favor of me, baby doll?" His voice was thick with need.

She put a hand on her hip and narrowed her eyes. Before the smart quip he knew was on the tip of her tongue could leave her mouth, she sighed.

"It's more a favor for you."

Intrigued, he sat forward, his elbows on his knees. It put him even closer to her face. Their breath mingled and Levi wanted nothing more than to kiss her.

"Do tell."

"The Akachi piece. If you'll allow me. I can help you shield it in a way that will allow you to keep it, but also keep you from feeling the ill effects of it."

He tilted his head, curiosity momentarily tapering off his lust.

She continued, rushing her words out. "I understand why you feel the need to have it. I don't know the first thing about running a coven, or any group of people for that matter, but I do know what I feel when I allow myself to touch your mind." She bit her lip, the first sign of her nervousness. "My mother has those same scattered thought patterns and they will only get worse if you don't do something with the Akachi."

"Are you worried for me, baby doll?" He lowered his tone, his eyes watching her mouth, the lust back tenfold.

Amaya was worried about him? Did that mean she was softening towards him? Had his distance from her worked?

She sucked her teeth. "Do you want my help or not?"

He couldn't help the smirk that lifted his lips. There she was. The meekness Amaya had entered the room with was completely gone and in its place, the fire that he'd become accustomed to when dealing with his mate.

"I will consider it." He acquiesced.

After all, it was already something he'd been considering. Her offer was timely. It would allow him to keep his pride at the very least. But...

"Would it still give me access to its power?"

Amaya reared back in surprise. Smoothing back her hair, she considered his question.

"I'm sure there is a way...I'll work on that."

He nodded and leaned back in his chair in satisfaction. He reached out his hand, tugging on the waist of her pants to pull her up the stairs to stand between his legs. His hands skimmed her hips.

"Then I thank you, Amaya."

She smiled at him and the entirety of his bad mood dissipated. He would say yes to almost anything to have her smile at him like that on a regular basis.

"Give me a kiss, baby doll." He said softly.

Their eyes met, and he watched the progression of her emotions as she debated his request. He saw the moment she fell back onto teasing to break up the intensity of the moment.

"Is that how you ask, King?" She licked her lips.

Levi tugged on her shirt until her head lowered and their mouths aligned. He took the kiss he wanted, unwilling to wait on her answer. He sucked on her bottom lip, sliding his tongue inside. She sighed and lowered her body to his legs, perching on the edge of his lap. He braced her and deepened the kiss, his need consuming him. He lost himself in the kiss, cradling her head as he devoured her mouth. A moment later, Amaya's hand went to his chest and she pulled back.

"I need to go," she said softly, scrambling from his lap.

Levi allowed her to go, fighting to keep the hunger inside of him corralled. He watched the way her hips swayed as she headed to the door, his body an inferno. She left the room without another word and the moment the door closed behind her, the shadows of his mind crept in and wiped away that euphoria. He sighed in frustration. Yes, it was time for him to deal with the Akachi stone. But more importantly, it was time to stop being passive about his mating. He wanted Amaya, and he was done waiting on her timing.

CHAPTER
SIXTEEN

Concentrating on work was hard. The kiss with Levi was circling her brain in an endless loop. It was different from any of the other kisses they shared. In this one she was a willing participant. They'd shared a kiss the night they'd walked together, but that was different. Levi had been angry, trying to shut her up but this one...

Her body was flushed with heat and it had nothing to do with the magic flowing through her as she worked. She'd made so many simple mistakes today that she gave up and took her lunch early. She could feel the phantom touch of his lips on hers, and even his grip in her hair. She shivered at the hard slam of need that hit her as she sat down in front of her locker. She shouldn't have let him kiss her. It was inviting trouble and temptation. Every day under his roof it was getting harder to resist the king.

Their teasing was becoming second nature to her. There was no longer any real bite to Amaya's sarcastic quips. Half the time she did it to see that small smirk that graced his lush lips. She was in so much trouble.

"Amaya."

Malik's voice startled her out of her thoughts. She gave him a small smile. He was in the doorway of the dressing room.

"Ms. Sophia wants to see you in her office."

Her eyes widened in alarm. What did the director of the archive want with her? She hurriedly stripped from the clean suit and hung it up for use after lunch. She walked up to Malik.

"Did she say what she wanted?"

Malik shook his head and gave her shoulder a reassuring squeeze. "She didn't seem like it was bad, though."

Though her heartrate was still thundering, his words helped. She nodded and headed towards the third floor where Ms. Sophia kept her office. She smiled at her assistant and was waved to go back. She knocked to announce her presence and opened the door at Sophia's prodding. The office was small, but the elegant space was filled to the brim with bookshelves. The windows in the office were narrow and lined the top of bookshelves behind the desk. They let in just enough light to make the place cozy, but not enough to ruin any of the ancient texts that Ms. Sophia liked to surround herself with. Amaya was sure the director could have access to a bigger office, but it was indicative of the kind of person Sophia was.

"You wanted to see me?" Amaya stopped just inside the door, not wanting to intrude in the space.

Ms. Sophia stood, a warm smile on her face. The woman looked like a librarian plucked right out of novel. She wore a brown plaid dress, cinched at her waist with a thick leather belt. The skirt swept the floor, the square-neck top of the dress demurely caressed the collar of her neck. A large pair of glasses adorned her angular, beautiful face.

"Yes, have a seat." She waved to the chair in front of her glass desk.

Amaya sat, and looked around, anxious energy had her stomach fluttering.

"Relax, Amaya." Sophia settled in her chair and leaned forward, her elbows on the desk.

The older woman studied her. Amaya fought not to squirm under her attention. Sophia was the director of this archive and head director for all of the archives across the south. The only thing she required of those under her was that they did their jobs as outlined. Amaya didn't understand how being called into her office could be anything but serious.

Sophia's eyes softened and she sighed. "There are rumors that you've gotten yourself into a bit of trouble."

"Me?" Amaya pointed at her chest. "What kind of trouble?"

"It's going around that you're being kept against your will by King Levi."

Amaya swallowed, and forced her racing heart to slow down. "Not against my will."

At least not technically. And certainly not now. As everyone kept pointing out to her, she'd willing given herself to the king. Sure, her uncle's life was in the balance, but a month under Levi's roof and for some reason, it felt unfair to categorize her stay as 'against her will'. Sophia studied her before sitting back in her chair.

"Your uncle has told the elders of your compound otherwise," Sophia said.

Amaya took a deep breath and rubbed a circle around her temples. Paul wouldn't be satisfied until Levi yanked his heart from his chest.

"That's funny. Did he tell the elders that we are in the position we're in because he stole from King Levi and tried to sell the item to the Buru?"

"What?!" Sophia threw her hands up in shock. "What did he steal?"

Amaya shook her head. "It's not my place to tell King Levi's business. But, because of Uncle Paul's actions, Buru were spotted at our house more than once. If anything, King Levi is keeping my mother and I safe."

Saying it out loud gave Amaya paused. She didn't know if the Buru were still circling their house, but regardless, she felt safe at

Levi's house. She and her mother were well taken care of, and despite Levi's reputation, nothing had happened to Amaya that would justify getting him in any type of trouble with her family's elders.

What did that mean?

She was softening on the idea of staying with Levi. When was the last time she'd asked him to let her go? Even when he'd given her a chance to do so?

"So, the rumors that King Levi has a piece of the Akachi are not true?"

Amaya fought to keep her face from betraying her and in turn Levi.

Sophia removed her glasses and rubbed her eyes. "Amaya. I don't have to tell you how this all looks."

"King Levi saved our lives." Was her answer to that.

"If it's true. I would hope that you of all people understand the danger that poses to not just King Levi, but anyone around him. I'll let you keep his confidence, but if it is true, then please talk him into bringing it here."

"Taking on the Buru can't be an easy job. I can understand if he thought have the extra power was worth it."

And now she was full on defending him. But, she couldn't tell her boss that she'd already offered to shield the Akachi for the king without admitting that he was in possession of a piece of the meteorite.

Sophia's hand cupped her own chin as she looked away in thought. After a few moments of silence, she turned back to Amaya.

"In that case, shielding it would protect Levi and the Bayi under him."

Amaya nodded, understanding what Sophia was saying.

Her boss sighed. "So, then I don't have to worry about you? How is Ms. Anita?"

"My mother is fine. Better than fine actually. I don't know what it is about the Bayi compound, but she has more lucid days than not."

"Are you sure this is a good idea, Amaya? Your family has offered to take you and your mother in."

Amaya bit her lip, this was where it got tricky. Before, pride had kept her from accepting her family's help, but now, with how well she and Levi were getting along and how her mother was doing, she didn't want to risk her mother at their family's compound.

"All my life, mom has stressed how much she never wanted to go back to the family compound. I don't think I could do that to her."

Sophia nodded. "Stress can make her condition worse."

"Exactly. I don't know what it is about the Bayi compound, but some days she even feels like her old self."

Her boss frowned. "One would think that being in the middle of a coven of vampires would stress her more. You know how the Chawi are about vampires and witches mingling."

"Trust me, I understand the risk."

Sophia leaned forward and rested her chin in her hand. "Is there a possibility of you mating with King Levi?"

Her cheeks heated at the blunt question. "I've explained to the king the outcome of something like that happening."

"That's not a no, Amaya," Sophia said softly.

"It's all the answer I can give you. The way we met...it's not something that's conducive to mating. And besides, I have no desire to add a curse on top of all this other business."

"A curse?" Sophia's eyebrows furrowed. "Is that what the Chawi are told?"

"Is that not true?"

Sophia shrugged. "I don't have a clue. To my understanding of Bayi/Chawi relations, it's a dangerous combination, but a curse...I've never heard that."

It was Amaya's turn to frown. "We're told that matings between the Bayi and chaos Chawi specifically can result in a curse."

"And yet, in their presence, your mother's condition has not deteriorated."

It wasn't a question. Sophia's eyes darted around the room as her face turned contemplative. Amaya was afraid to voice a thought that had been circling her mind for weeks. She'd been observing her mother, and Anita had been improving. In small ways at first, but these days, according to Levi, he was having full-fledged lucid conversations with her mother. That was impossible weeks ago.

Sophia's eyes speared her. "You think being at the Bayi compound is the reason?"

Her heart thumped a hard rhythm. Amaya wiped her sweating hands on her pants and cleared her throat.

"Anything I have is purely anecdotal."

Amaya knew how Sophia was when it came to information and facts. There was no room for feelings in research according to her boss. Sophia barely allowed speculation when solving problems.

Sophia hummed. "Do you imagine King Levi would allow for me to visit your mother?"

Amaya shrugged.

"This is incredibly dangerous speculation." Sophia insisted.

"I understand," Amaya assured her. "I wouldn't do anything that put my mother at risk."

Sophia sighed. "I'm gonna put Raven on this curse business. You know how I am."

Amaya nodded, Sophia liked to be two to three steps ahead of information.

"I'll quiet any rumors on my end. The last thing I want is for the Collective to become involved. They are rabid about pairings and I can only imagine how they would react to a chaos Chawi living with a vampire."

"There is nothing going on between me and King Levi," she hastily assured Sophia.

How long that statement would stay true was anyone's guess. After that kiss this morning, Amaya would have to be vigilant, because Levi was slowly breaking her down. With every interaction between them, they were getting closer.

Her boss eyed her skeptically. "Just do what you can about

shielding the Akachi allegedly in his possession and I will see what I can find out."

Relief relaxed Amaya's shoulders. "Thank you, Ms. Sophia."

"Mating is…It's not something that can be denied and while I share the collective's worry, I don't have the same pessimism. I would never want you to miss that blessing."

Her throat clogged. "It's not gotten as far as that." Amaya whispered.

"Let's hope it stays that way until I can be sure you won't be endangered by whatever this…turns out to be."

"I can do that," Amaya said softly.

She got up and left, feeling buoyed by the conversation. It felt good to have someone on their side, even if she hadn't decided whether or not she would even attempt a relationship with Levi. One thing Sophia was right about…she needed to shield the Akachi. If Levi still felt the same about her after the influence of the meteor was gone, then…maybe she would consider whether a mating to a vampire was worth ensuing trouble.

CHAPTER
SEVENTEEN

It took two days of research and then another day for Amaya to formulate her plan. With a bit of finessing and promising Bronx that she would be on her best behavior, she was finally ready to go to King Levi with her plan. Excited, she rushed into the mansion, hoping to catch him before he left for the evening. It had taken her a little longer than she'd planned to finish everything.

The first person she ran into was Sebastian as she slid her shoes off at the foyer. "Is the king available?"

Sebastian nodded and tilted his head for her to follow him. She clutched the small box against her chest. She'd gotten permission from Ms. Sophia to take some of the shielding sand from the sacred garden for the 'hypothetical' stone in King Levi's possession. Her boss had quickly agreed, happy that some part of their conversation was being dealt with. Raven was coming out of the dining room when she spotted them.

"What's going on?"

"I'm going to try and convince the king to allow me to shield the Akachi." She answered distracted.

Her mind was on the steps she would have to take to actually shield the stone. She had a feeling that her plan would work, but there was always the possibility that it wouldn't. The border mages had come to the archive a couple days ago for their yearly sabbatical to the sacred garden. It had given her an idea that would hopefully work for the meteorite piece Levi had.

Sebastian's steps stalled and he stopped walking, focusing his attention on Amaya. "You've spoken to Levi about it?"

She nodded. "The other day. He agreed if I could still give him access to its power."

"And you think you could to that?"

"I can absolutely shield it and take away its ill-effects on the king. The other part is a little trickier, but I'm fairly certain it will work."

Sebastian studied her before sharing a look with his mate. Amaya knew that he and Raven were probably talking telepathically. She waited them out.

Raven turned her gaze to her. "I'll come with you."

Amaya nodded because it wouldn't make any difference with what she had to do. Instead of the throne room, Sebastian led them to a door down the hallway from it. When the door opened, Amaya realized it was Levi's office. It was different than his throne room. There was nothing ostentatious about this space. She'd expected it all to be dark and intimidating, but his office was warm. The walls were dark gray, somewhere close to blue, where it felt both cool, but welcoming.

Behind his oak desk was a book shelf that went to the ceiling, but none of the books were in any discernable order. They looked well red and loved on, the spines varying in thickness and color. There was a section of obvious serious tomes, but the others looked like journals and fiction books. It surprised her. His desk was clean, a small lamp, his desktop computer and a couple of notebooks. There was a plush carpet under the desk that softened the marble floors in the room. A tv on the wall behind them was on, the low hum of the news running.

Levi watched the trio of them as they entered his office. 'What's up?"

Raven and Amaya sat in the chairs in front of his desk. Looking around his office, she was impressed. To the left of her in its own alcove was a softly lit area that held a gold service set covered with glass decanters of various liquors. The dark rich burgundy of the liquid told her that it wasn't just wine or cognacs.

"Baby doll," Levi prompted, drawing her attention.

Amaya set the box in her arms down on his desk. "Remember what we talked about the other day?"

He nodded.

"Well, I found a way I think will allow you to access the power of the Akachi and keep you mind shielded."

Levi leaned back in his chair, his eyes betraying his surprise. Amaya opened the box on his desk, passing the lid to Raven. She pulled out the smaller box inside, moving aside the small bag of sand. She stood and handed him the smaller box. Levi opened the box and his eyes softened.

"You bought me a pocket watch, baby doll?"

Her cheeks heated under his intense scrutiny.

"It wasn't that much. I got it from this..." she tapered off her words. "Yes, I did."

He didn't need to know where she'd gotten the watch. It was clear for anyone to see that the piece of jewelry wasn't expensive. She'd had the shopkeeper clean it so that the antique gold shined brightly.

His eyes warmed as he fingered the chain, stopping at the opaque stone she'd attached to it. "What's the stone for?"

"It's called a heartstone. Mages use it to carry the power of the Akachi with them. It amplifies their power without the side effects of the meteorite."

"And you can tune his piece to do the same?" Sebastian asked from his position from behind Levi. Bright interest lit his eyes.

Levi smiled at her and Amaya's stomach fluttered in pleasure. It pleased her to please him. That was scary, but she was resigned to her fate at this point. No, she couldn't mate with Levi, but that didn't stop her from enjoying his company and this push and pull between them. Levi stood and turned to his bookshelf. Hidden behind Sebastian, she couldn't tell what he was doing, but a few moments later, a small snick sounded and the book shelf behind him opened.

Raven gasped. "A secret room."

Both women leaned forward, scrambling from their chairs when Levi motioned for them to join him. Amaya grabbed the bag of sand, anxious to see what Levi hid. They entered the room, its cool temperature coupled with the magic thrumming in the room. It sent a small shiver down her spine. Without setting eyes on it, Amaya knew he hid the Akachi somewhere in this room. The cold touch of chaos magic skimmed her skin, calling to her own power.

How had her uncle found this room?

"He didn't," Levi told her. Always a ghost in her mind. "The Akachi was once in my throne room."

Amaya glanced around the room. Lined along all three walls were lighted shelves. Some held weapons...a lot held weapons, but some were walled off with glass, varying artifacts and antiques displayed behind the cases. Power thrummed throughout the room and it took her breath away. Levi stopped walking and stood to the side. In the center of the floor was a waist high cabinet and on it sat the Akachi stone. It was on top of some kind of cloth. Amaya narrowed her eyes and studied the cloth, realizing it was supposed to serve as some type of shield. She shook her head and gave Levi a small smirk.

He returned her smile. "Blame it on my arrogance. Firefly warned me."

Raven sighed behind her.

"Is this where you want to keep it?" Amaya asked, gripping the small bag of shielding sand.

At his nod, she upended the bag of sand in front of the meteorite. Immediately the stone flared and power pulsed out.

"Shit," Bas cursed, stepping back. He pulled his mate back with him.

Blocking them out so that she could concentrate, Amaya spread the sand around the small stone until it was completely surrounded. She infused the sand with her power, building the shield up until the power was walled inside. Raven and Sebastian breathed easier behind her, even though the power still resonated throughout the room, it had gone from a roar to a whisper.

Next, she worked on the meteorite itself. Probing its power, she saw the tendrils connecting Levi to the Akachi. The ropes were thick and bright, the vampire's power feeding the stone as much as it was feeding Levi. She'd never seen anything like it. Her magic flared to dig deeper and Levi grunted. She sent him an apologetic grimace.

"The watch," she requested, holding out her hand.

Levi placed it in her palm, stepping closer to her.

"I need you to touch the stone, please."

He didn't ask questions and for that she was relieved. She didn't think she could quite explain what needed to be done. Taking a deep breath, she lowered her mental walls to take advantage of the blood bond she had with the king. It made this next part easier. Carefully, she worked to untie and separate the tendrils connecting Levi to the Akachi. There was some resistance, places where their magic was so similar that the power was fused together. Amaya lost track of time as she worked, but eventually, she was able to remove the traces of the Akachi from Levi's mind. His sigh of relief brushed her temple, but she kept working, moving on to the next part of her plan.

If she took even a moment's breath, the Akachi piece could reach for him again, or worse, one of the other of them in the room. Most likely her as she carried the same type of power within her. Biting her lip in concentration, Amaya fed the Akachi's magic into the heartstone. It heated in her palm, glowing softly as it absorbed it. The crystal was capable of taking a much bigger magical load, so the small stone in Levi's possession wasn't too hard.

Her breathing was labored as though she ran a mile flat out, but she pushed passed the exhaustion and continued to feed the power. When the crystal was saturated, Amaya tapered off her magic. The once opaque heartstone was now blood red, the color swirling with gold. Levi removed his hand from the stone, his shoulders slumped, sweat on his brow. As hard as it was for her, she knew he'd also gone through it.

Rolling her shoulders, Amaya turned her attention to Levi, handing over the pocket watch. He was staring at her with awe on his face.

"What happens next?" He asked softly.

"Keep this on you. It's tied directly to you, so even if someone tried to steal it, the heartstone won't work for them." She wiped her forehead and closed her eyes to steady her body. "From what I can discern from the mages who use the heartstones, it amplifies their power. It should do the same for you, without the madness."

Her eyes popped open when Levi pulled her into his arms. He kissed her, and unbidden her heart soared. With the protections down around her mind, and her body vulnerable due to the expended magic, Amaya couldn't fight the feelings swamping her. An ache built within her, her stomach clenching, and a thud between her leg that matched her heartbeat. His kiss swept her under a tide of need and the whine that left her mouth was the closest she could come to begging him for more.

It wasn't until Raven cleared her throat that Amaya remembered that they weren't alone. Levi stepped back first. Amaya's knees were weak, so she clutched his arm tightly, keeping herself upright. Levi laid his forehead gently against hers.

"I owe you, baby doll." He whispered against her lips.

She started to ask him if the price was her freedom, but something stopped her. Where would she go? Back to the life where she struggled and her mother deteriorated under the stress. Amaya stepped back, conflicted with what her heart wanted and what was right.

"Whose journals are these?" Raven asked, breaking the moment between them.

Amaya straightened her clothes, gathering her wits together.

Levi cleared his throat. "My grandmother's."

"Can I?" Raven rand her fingers over the spines of the worn leather books.

Levi nodded, and Amaya watched her friend, just to keep from getting lost in the king's eyes. She was precariously close to breaking apart. Her emotions were raw, her mind conflicted. She tucked away her magic, but was too exhausted to erect the walls over her thoughts. Her hands shook as she brushed a hand down her face.

"Levi..." Raven looked at the king with wide eyes. "Your grandmother was Bria Cauly?"

Levi gave Amaya one last lingering look before giving his attention to Raven. "Yes. The journals are hers. There were more, but they were all I could save when war with the Buru ran us from our home."

"How many do you have?" Excitement threaded Raven's voice.

Levi looked around. "The four there are the only ones that are left. There are some from others."

"Do you mind...can I take them to the archive to study them? I'll bring them back when I'm done."

"What is so interesting about the journals?" Bas asked, weighing Levi's weapons in his hands.

"Bria Cauly is the last true Bayi hybrid. She's the reason the Collective was started." Raven informed them.

Levi frowned. "The Bayi were banned from the Collective."

"Levi is the first they've allowed in a hundred years. Why would the Bayi be kept out of an organization they started," Bas asked, stepping closer to his mate so he could read over her shoulder.

"It has something to do with her father," Raven shrugged. "But, I can probably give you a better answer if I can study the journals. Do you know what years they are?"

Levi shook his head. "Bas and I grabbed what we could."

"I was more focused on weapons and the gold his father had hidden." Sebastion said.

"Those served us better than the journals have," Levi told his friend with a smile. "You understand how private I am, firefly."

Raven nodded. "I'll keep these to myself. Maybe I can find out why the Collective hates Bayi."

Bas snickered and Levi scoffed.

"You already know?" Amaya asked, curiosity getting the best of her.

"Bria Cauly single-handedly saved the south from the tyranny of her father, and as payback, the survivors shunned her. My father never told me the full story, but he said they blamed his mother for something they lost. What they lost, I don't know, but they used my great grandfather's destruction as a reason to keep the Bayi out of the Collective."

"Until Levi gave them no choice," Bas's sinister smile held both threat and pride.

"So, you haven't read these?" Raven asked.

"Over the years, I've read my grandfather's and fathers. I wanted...needed guidance on how to run a coven. Bas and I were, what, fourteen when the Burus swept through our coven?"

Bas nodded in agreement.

"Survival was my single focus for past six or seven decades."

Amaya's eyes widened, doing the math in her head on Levi's age.

"Not one hundred, my ass," Raven gave her mate a narrow-eyed look.

Sebastian laughed. "it's too late, Red. You're stuck with me."

Amaya didn't understand the joke, so she let it go. Raven gathered the journals, gave Levi a grateful smile and escaped the room before he could change his mind. It left Amaya and the king in the privacy and intimacy of the secret room alone. She took a shuddering breath, suddenly very tired.

"Let me take care of you tonight," Levi said softly, tipping her chin up to look at him.

Her eyes widened. "That's not a good idea, Levi," she whispered.

"I like it better when you call me King," he told her, kissing her softly.

Her stomach fluttered and a soft shiver trickled up her spine.

"Come." His tone left no room for argument.

He guided her from the secret room and out of his office, locking it behind him. Amaya's breath hitched when he bypassed the hallway that led to her room and kept going. She'd never been in this wing of the house. Levi opened the door to a room that was twice the size of hers. The black she was expecting in his office was present here. Dark luxury was the only way she could describe the room. Was she really doing this? Her body disobeyed her mind and stepped further into his bedroom. Gods protect her from her impulsive decisions.

CHAPTER
EIGHTEEN

L evi didn't know how to feel. Amaya was finally in his bedroom. He slid his hands in his pocket and watched as she wandered through his room lightly touching his things. He tried to see the space through her eyes. His king-sized platform bed took up the middle of the room, the bedding was dark gray. The wall behind it was black, with gold marbling, warmed by the shelves and lighting on either side of it. To the right of his bed was his sitting area, the fire place electric, control by a switch.

His room was comfortable and his sanctuary. He led her into his bathroom, satisfied with the pleased look on her face. Her eyes took in the sunken tub and the oversized shower with three shower heads. There were fresh towels folded under the floating sink, which he grabbed for her.

"I'll bring you something to sleep in," his told her.

"Levi," she started.

He closed the distance between them. Her exhaustion was evident in the simple fact that she hadn't yet erected the shield over her mind. Levi didn't feel a twinge of guilt for greedily exploring her thoughts. He read her wariness, but underneath that was her own need that she was actively fighting. It soothed a part of his ego that worried none of his efforts were getting through to her. Instead of taking advantage of it, he simply pulled her into his arms.

Amaya sighed, resistant for only a moment before her arms went around his waist. She rested her head against his chest and Levi closed his eyes, savoring the closeness.

"No shit tonight, baby doll. I just want this with you." He assured her.

She nodded, and he relaxed.

"Shower and I'll have clothes for you when you come out," he murmured against the top of her head.

She raised her head and Levi couldn't resist. He kissed her lips softly, no heat, just comfort. He unwrapped his arms from her and stepped back, leaving her to take a shower. His body yearned for hers, but he would not go back on his word to her. When he re-entered his bedroom, he felt Bas prodding at his mind. He sat on the edge of his bed and tuned into his friend.

"What's wrong?"

"That meeting with the Collective...they've called it for tonight."

Levi sucked his teeth in aggravation. It wasn't as though he didn't work at night, but still. He had plans. He looked towards the bathroom door, and resigned himself. Ignoring a summons from the Collective would invite more trouble than it was worth. Levi had no desire to be fighting on two fronts.

"Let me settle Amaya," he told Bas.

His friend pulled from his mind and Levi closed his eyes to stave off the anger building in his chest. He opened them a moment later, realizing that two hours ago, before Amaya had shielded the Akachi, a summons like this would've sent him off the deep end. There was still residual anger rumbling around in his mind, but in the last few months, that anger would've swelled until he blacked out. Already he was feeling the effects of her shielding. Cloudiness still hovered around the edges of his consciousness, and were it not for his single focus on caring for Amaya, he was sure his thoughts would be jumbled. But, there was a distinct difference. He put his head in his hands, leaning forward on his knees.

Fuck.

Amaya had saved him.

He summoned a maid with instructions to go to Amaya's room for her clothes as well as the dinner she'd skipped to help him. Ten minutes later, the small knock on his door signaled that his order had been followed. He allowed them entrance, his mind already getting into work mode. The maid left as quiet as she'd arrived.

He looked up at the door to the bathroom opened and she stepped from the steam filled room. Her skin was dewy, the towel wrapped tightly around her voluptuous body. A red haze of lust took over his mind, and his teeth ached.

"Come, baby doll," he called to her, unable to stop the power infused in his voice.

The indecision was all over her face. She bit her lip, her thoughts racing.

"No funny shit," he promised, holding up his hands in surrender.

She nodded and walked over to him. He gripped her waist once she was within touching distance.

"You're so fucking beautiful," he whispered, kissing her soft stomach through the cloth. He stood and towered over her, leaning down to put his forehead against hers.

"I have to go handle some business, but I want you here when I get back."

Her eyes widened, relief one of her central emotions. There was some regret, but Amaya quickly pushed it aside. It was fascinating finally being able to see the way her mind worked. She compartmentalized better than anyone he'd ever observed, moving her feelings and thoughts around easily. It seemed her top priority was her and her mother's safety. He fucked with that and knew that talking would never get him anywhere with Amaya. She needed to see action, feel security. He would make sure that she felt that and more going forward.

"I can just sleep in my room."

"Please, baby doll."

Her eyes softened and she nodded. "Be careful with your business."

He smiled and kissed her collarbone. "You worried about me, my baby?"

She mushed his forehead. "Where are my clothes?"

"The middle of the bed. You'll be here when I get back?"

She moved from between his legs and leaned over to grab the underwear and gown that had been left for her. He growled as her towel lifted, giving him a small glimpse of her ass. Gods above, he was seconds from jumping on this woman. He needed to leave before he fractured all the good will he'd gained.

"I'll be here, King." Was her sarcastic reply.

He chuckled, headed towards the door. "I had your dinner brought up. Eat, and then rest, baby doll."

Her impish smile buoyed him on the way out. By the time he reached the bottom of the stairs, the lightness of his interaction with Amaya was gone. In its place, the anger that he'd tried to set aside flared. Bas and Lucas met him at the door. Less than an ago, he was in a place where not even aggravation could touch him, and now, as he pulled up to the archive where the meeting was taking place, Levi prayed he could hold on to his temper. His mate was going to sleep in his bed and he wasn't there to enjoy it. His hand slipped into his pocket and he caressed the ridges of the antique watch Amaya had gifted him. It was inexpensive, but the gesture...it pleased him. It meant that she was thinking of him, even when they were separated. One more sign that his effort was paying off despite their bad start.

"Do you feel different?" Bas asked as they slipped into the armored SUV.

"Hell yeah," he answered his friend.

"Then maybe there is something to kidnapping your mate," Bas joked.

Lucas laughed from the front seat.

Levi shook his head. "I'm in a good mood, so fuck both y'all."

Bas snickered.

"How we doing this?" Lucas turned and asked, his face back to serious.

"I don't care what the fuck they want, I'm not letting baby doll go."

Bas sighed. "Okay. We matching energy then."

Levi nodded. They get to the archive where the meeting was being held. It was considered neutral territory since none of the leadership in the Collective trusted the Bayi on their compounds.

He scoffed. Fucking cowards.

Sophia, the director of the Archive met them at the door. She nodded her head. "Your highness."

"Ms. Sophia," Lucas said. "How you doing this evening?"

"Don't start your shit, Lucas."

"Not you recognizing your baby under the mask," his friend taunted.

Sophia's light skin flushed. Levi could only shake his head. She led them to the conference room on the ground floor where they were meeting. They entered the windowless room and it was already full. Slated wood panels covered the walls, matching the décor in the atrium of the Archive and the room was filled with tall green plants in the corner to soften the starkness of it. A long oak table was in the middle of the room polished to a bright sheen, reflecting the warm light from the sconces floating over it. Leather chairs lined both sides of the table, and all seven on the right side were full, leaving the entire left side reserved for Levi. It seemed he was in the hot seat tonight. Lucas and Sebastian were behind him as he sat and faced the stern looks of the elders gathered.

The Collective was comprised of the heads of the oldest families in the South. There were representatives for the Chawi tribes, one for the witches, the other representing the warlocks. Four elders from the Mujaji were seated, the storm gods electing one representative for each element. Raven's grandfather was the head of the fire Mujaji, and that motherfucker already had a grudge against the Bayi, thanks to her mating with Sebastian. The last representative was from the Border Mages and his warden. The supernaturals were in charge of securing the borders of the entire Southern United States and operated in pairs for some reason.

None of these bastards liked him, but if asked, he would say that Lucian hated him most. It could be as simple as the two of them butting heads at the docks or maybe that bitch had a personal beef with Levi. He didn't know and he didn't care. Fighting with Lucian was tiresome, and were it not for his spot on the Collective, Levi would've been buried him somewhere in the woods. Their various staff members stood scattered behind them and around the room, some taking notes, some looking bored.

Levi eyed them all with barely concealed disdain and waited to see who would speak first. It didn't take long. The Chawi representative sitting forward in his chair.

The male glared at Levi. "You've been accused of kidnapping a young chaos Chawi."

Levi sucked his teeth at the male's emphasis on young. Tried to make his shit sound sinister, he wasn't falling for the bait, thanks to Amaya. He gripped the heartstone in his pocket to ground himself. Before he could answer the doors opened and a young female entered bringing in drinks.

"*They acting like we at a fucking tea party.*" Lucas complained.

"*Gotta play the game,*" Levi told them, accepting the wine from her.

"I haven't kidnapped anyone." Levi answered the accusation after he'd taken a sip of the wine.

He frowned at the taste, pushing it aside. The warlock eyed him before shaking his head. He waved for the staff to open the door and Paul walked in, fear and defiance on his face. Bas scoffed behind him.

"This finna go to shit quickly," Lucas warned them.

"Thanks to Amaya it won't," Bas assured his friend.

Levi tuned out their conversation focusing his attention on Amaya's uncle. What did he think going to the Collective would accomplish? Every time he saw this motherfucker he regretted his promise to Amaya not to kill him.

This time it was the witch who spoke. "This male has accused you of not only kidnapping his niece, but also her mother, his sister. He claims you are holding them hostage."

Levi shrugged. "Amaya has taken refuge in my home, yes."

"You forced her!" Paul interjected.

"you want to tell the class why?" Levi challenged.

Paul swallowed and lowered his gaze.

"Nah, don't get quiet now. You been spreading my business all across this fucking city. Speak up. Have you told your elders that your sister and her daughter are at my house because you stole from me and tried to sell to the Buru, making it unsafe for them to go home?"

The whole of the Collective turned their attention to Paul then. He blanched under their scrutiny.

"What did you steal?"

"An Akachi piece."

Levi speared him with a look that promised retribution. He would have one more thing to beg Amaya's forgiveness for, because as soon as he left here, he planned to put her uncle in the dirt.

"You have an Akachi piece?" Lucian snapped.

"What goes on in my compound is of no concern to this council." Was his answer.

Lucian growled, his eyes turning cagey. "It's against the rules for a chaos witch and Bayi to fraternize."

He said that shit like it meant something to Levi. Shaking his head, he leaned back in his chair and eyed Lucian.

"This collective wanted to keep excluding the Bayi. Ya'll gotta pick. You want us to abide by your rules or you don't want us here? You can't have it both ways."

"We've invited you to a seat," The water Mujaji elder spoke.

Levi nodded. "the negotiations were only finalized weeks ago. If I remember, there were still objections."

The elders grumbled.

"You will release the girl." The warlock demanded.

Levi laughed. He had to. It was either that or crash out. They would take Amaya out of his house over his dead body.

"Amaya stays with me and I won't be debating that. So now what?" He sat forward table, hands clasped.

The collective shared another look.

"Mating between the Chawis and Bayi are forbidden. that is non-negotiable." The witch declared.

Levi said nothing. He would have her and wasn't shit they could say about it.

"If it's about the girls safety she can be protected at her family compound." The Earth Mujaji spoke.

"Thats not happening." Levi said.

She and her mother would be appalled to know that the council wanted to ship them both to their family compound. From the way Amaya talked about it on their walks, he knew she would never voluntarily go. The grumbling around the room started again.

The witch narrowed her eyes. "You won't budge on this?"

"You're being unreasonable about this." This from the fire Mujaji. There was nothing but hate in his gaze.

"Was there any other business we needed to discuss this evening?" Levi asked as politely as he was able to.

"I told you, we should've never allowed the Bayi into this Collective. They are completely lawless." Lucien snapped.

"Not completely," Levi warmed him softly.

He could show them lawless if it came down to it. The elders read the threat in his words.

"This is getting us nowhere." The warlock said.

"On that we agree." Levi stood. "Perhaps we can discuss this more rationally on our next meeting."

Levi left the room ignoring their yelling.

"I thought you would lose your shit in there," Bas told him.

"The thought had occurred to me, but then they would use it against us all." Levi reminded his friend.

"Facts." Lucas chimed in. "What are you going to do about Paul?"

"Ask Amaya for forgiveness after I bury his ass." Levi promised.

Lucas chuckled and they all got back into the car.

CHAPTER
NINETEEN

Deep in his gut, Levi knew something was wrong. He couldn't quite pin down what it is, but his head was spinning, and his instincts were telling him that something wasn't right. So, when a black SUV blazed through the stop sign and rammed into his armored truck, his body was already loose, expecting it. Sebastian cursed next to him as the truck spun. No one in the car panicked, simply braced for the attack they knew was coming.

They could've easily stayed in the car, it was reinforced for this very type of situation. But, Levi didn't relish sitting still while motherfuckers played in his face. Skipping the gun he kept in the holster at his waist, he reached behind him for the short sword he kept in the car. He watched as another SUV sped towards them, tapping their bumper to pushing them towards the embankment on the side of the road.

"Ain't this some shit," Lucas called from the front seat.

Levi could only shake his head as the SUV finally came to a stop from its spin. Vampires rushed from the other SUV, and from their red eyes, he knew they were dealing with Buru. They immediately started firing at the Bayi's truck, their bullets slamming into the plated metal and reinforced glass. Next, footfalls sounded on the roof and Levi smiled in anticipation. He made eye contact with his driver in the rear view mirror.

"On my count, release the emergency seal on the sunroof." Levi ordered softly.

James nodded and they all tensed as the footsteps stop. Levi opened the sunroof cover and watched as the Buru lifted his foot.

"Now," he ordered softly.

And as the Buru stomped down, Jame released the seal. The Buru dropped from the roof and Sebastian shot him twice, heart and head. The silver in his gun guaranteed the vampire wouldn't get back up. Levi tossed the Buru's body into the air and as predicted, the hail of gunfire followed its progress. Using the distraction, Sebastian and Lucas rolled from their seats and out the door, returning fire the moment their feet hit the pavement.

The return fire was then directed at his men, leaving Levi open. Instead of going through the door, he propelled himself from the sunroof, flying towards the other SUV, smoking in the middle of the intersection from its collision with Levi's armored vehicle. The occupants had their windows down, firing, but Levi was quicker, darting straight for the driver. By the time the male registered Levi's trajectory and tried to lean out and fire, Levi had already drove his hand into the driver's chest. Still, the male managed to get one shot off, his bullet grazing Levi's arm. The back passenger tried to exit, but Levi slammed his foot into the door, closing it on the Buru's leg.

The force of the kick, coupled with the metal of the door crushed it and the Buru howled out in pain. The vampire fell on his back. The Buru in the front passenger seat lifted his gun to fire, but was blown back by the sawed-off James fired at him. Levi nodded at his enforcer in gratitude and turned his attention to the backseat and the Buru writhing in pain. Snatching off the destroyed back door, Levi locked eyes with the Buru, his magic immediately ensnaring the vampire.

Heat from the heartstone in his pocket was Levi's first clue that his power was being amplified just as Amaya had suggested. It took less than a second for Levi's magic to take hold of the other vampire's mind.

"Quick question. Who's in charge here?"

The Buru, stared at him with glazed eyes and a slacked jaw. "You are," he answered in a slow cadence.

Levi chuckled. "No doubt. But who sent you here?"

The Buru shook his head, confusion clouding his features. Sucking his teeth, Levi sent two silver bullets into his skull and backed away from SUV.

"Boss. We got more company!" Lucas called out.

Sebastian finished off the last two Buru and cursed. "I'm not doing this shit all night."

His best friend went around to the back of their SUV and popped the trunk. When Sebastian lifted, he was balancing a rocket launcher on his shoulder. He fired it at the speeding SUV and they all watched dispassionately as it hits its mark, sending the SUV flipping as it exploded. Sirens sounded in the night and they all shared a look.

"Into the car, your highness," Bas said, rushing to put back the launcher.

They rushed into the SUV, and it took some maneuvering, but James navigated around the now decaying bodies, speeding them away from the scene.

Lucas looked back at the carnage. "What are the odds that a bunch of Buru attack us as we're leaving the meeting?"

"It's definitely not a coincidence," Levi muttered.

Adrenaline was still pumping in his system, making his heart race, but he frowned. The fight was over and they were well away, why then was his body still tense. He rolled his shoulders, trying to shake off the feeling of impending doom. Levi took deep breaths as Lucas and Bas talked around him. Their voices sounded muffled, and a cloudy film of confusion separated him from reality. He had become accustomed to that feeling ever since he'd taken possession of the Akachi. Had Amaya's shielding worn off?

"Levi."

Bas's voice cut through his thoughts, and Levi shook his head to focus. Heat filled his body, searing the blood in his system. Sebastain leaned over him, his face swimming in and out of Levi's vision. He looked down and tried to lift his hand, but nothing happened.

"Your highness," Lucas's tone was sharp. "Speed this shit up, James."

Levi wanted to tell them that he was fine, but no words left his mouth. He reached for them on the mental link they shared, but even that was hard to grasp. What was happening to him?

"Levi." Sebastion called out to his mind.

"Wrong." Was all Levi could manage.

Their panic rose, feeding his own, and Levi closed his eyes, fighting through the heaviness invading his body.

Sebastian tapped his cheek. "Keep your eyes open, Levi."

He nodded? Maybe? Everything was swirling around him, his vision swimming and he was fairly certain keeping his eyes open was going to be impossible. He felt his body lifted, and all around him, loud voices tried to break to through the fog overtaking him. Time lost all meaning, as Levi fought to hold onto to some semblance of sanity. His vision had gone dark around the edges, even as he wrestled to keep his eyes opened.

Chaos seemed to surround him. His body was jostled, and more voices joined the others rising and falling around him. Soon though, one voice stood out, his pulse instantly slowing, a calmness filling him. Next was a scent. One that raised the beast inside of him as hunger gripped his body. Need consumed him, feeding the fire already burning through his system. A moan sounded. Was that him?

"King."

Levi leaned towards that voice as it cut through the disorientation. Soft hands touched his skin and his muscles tightened. His fangs descended and a ravenous craving seized him. A face, blurred and soft drifted into his line of sight and Levi whimpered, the hungry sound the only one he could make as his body betrayed him. He fought the paralysis in his limps to reach for her.

Amaya.

He would know her anywhere across any timeline.

He'd longed for her to touch him with the tenderness she was now displaying. Even through the fogginess he could see the distress covering her face. Since he couldn't touch her physically, he reached for her mind, frustrated when even that path was blocked to him.

"I got you, King." Her soft voice washed over him and comforting him through his anguish.

Instead of fighting, Levi relaxed into her solace and closed his eyes. If it were for the last time, at least he'd gone in her arms.

CHAPTER
TWENTY

What was a stronger word for despair? What could she use to describe the fear that had nausea churning in her belly? Amaya could think of no words as Sebastian and Lucas led an overheated, thrashing Levi into his bedroom. She'd awoken ten minutes ago in a cold sweat, unsure of the source. There were long moments of confusion until she realized that she was in Levi's bed, waiting on him to come home.

She scrambled from beneath the covers and Lucas and Sebastian carefully put Levi into his bed.

"What happened? She shook off her grogginess, her focus solely on Levi.

"We were attacked." Sebastian informed her. "A healer is on her way up."

Amaya nodded and moved closer. The king was sweating, his copper skin flushed and heated. She rushed to the bathroom and wet some wash cloths with cold water. A healer chawi woman was coming through the door as Amaya reentered the bedroom. With brisk movements, the witch examined Levi.

"Was he bitten by a Buru?"

"Fuck no," Lucas told her.

Amaya stayed back as she examined him, sick with anxiety.

"Call for your mate, Sebastian," the healer ordered. "He has been poisoned."

"Poisoned?" Angered rippled through Amaya and she rushed to the other side of the bed, pushing Lucas away.

Wash cloths forgotten, Amaya reached for Leve's forehead, closing her eyes to concentrate. He was hot to the touch. Sending out her magic, she felt the foreign poison all throughout the king's body. Who would do this? Who had gotten close enough to do this?

Raven entered the room and Amaya moved her hand, but didn't give up her spot next to Levi.

"What's happened?"

"I need you to burn the poison from the king's blood," the chawi ordered.

Raven's eyes widened but she rushed to the bedside to do as the witch requested.

"Your fire won't burn him?" Lucas asked her.

Raven shook her head and tilted her head as she tried to figure out logistics.

"The king is tied to her," the chawi explained. "but, the healing fire wouldn't hurt him regardless."

"What do you need, Red," Sebastian asked.

"I need him moved, because I don't want to set fire to the bed."

"I can fix that," Amaya interjected, happy to have some way to help.

Using her magic, she wrapped Levi into a protective circle, his body lifted, hovering over the bed. The Chawi frowned, but backed away so that Raven could work.

"What the fuck," Lucas whispered.

Amaya nodded for Raven to continue. The fire mujaji lifted her hand and blue flames engulfed the king, burning off his clothes. The fire licked across his skin for a second before it seemed to seep beneath the surface. Levi's body glowed, his veins a red path throughout his body. There were dark spots along that path that signified the poison. Amaya held her breath at the sight of how close the poison was to reaching the king's heart. She'd never seen anything like it.

Levi thrashed, a moan releasing from him that brought tears to her eyes. The Chawi stepped forward as Raven worked, using her magic to monitor the progress. The room was silent as they all waited with bated breath for Raven's fire to obliterate the poison. Dawn was approaching as they worked, the noise of the shutters rumbling shut the only sound in the room.

Holding the shield was exhausting Amaya, so she could only imagine the amount of power Raven was expending. Sebastian stepped forward as his mate stumbled, his hand going to her shoulder. That boosted Raven's power and it flared brighter as the Mujaji doubled down on her effort. An hour later, the sound of the Chawi's voice broke the heavy silence.

"it's done." The witch announced.

Breathing out in relief, Raven released her magic and Amaya slowly allowed his descent onto the bed. Covering him quickly, Amaya used the washcloth she'd discarded to wipe the sweat from his face. She watched patiently as the witch examined Levi for a final time, nodding that her work had been completed. Sebastian led his mate from the room, promising to return once he had her settled. The Chawi took her leave along with him, leaving her and Lucas to watch Levi.

"Can you bring me some warm water?" Amaya requested. "And a towel."

She wanted...no needed to care for him. It scared her to think of the frustrating male she was falling for in so vulnerable a position. She paused and blinked, realizing where her thoughts were taking her. How did she get from barely tolerating to falling?

"Do you need anything else?" Lucas asked, setting a storage container full of water down on the bedside table.

"I'm just going to clean him off so that he can rest better."

Silence descended between them as Amaya wiped down the king with trembling hands. Every now and then, a soft whimper would escape Levi and her heart clenched. Was he still in pain? She pulled the sheet back and swallowed as she got her first clear look at Levi naked.

She wasn't even gonna go there.

Lucas chuckled behind her but said nothing. All the same, her cheeks flamed and embarrassment churned within her. Instead of focusing in...that area, she started at his feet. Gently, with care she was becoming to realize she had for the king, Amaya cleaned his body. She was sliding the blanket back over his body when Sebastian reentered the room.

"How is Raven?" She asked him.

"Sleeping, which is where I'm headed next. Has he awakened at all?"

Lucas shook his head. "He needs to feed. He hasn't been feeding for shit."

Both their eyes turned to her.

"Why hasn't he?" She finally asked, unable to take the weight of their stares.

Sebastian gave her an incredulous look. "Shawty, be fucking for real. His mate is under his roof, I'm sure he can't feed from someone else."

Her mind immediately went back to a conversation with Levi when he'd told her as much himself. Guilt wiggled its way into her mind, fighting with her justifications. After all, it wasn't her fault that the king couldn't feed, despite what they said. Circumstances outside of her control had put her in Levi's path, and she wasn't to blame for the tumultuous start to their relationship.

"You need to try and get him to feed from you." Lucas interjected, his tone a lot nicer than Sebastian's.

She nodded and scanned Levi's face, her heart softening more towards him. Though she was sure he would hate being described as such, there was a beautiful innocence to him as he lay recovering.

The power and authority he commanded while awake was dulled, though still apparent. His thick lashes lay against his cheeks, his lips parted slightly as he slept, his countenance serene. In spite of their start, she was in a position to help and her heart wouldn't allow her to deny him.

She took a deep breath. "Do I need to cut myself, or..."

The logistics of feeding the king while he was unconscious eluded her. Sebastian gave her an exasperated look and her temper flared.

"How the fuck am I supposed to know how vampires feed?"

"What I told you 'bout that tone, shawty," Sebastian snapped.

Lucas stepped between them. "Go to your mate, Bas, I got this."

"What am I supposed to do?" Amaya asked helplessly.

For the entirety of her life, her mother had warned her to stay away from vampires. Her first encounter had been when the Bayi had picked up her and her family. She hadn't the first clue how they fed.

"Call him using the bond he forged. His instinct should do the rest."

Nodding, Amaya crawled into the bed with Levi, sliding beneath the covers. Biting her lip, she wrapped her arms around Levi, bringing his body into hers. Lucas moved to the end of the bed.

"You're going to watch?"

Lucas sighed. "Girl."

"Alright, alright," she mumbled, settling Levi's head into her neck.

Amaya caressed the back of his head and searched her mind for their mental connection. It was much easier to get to now than it had been when his body was fighting the poison.

"King."

He stirred in her arms, his face nuzzling into her neck. She held her breath, anticipation of his bite tightening her body.

"He won't be able to use his pheromones," Lucas warned.

That made Amaya even more nervous, but she prodded Levi's mind again. This time she felt an answering pulse from him.

"Feed, king." She ordered him.

Levi licked across her throat and her breath hitched. He moaned and his arms went around her waist. A whimper escaped Amaya and there was a small nudge from Levi's mind. Even incapacitated he was trying to reassure her. Relaxing her body, she called to him again.

"You have my permission to feed, King."

It was as though that's all he was waiting on. His teeth scraped along her skin and goosebumps trailed her arm. A wave of need crashed over Amaya and her body heated. Levi bit down and the initial pain made her gasp. It didn't last long. The moment Levi began to suck on her skin, there was an answering tug low in her belly. Levi gripped her tight, a deep moan releasing from him. It was then the depth of his yearning was revealed.

The more he drank, the clearer his mind became and the stronger his body grew. Amaya knew the exact moment the king came back to himself. His touch gentled and the sucking movement on her neck became decidedly more sensual. Hunger filled the connection between them, his ravenous appetite overtaking her senses. She understood what both Sebastian and even Levi had been telling her prior to this point. Levi had been starving himself in his wait to have her. It brought tears to her eyes and Amaya curled her leg around him to keep him tethered to her.

"Take what you need," she whispered through his mind.

"Mine." He declared, his hands sliding up her back until he gripped the back of her neck.

Amaya couldn't deny his claim. Not while she was immersed in his thoughts, reading his aching desire for her. If what he felt was only physical, perhaps she could fight the draw between them. But, no. There were tender feelings that she'd missed in their interactions. Yes, there was craving there, lust for sure, but underneath all that... was devotion.

It softened her heart and erased the doubts she harbored about their situation. Levi took immediate advantage of that softening, opening his mind further to her. She saw the good and the bad, the frustrations he harbored, and the peace she alone brought him. In turn, she did the same, allowing Levi past the shields she'd built over her mind. It tightened the bond between them. Amaya could feel it, the strings them once tentative now inflexible and solid.

"Your highness," Lucas called out.

Levi ignored his friend and fed more, deep pulls that had her clit pulsing along with her heartbeat.

"Give it to me, baby doll." His command was uncompromising.

Her body obeyed, and her thighs trembled as an orgasm slammed into her, bowing her back. Pleasure had Amaya floating, a soft cloudiness that scattered her thoughts. A small whimper escaped her as she bit down on her bottom lip to trap louder moans.

"Too much."

That warning came from Lucas somewhere far away. Nothing could reach her in her current state. A drowsy smile tilted her lips. The king had done that from a simple bite. How much more pleasure could he give when he was focused? It was the last thought Amaya had before everything went dark...

CHAPTER
TWENTY-ONE

Levi closed his eyes and forced the voracious beast that had risen in him down. He was satiated and full for the first time in months. Even before Amaya had set foot in his home, he hadn't trust himself to fully feed. He'd been afraid the madness would make him go too far. With Amaya under his roof, the desire to use another to satisfy his needs had diminished. The hunger had still been there, it was just pointed solely at her.

Retracting his teeth, he pulled back from her neck and stared down at her beautiful face. Her body was lax in his arms, her mouth slack, soft breaths stirring the air between them. Using his index finger, he lightly traced her face, wholly in love with this woman. But even with his obsession, he hadn't expected this depth of feeling.

"Your highness."

Lucas brought Levi's attention to him. He'd been so enamored with Amaya that he hadn't realized his enforcer was still in the room.

"She's fine," Levi assured Lucas, extricating the worry from his friend's thoughts. "I didn't take too much."

Besides, the moment she awoke, Levi planned to give her more of his blood to seal their bond. Her allowing him into her heart and mind had started it, and he would complete it. It was greedy of him and he didn't care.

"How long have I been down?"

"Three or four hours." Lucas assured him. "If you two are okay, I'm going to bed."

Levi gave him an absent-minded nod, his gaze steady on his mate as his friend left the room. She had willingly given him blood, even after she claimed she would never. During his healing, he felt Amaya tethering him to this side of the veil as the poison worked through his system. How did he thank her for helping to save his life? Careful not to jostle and wake her, Levi unwrapped himself from her.

He padded to his bathroom, needing to wash everything that had happened tonight off his body. Well, last night, as the shutters being down announced that it was a new day. As soon as his baby woke, he would get them to change the sheets too. As he bathed his body in the scalding hot water, his mind went to the events of the night. Someone had tried to kill him.

Twice in one night.

Was it a coincidence?

Hell nah. Muthafuckers were trying to play on his top and he would bet money that the attacks were coordinated. He was poisoned during the Collective meeting, did that mean one of the elders were working with the Buru? That didn't bode well for the south if someone on the Collective was going outside of their territory and bringing in their enemies. Going toe to toe with the council hadn't been in his game plan, shit, plans could always be adjusted. He reached out to his best friend.

Bas answered his summons immediately, his voice groggy with sleep. *"Yeah."*

Shit, he realized the time of day. *"Never mind. We can talk this evening. Thank Firefly for me, please."*

"Will do."

Bas withdrew from his mind and Levi was once again left alone with his own thoughts. That brought a startling realization to him.

The fogginess of the Akachi was completely gone from his mind. Had Raven's healing fire destroyed what the Amaya's shielding hadn't been able to reach? He could think straight for the first time in months. With that thought, came an immediate sense of guilt for the way he'd started his relationship with his mate. There should never be any doubt on her end that he would care for her.

But, he'd seen firsthand from Amaya's mind how she'd been affected by their interactions. He lowered his head and braced his hands on the tile wall in front of him.

He'd fucked up.

There was no question about it. Even the warnings and admonishments from Lucas and Sebastians hadn't gotten through to him. He'd seen so much in his mate's heart and mind when she'd opened up to him. There had been a sense of forgiveness, but she was still wary of him. Even as she gave herself freely to him, a small part of her was held back because she was unsure of Levi. He couldn't fault her. Seeing his madness from her eyes brought home just how erratic his actions had been lately.

He owed all of his coven an apology.

Finishing up his shower, he got out and wet a wash cloth with warm water. Carrying it out to the bedroom, he paused at the foot of his bed and just watched his sleeping baby doll. She rested peacefully.

Fuck.

He would make it all up to her, no matter how long it took.

He joined her in bed, lifting the hem of her gown. The evidence of her climax was all across her thighs, re-igniting the hunger in him. Before using the cloth, he leaned down and licked across her skin.

"Amaya." Her name was a whispered plea from his lips.

She shuffled a little, but still didn't awaken. He kissed the inside of her thigh, hunger clenching his stomach. It was too soon to feed from her again, but he promised himself that would be his first stop. Gently, he wiped the cloth across her sex, pushing down the lust making his mouth water.

Temptation proved too much though, because no sooner than he'd promised himself he would behave, he was trailing kisses up her thigh. They started out innocently enough, but he was intoxicated by her, there was no other word for it. He licked across her skin, dragging open-mouth, pleading kisses up her thigh.

"Levi." She whispered his name softly as she fought through the fog of sleep.

He raised his body over hers, dropping soft kisses on her lips and all over her face.

Obsession.

He was obsessed with his mate, and damn if he cared. Amaya's arms snaked around his neck and she pulled him down until his weight held pinned her to the bed.

"You saved me, baby doll," he said softly, nipping her ear.

She nodded, her eyes still closed. "You're welcome."

Chuckling softly, his bite to her chin was a little rougher. "Can I have you?"

Her eyes opened then, the debate written on her face. Lust and longing flitted across her gaze also, and that gave him hope. Her heart and mind were still open to him, and Amaya wanted him just as much as he wanted her. Allowing her time to ruminate on her answer, he slid down the strap of her gown. Unable to resist the expanse of skin, he kissed her rounded shoulders, indulging in her softness. Her bountiful breasts spilled from the gown and Levi lifted one, sucking her nipple into his mouth.

Amaya squirmed beneath him, whispering his name.

"Say yes, baby doll. You've already started our bond, let me seal it. I'll take care of you. You'll never have to want for anything. You've seen my heart and know how I feel about you." He stared into her eyes, willing her to see his sincerity.

Her eyes watered as he reached out to her mind and once again allowed her entrance. She cupped the back of his head and, holding him to her breast.

"*King,*" she whispered across their bond.

He slid his fingers down her soft stomach and it hollowed as she sucked in a breath. He rubbed his face into her chest, her soft skin soothing and riling him. The peace she brought him clenched his chest, even while it made his dick hard. He reached her sex and slid his finger through her heated folds.

"So fucking wet," he murmured, playing softly with her clit.

She whimpered and Levi damn near vibrated with anticipation. He knew the moment he pushed through her walls the obsession he already had would double.

"Let me in, lil baby," he cajoled. He was careful to not use his glamour, wanting his mate to choose him herself.

Amaya cupped his cheeks, bringing him up to kiss him. Their tongues danced as her hips lifted to grind against his. Need was building between them, taking hold of his control. She reached down and removed the towel around his hips while her fingers sought his erection straining between them. Her soft hands gripped him slipping up and down his shaft. Levi dropped his head to watch, frantic hunger making his stomach clench.

"I say yes, King." Was her whispered reply.

Levi didn't give her a chance to change her mind. He used her hand to guide his dick to her center. Amaya canted her hips and he sank in. Warm and tight, her pussy welcomed him in.

"God damn, baby doll," he hissed as he fought through her clenching walls.

Spreading her legs out wider, Levi sank deeper, lust clouding his mind. Leaning forward, he joined their lips, their kisses frenzied. He thrust in and out of his mate, closing his eyes to luxuriate in the silken feel of her skin sliding against his. Tucking his head into her neck, he pulled her hips closer as he drove into her. Before he lost himself in her, Levi wanted their bond sealed. It had to happen now, since he'd just fed from her. Any longer and they would need to start the process over.

With that in mind, he grew out his nail and sliced it against his neck, careful not to go too deep.

"Drink," he ordered.

Amaya's head raised and she latched onto the side of his neck, sucking on him. His back bowed, electricity raising the hair on the back of his neck as his mate fed from him. She tried to stop, but he held her head in place so that she could take enough for the mating bond to activate. The little amount of blood he'd taken when they'd first mated wouldn't be enough.

She needed more.

The feel of her mouth against his skin was heating Levi from the inside out. Keeping his strokes leisurely, he used his magic to finish the job Amaya had started fusing their souls together. Their bond was bright and vibrant, testament to how deep their love could develop. He was already there, but that gave him reassurance that his mate wasn't too far behind him.

She moaned beneath him, the pressure of her sucking driving up his need.

"Enough," he managed to whisper, his hips driving forward to get deeper.

Amaya pulled back and her nails scored his back as she arched beneath him. "Don't hold back from me."

"With pleasure," he growled, lifting his weight from her.

He pulled out and flipped her body, lifting her hips until her back arched deeply. The sight of her ass up, her center dewy and waiting for him released the monster waiting to devour her. Driving forward, Levi plunged in her with desperate strokes, insatiable hunger filling him. She was now his, tied irrevocably. His heart soared as he rocked against her. His gums ached, his fangs sliding down as he rode his mate. The prettiest sounds escaped Amaya, feeding his ego as she pushed her hips back into his.

"More, King," she panted.

Levi rotated his hips, bottoming out in her pussy over and over. He gripped her hair and pulled her head back. The pain had her whimpering, her walls clamping down on his shaft. All sense of logic faded and in its place was pure, heated craving. They moved together as though they'd already spent a lifetime together, both answering the other's needs before they could be voiced.

He lost track of time in her body. There was no room for anything but satisfying the aching need between them. Soon though, a tingle started at the base of his spine. Holding back his orgasm was impossible. Wrapping his arms around her his, he used his fingers to tease her clit. Amaya screamed, as her climax flooded their mating bond, dragging him under with her. Instinct had him driving his teeth into her shoulder as he came.

Her body shuddered beneath him, the keening cry she released signaling that she'd come again. Levi tightened his hold on his mate and released her shoulder, licking her skin to close his bite.

Fuck. This woman.

He was hers, in every way and he already knew she would run him.

"I'm glad you know," she murmured sleepily beneath him.

Smirking, he gently extracted from her body. "Shower, then you can rest, my love."

She hummed her agreement, her body pliant in his arms as he gathered her. His life was changed, hell, had been from the moment he'd set his eyes on this witch. But now that they were bonded and her heart and mind open to him, Levi understood the responsibility that came with holding her soul within him. It was a closeness he'd never experienced before and if the world thought he'd been rabid before...the would not be ready for what he'd do to protect and keep this woman.

TWENTY-TWO

G oing into the office after the morning he'd spent with his mate was out of the question. Especially since she was off work today. Every instinct in him wanted to be upstairs in bed with her, savoring in their new found bond, but Levi knew he wouldn't rest well until he found out who was trying to have him killed. So, with a relaxed body and a clear mind, Levi was meeting in his office with Lucas and Sebastian, his most trusted enforcers and best friends. He didn't trust anyone else at this point.

"Congratulations." Lucas told him, stretching out in the chair in front of Levi's office. "Can't believe you pulled it off."

Sebastian snickered. "I just knew she was finna give us all hell for another month."

"Don't talk about my baby like she difficult. She just one of them ones who can't be handled by just anybody."

"Whatever you gotta tell yourself to feel comfortable closing your eyes in bed next to her," Lucas said.

The three of them busted out laughing. Levi knew better than to have Amaya sleeping anywhere near him those during the days that she'd hated him. Especially after her escape attempt. He was almost certain she would've tried to kill him.

"Focus, man." He needed to change the subject befreo he left his friends to go upstairs.

Sebastian crossed his arms over his chest. "Someone tried to kill you."

"Twice," he added.

Lucas nodded. "I want to know who poisoned you. That Buru shit will get handled like it always does, but someone getting close enough to slip Buru blood in your drink is a problem."

"It had to have happened at the meeting, but you barely took a sip of that drink." Bas said.

Levi frowned. "You're right. It tasted weird, so I set it aside. Damn." The thought of what could;ve happened to him had he kept drinking pissed him off. "I want that server and anyone who worked with her found."

Lucas pulled out his phone, going to work. "I remember her face. You know I memorize anyone floating around you."

That was a given. Lucas had been with Levi since the moment he'd started making moves to take over the city. Thirty years together and not once had Levi questioned his loyalty.

"We need allies in the Collective," Bas broke the tense silence.

Levi leaned back in his chair. "Who do you think is the most likely candidate. The Fire Mujaji elder hates your guts. Lucian will most likely try and get me kicked out that shit at the first chance, that leaves four others."

"With the current elders? None of them motherfuckers are siding with us." Bas informed him. "That's why we gotta shake that shit up."

"What are you thinking?" Lucas stopped his typing.

"Lucian gives us the most trouble and his voice is the loudest. We should replace him," Levi grumbled.

Sebastian's face turned thoughtful. "The Lathams are the next powerful family of border mages."

"Their patriarch is fair," Lucas added.

"Then reach out and see if we can get a meeting with one of them." Levi ordered.

He didn't care which of them accomplished that. He went to the next thing bothering him. "Did you find her uncle?"

"That bitch hiding at his daddy's compound. If we bust in there, we'll have a lot more problems than I feel like tackling at the moment." Lucas said.

Levi sighed and shook his head. There was no use in stressing about it at the moment. There wasn;t much more trouble Paul could put him in.

"I need to be seen out." He announced. "I can't for one second let a motherfucker think they got the drop on me."

Sebastian sat forward. "Agreed. It needs to be somewhere the Collective can see you."

"You sure you want to announce to the world that you just said 'fuck you' to a Collective decree."

"I think that's exactly what I want to do." Levi smiled.

Lucas shrugged. He would ride regardless of what Levi did. "They like that lil swanky shit down on Fischer."

"The fusion place? Red been wanting to go." Sebastian rubbed his hands together.

"I know the Native fire bird that owns the place. We'll be safe to send men ahead in case shit gets active." Lucas told them.

Levi nodded. He knew for a fact that he'd had a few dresses delivered to Amaya when Raven demanded he get clothes for her. A fun outing with his mate and his friends could fun.

"*Amaya,*" he called out.

Her presence warmed his mind and made his heart stir. "*Yes, King.*"

"*We're going out tonight on a double date with Bas and Raven. How long will it take you to get dressed?*"

There was a moment of hesitation on her part. Did she regret their mating now that she was up and moving? Before he could comment on it, she answered his other question.

"I'm in the shower now. An hour?"

"You're in the shower?" This time it was his dick that stirred. *"I can be up in a sec."*

She laughed, the husky sound filling his mind. *"Then it will take longer than an hour."*

"Fine," he pouted. *"I'll shower and get ready down here."*

"See you soon." She withdrew from his mind.

He focused his attention back on his friends. "Baby doll is good to go. Send a call out to the coven for a meeting in an hour."

Sebastian smiled. "Ah shit. You making it official. The King of the Bayi is mated."

He smiled at his friend. "If they thought I was a problem before."

CHAPTER
TWENTY-THREE

Amaya was in all black. From the silk wrap around skirt that tied at her waist and left her right thigh exposed nearly to the top, to the leather corset that cinched in her waist. The only bits of color on her came from her matte red lipstick and the gold stilettos strapped across her feet. She pushed her mass of hair up into a knot, allowing a few tendrils to caress her face. Satisfied with the beat on her face, she sent kisses at the mirror and left Levi's room.

She felt different.

But that was to be expected. She was a mated woman now. Though she felt more secure now that she was tied to Levi, there was still that fear in the back of her mind. They had gone against every warning her family had given her. Mating between the Bayi and the Chawi was strictly forbidden. And Amaya had no idea what the fallout would be.

When the king had asked her to go out, she'd had a moment of hesitation. Were they doing the right thing? It wasn't the mating that she doubted, it was flaunting it that gave her pause. Were it up to her, Amaya would probably hide out at Levi's compound and pray the elders of her family didn't find out. Clearly, she'd forgotten who she was mated to.

The king of the Bayi didn't hide, and he certainly didn't cower from anyone.

Rolling her shoulders and lifting her head, Amaya decided then and there that she would be the same. Hell, she'd been kidnapped by her mate and hadn't broken, with him by her side, she could take on the rest of the world. Still, there were butterflies in her stomach as she reached the end of the hallway and the top of the stairs. Below her Levi waited in the middle of the stairs and below that, his coven filled the space of the foyer spilling into dining and living room on either side of that. Her stomach fluttered.

"What's going on?"

He smiled but didn't answer. He grabbed her hand when she met him and lifted it to his lips. His soft kiss sent a shiver of want throughout her body.

He turned and face his coven. "I'm sure all of you felt the change in me but let this be the official announcement and introduction to your queen."

She sucked in a surprise breath, her hands getting sweating.

"Allow me to introduce Queen Amaya Cauly of the Bayi."

Whistles and cheers went up, the applause flooding the space with sound. Her once nervous smile widened, as she was swept up in the goodwill coming from his coven. Through her tie with Levi, she could feel it all.

It was a heady power.

Levi's eyes speared her and heat flushed her cheeks. Her legs weakened when he smiled, his gold fangs in. Gods this man was too fine. Privy to her thoughts, his smiled turned lascivious. Winking at her, he turned back to face his coven.

"Along with the introductions, I want to say something to you all. Under the influence of the Akachi stone, I was not myself these past few months. I want to apologize to you all that my arrogance had our coven in disarray. Thanks to your new Queen, I'm back to myself, and back to the business of taking this coven to the top of all this shit."

A deafening roar of agreement went up and Amaya laughed. Her mate's coven was filled with both males and females who were as bloodthirsty as their master. She prayed she was enough to live up to their expectations.

"I don't expect anything less from you, baby doll." Levi encouraged, pulling her into his arms.

The king held up his hand to quiet the noise. "It's a new time in our coven's existence. We gon' claim back the power stolen from the Bayi and ain't nobody standing in the way of that. With every new mating in this coven, our power is expanding and that's a good thing for us. We're done hiding in the shadows, accepting scraps. We're no longer allowing the Collective to tell us who we can and cannot mate. They've starved this coven and others like ours and that ends now."

He leaned down and kissed Amaya until everything around her disappeared. His tongue swept into her mouth and she wanted to melt on the spot. Now that they were mated, Amaya understood his obsession with her because she now felt it for him. She would follow this man to the ends of the Earth and clearly his coven felt the same.

His loyalty was well earned. She saw the way he moved for the Bayi, and the sacrifices he'd made over the years. It all been there in his heart and mind when they'd merged. The Bayi were lucky to have him as their leader.

Giving Amaya one final kiss he turned back to the crowd and touched his fist to his chest. "Thank y'all for riding this out with me. We're going out tonight, because clearly muhfuckas forgot who I was. But, in the upcoming days, feel free to make yourself known to my queen. Dismissed."

Levi guided her the rest of the way down the stairs and though he'd dismissed the coven, some still stuck around to greet her as they headed to the door. She waved and smiled, accepting their hand kisses as she passed through the crowd. She looked forward to getting to know everyone. Bas and Raven were waiting at the SUV when they got outside.

Raven pulled her into a hug. "Congratulations!"

There was still worry in the other woman's gaze, but Amaya could still feel her happiness for the mating and that relaxed her.

"Thank you, Raven."

"Are you ready for tonight? We're going to get stares," Raven told her and they both shuffled into the very back of the SUV.

Amaya nodded. "If I can survive Levi's bad temper a few stares should be easy."

Sebastian chuckled as he buckled in in the seat in front of them.

"Not too much on me, baby doll," Levi said dryly as he did the same.

She smiled rubbing her mate's shoulder. Headlights illuminated the interior of their SUV so she turned in curiosity. There were two other SUVs being loaded behind them.

"All these people are coming with us?" She asked.

"Just the one behind us. Lucas already sent enforcers ahead to the restaurant." Levi told her.

On cue, her stomach grumbled. Food sounded good.

HALF AN HOUR LATER, they were pulling up to a swanky restaurant in downtown Black Hollow. Levi and Sebastian got out of the truck first before helping them out the back. By the time they came around to restaurant entrance, the four of them were surrounded with balaclava clad vampires. It was intimidating to say the least. Pride for her mate filled Amaya and she straightened her shoulder, the sway in her walk one that matched her king's.

She was on the arm of the most powerful man in the city, and damn that felt good. They were guided to a private dining room, and just as Raven had predicted, all eyes were on them. The staff was over gracious, pulling out all the stops for the King of the Bayi.

Amaya couldn't hide her smile when they were finally seated at the elegant table.

"This is fancy," she murmured.

Raven snickered. "I was thinking the same thing. I've been asking Bas to bring me here for a lil minute."

"Where are the menus?" Amaya asked, searching the table.

"You won't need them. Bas spoils firefly, so we're having the chef's menu. It's six courses, so you'll get a little bit of everything." Levi said, waving the waiter over.

He ordered wine for the table and Amaya bounced in her seat in excitement. The waiter brought two wine bottles to the table. One of Levi's enforcers stepped to the table and watched like a hawk as both bottles were opened for the first time. Still, the male tasted both before nodding to Levi and Sebastian. It dampened her excitement just a little at the reminder that someone had tried to kill her mate two nights ago.

Levi slid a reassuring hand up her thigh. He kissed her exposed shoulder. *"I'm not going anywhere any time soon, baby doll."*

She nodded and took a deep cleansing breath. Amaya eyed the bottle as Levi poured it into his glass. The wine was more viscous than that which he'd poured into hers and Raven's glasses. Clearly it contained blood and why did that make her possessive. She wanted to be the only one to provide for him. She was almost jealous of that unnamed donor who gave for that bottle and that's when Amaya realized she'd gone off the deep end. She sipped her wine and chuckled to herself.

Their dinner went well. The four of them got along and the conversation flowed between them easily. Levi's hand never left her. His power along their connection heated her from the inside. That, coupled with his attentiveness had Amaya smitten. From small touches to her thigh and shoulders or soft kisses, he was affection-ate, Levi made his presence at her side known. By the time they wrapped it up and stood to leave, her whole body was flushed.

"Have I told you how amazing you smell?" Levi leaned into her neck and shivers went down her spine.

He guided her from the private dining room, his hand on the small of her back, sending little pings of awareness flitting across her skin. She was so wrapped up into the king that she nearly ran smack into her grandfather who was standing at the hostess table, his steely gaze on her. As always, Bradford was dressed crisply, not a wrinkle or stitch out of place. His salt and pepper hair was the only indication that he was over the age of fifty. Like all supernaturals, with the long lives they lived, it was hard to ascertain their age.

The disapproving look stopped Amaya in her tracks. Surprise momentarily had her mute. Her grandfather hardly ever left the compound, complaining about the way the world around him had changed. To see him not only out, but with two of the other elders of her family was shocking to say the least.

"Grandfather."

"Amaya. How is Anita?"

She blinked at his brusque tone. "She's better these days, actually."

He looked shocked. "Really? Paul said she was in trouble."

"The opposite. No thanks to Uncle Paul, we're staying somewhere safe after his latest scheme. The lack of stress has done wonders for her."

He frowned at the slight censure in her tone. "And you?"

"Wonderful."

His eyes went directly to King Levi and Amaya ignored his pointed look. The king wasn't haven't it though. He nudged her with the hand on her back and she swallowed a sigh.

"Grandfather, this is my mate, Levi Cauly. King, my grandfather, Bradford Armstrong."

All three elders gasped, sharing a look between them. Amaya knew what that look meant and knew it would only be a matter of time before she or her mother were called before them. She looked around and noticed all eyes were on them, watching this conversation play out. Levi's soothing touch in her mind grounded her.

In no mood to deal with it tonight, Amaya injected levity into her tone. "Want me to tell mom to call you?"

"Don't worry. I will be in touch with you both." Her grandfather's eyes were hard, his jaw tight with anger.

"Then goodnight," Amaya rushed out and grabbed Levi's hand, leading him out of the restaurant.

Her grandfather wouldn't make a bigger scene and for that she was thankful. Bradford's presence was a slap in the face, reminding her why she was not supposed to be mated with a Bayi vampire. Payment would come due for her betrayal, but she would gladly pay any price to be with Levi.

"Breathe, baby doll," Levi whispered, kissing her shoulder as the SUV slid to a stop in front of them.

"I'm fine," she promised him.

And she was. For now, at least. Tomorrow, when the rest of the supernatural community found out what they had done was another separate problem.

CHAPTER
TWENTY-FOUR

Amaya had thought she'd been ready for the world to know about her mating, but realistically, she hadn't been prepared. Luckily for her, she worked alone for the most part, so while she'd had to answer questions at every stop along her day, it hadn't been so bad. What had given her pause was the way the people with whom she'd worked for years had looked at her. Some had outright treated her like a pariah while others had given her a wide berth.

Some part of her could understand their wariness. Punishment would come from what she had done, and no one knew what form it would take. Keeping away from Amaya kept them safe from any fallout and she couldn't blame her co-workers. Still...it had been uncomfortable.

She was used to spending her days being unperceived. No one outside of the sacred garden staff knew she existed and now, just walking through the Archive, all eyes had been on her. Being who she was, she didn't let it phase her. She kept her chin up and her shoulders back, but now that she was home, her body wanted to collapse from the stress. She frowned when she passed the foyer. The house was quieter than usual. The staff was usually setting up for dinner this time of night. Curious, she rounded the corner into the dining room and gasped.

The whole dining room had been transformed. The lights were off, and the only illumination came from the table. Thin gold candle holders covered the surface from one end of the table to the other, the small candles giving the whole room an intimate vibe. Flowers were set up in every corner, roses shades of red and pink scenting the air. There were only two place settings set. Heavy crystal dinnerware and a plethora of silver cloches in middle of the table. The smells were heavenly. Her day was forgotten as she stepped further into the room. Levi stepped from the shadows, holding out a glass of wine for her. She happily took it, dazed.

"What is all this?"

He stepped closer to her and pulled her into his arms. "I realized that our mating was something that happened more as an accident and I wanted to replace it with a new memory. One where we choose each other."

A lump formed in her throat. "Levi," she whispered, her eyes trying to take it all in.

"Come sit, my love." He guided her to the head of the table, sitting her in the chair on the left.

He took her bag from her shoulder and placed it in the chair next to her, before sitting at the head of the table. Amaya was speechless. This was her first experience with romance, and it left her breathless. She looked up to find Levi's eyes on her.

"This is beautiful, King."

He smiled and his pleasure filled their connection. "I wasn't sure if you would like it."

Her shoulders relaxed for the first time today and she stretched out her legs under the table. "this is just what I needed after the day I had."

"What happened?" He grabbed her hand, nibbling on her knuckles.

"Well, it's safe to say that news of our mating is out."

"Does that bother you?" His gaze traced her face, his eyebrows bunched in concern.

Amaya shrugged. "I don't care who knows about our mating. But, I feel like the world is holding their breath to see what our punishment will be."

Levi growled. "I look forward to the first person that tries to step to me about you."

She pulled her hand back and brushed the top of her hair with a sigh. "No one would dare approach the king of the Bayi. Me on the other hand..."

"Do you honestly think I would allow anything to happen to you?"

"It's not about what you allow, King. You can't watch me twenty-four seven." She pointed out.

"That's what Bronx is for," he assured her. "They would have to get through him to get to you, and trust me, that shifter is good at his fucking job. It's why I entrusted your safety to him."

That comforted her and she adjusted in her chair, ready to put the whole topic aside.

"what's for dinner?"

"Pot roast."

She busted out laughing. "That's not romantic, King."

He smiled, his eyes sparkling. "But I asked Ms. Anita what your favorite meal and that's what she said."

Her cheeks hurt from how wide she smiled. Giddy happiness filled her and Amaya wanted to dance in her seat. It was hard to imagine they would've gotten here, from the way they started their relationship. He winked at her as he opened the cloche closest to him. Her mouth watered as he uncovered the lambchops inside. She could smell the garlicky goodness.

"Feeding me will get you big points every time," she told him clapping softly.

Levi chuckled. "Noted."

He uncovered the mashed potatoes and glazed string beans and Amaya smiled in appreciation. She had laughed at the pot roast, but she was a simple girl, and she loved that he catered to that. He fixed her plate for her and she wasted no time digging in. It amazed her how well the two of them carried a conversation. There were no awkward lulls or nervousness. Levi made her comfortable in way she never was around people outside of her mother and cousin.

After dinner, their dessert was a simple homemade pineapple sorbet that melted in her mouth. Amaya closed her eyes to savor the taste. When she opened them, she found her mate staring at her, abject hunger lighting his eyes.

"Good?" Was his husky question.

She nodded, her stomach clenching as he licked his lips.

"Let me see," he murmured, leaning forward.

Levi licked her lips first, before sliding his tongue between them. The coppery taste of his wine met with the sweetness of her dessert and somehow worked to amp up the lust between them. He gripped the back of her head and held her in place as he devoured her mouth. Lifting from her seat, Amaya sighed as Levi lifted her, sitting her on the edge of the table in front of him.

She reached back and pushed his empty plate back a little farther to give her space. "Are we done eating, then?"

"Oh, I'm just getting started." His voice was husky, his eyes darkening as lust tightened his face.

Levi tugged the back of her legs until she was on the edge of the table. Amaya went back until she was leaned on her elbows. She was happy to have worn a skirt today.

"Pretty ass pussy," he murmured.

Her mate unleashed his claws and rent a tear right down the middle of the maxi skirt. He kissed her knee before rubbing his face against her thigh. She released a contented sigh, happy to have him touching her.

He kissed her or dragged open mouth kisses up her thigh. Before she knew what was happening her king bit into her thigh, and started feeding from her. His pheromones were pumping out of him and taking her under. Levi's eyes were closed and he moaned, the sound tightening her womb as her center leaked.

Opening his eyes, he speared her with a hungry look as he sucked on her thigh. He reached up and his fingers traced the outside of her pussy before his fingers slid into her. Amaya threw her head back and rode his fingers. The sensation of him feeding from her while simultaneously fingering her had her primed for the climax making her clit throb in anticipation. She crashed into it, her load moan bouncing off the walls.

Levi licked his bite closed and stood, his eyes bright, the pupils red as the beast within him rose. Amaya tucked her bottom lip between her teeth in anticipation.

He fit his dick at her entrance and growled as the walls of her sex pulsed around him.

"Grip that mothafucka, baby doll," was his gruff order.

She relaxed her muscles, moaning as he pushed in further. "More," she panted.

He obeyed immediately, bottoming out, the bite of pain arching her back. Her pussy clenched, hard, sending goosebumps up all over her body.

"Greedy fucking pussy," he murmured, driving in and out.

Amaya could hardly catch her breath as her mate fucked her, his grip on her leg tight. He slowed his strokes and pulled her leg up onto his shoulder.

She hissed. "Too deep."

"Nah, you can take it, lil baby." He didn't stop, pounding into her body, setting her nerve endings on fire.

If she thought that was all he had for her, she was sadly mistaken. Levi gripped her waist tight with one hand and used the other to wrap around her ankle, bringing it closer to his mouth. His teeth pierced her skin, and Amaya fragmented, her release torn from her without warning. Her mate continued to piston in and out of her body, building another climax, one that felt too big for her body to contain.

Levi grunted as he fed, a dazed and drunken look on his face as he used her body for his sustenance. It was intimate, and sexy.

"King," she whispered as her body tightened with the force of her oncoming orgasm.

His eyes opened and the red had completely overtaken his eyes. A hungry animal stared down at her as he sucked on her skin. Full body chills went through her and Amaya canted her hips to take him deeper, letting him know that there was no part of him that she didn't accept. Levi separated from her leg, blood still staining his lips. He released her leg and leaned down to kiss her, sharing her life's essence with her.

She greedily sucked on his tongue, holding him tight as his strokes became erratic. "Come for me, King."

Levi cursed and gripped her waist tighter as he pumped into her until his body stiffened and he came, painting her walls. He shuddered with aftershocks as he buried his head in her neck.

"God damn you take my breath away," he drunkenly murmured.

Amaya slid her hand up his back and cupped his head, holding him tight to her. Emotion swamped her, heady and all-consuming. She knew the feeling tightening her chest was almost afraid to acknowledge it. Was she in love with Levi?

CHAPTER TWENTY -SIX

Levi shoved his hands into his pockets, his eyes on the dark water lapping at the shore. A few feet away were the busy docks of the Eastern harbor. It had taken them an hour to get here from Black Hollow, but he hoped the meeting he was waiting for would be worth it. His memories tried to drag him back to the nights he'd slaved away here while he and Sebastian had been trying to make a living.

It was at these same docks that he'd learned the importance of logistics and how to keep supplies moving throughout the south. It was one of the reasons Lucian hated him so. The border mage thought Levi beneath him since he'd started at these docks under his supervision. It galled Lucian that Levi had moved from unloading ships to owning them. He smiled to himself.

Fuck that border mage.

With this meeting, he hoped to do that and more.

A part of him reveled in the fact that he was about to have his current meeting on Lucian's territory. The mage elder no longer showed his face at the docks, preferring to run his little kingdom from the capital city behind a desk. Levi knew first hand that was the fastest way to lose control. People needed to see you...feel you, to know that fucking with you would always be a problem. Even at his trucking company, Levi made sure to show his face at least once a month.

His men were loyal, but all it took was once for a muthafucka to whisper the wrong shit in the wrong person's ear. Like tonight. If Lucian had control of his men like he thought he did, Levi would've never been able to step foot in this harbor without the border mage knowing.

Especially with another border mage.

The man of the hour pulled up in a matte black pickup truck, stopping about fifty yards from where Levi was standing. Both doors opened and two border mages stepped out of the truck. The male he was meeting with and the other who Levi could only assume was his warden. The male was way over six feet tall, nearly an inch taller than Levi's six-foot three body. He had long dark locks that he had piled in a bun on top of his head. His warden's locks were to his shoulder down loose, obscuring his face slightly. Both men were bulky and their power crackled around them.

"King Levi of the Bayi," the mage he was set to meet broke the silence.

"Khalil," he greeted. "I don't know your warden's name."

"That's a-ight." Khalil's voice was deep, his country twang very pronounced. "Bold to be meeting in Lucian's backyard like this."

"Fuck Lucian." Was Lucian's response to that.

The mage chuckled and nodded. Both men were on the same accord. "My father said you had a proposition for us."

"What would it take for your family to take over the mage position on the Collective?"

Khalil tilted his head, surprise flashing across his face a moment before he suppressed it. "Proof that Lucian ain't doing his job."

Levi considered his next words. "Two nights ago, I was attacked by a group of Buru. They've been getting past the borders and it seems strange to me that your representative in the Collective don't know shit about it."

"You sure about that?"

"About him knowing, or about the fact that my men have seen an uptick of Buru activity."

Khalil hummed but said nothing. The mage turned and faced the water, quiet for long moments. He turned back to Levi.

"My daddy won't move without proof."

"Fair. But again I ask: can you think of any other reason the Buru are getting through these borders without help?"

"They ain't getting through our shit," Khalil assured him.

"And yet..."

Khalil sighed and turned to look at his warden. They shared an indecipherable look. Levi decided to push the needle just a bit more.

"Your family has served the collective since its inception, if anyone deserves that seat it's you."

"I'll take it to Pops."

"If your family decides to go ahead with it, you'll have the support of all the Bayi in my coven as well as others loyal to me."

"Ah, but see, you just got your shit. What pull you got on the Collective?" Khalil asked, a small smirk on his face.

Levi shared the mage's amusement. "I'm making moves regardless."

"Bet. I'll talk to the family," Khalil promised.

That was all Levi could ask at the present moment so he let it go at that. The two men dapped him up and took their leave. Levi watched as they drove off until their headlights faded. Bas slipped from the shadows where he was hiding. Despite being out of eyesight, Levi knew his friend had been watching for any missteps by the mage.

One thing about his best friend, he never slacked when it came to his job.

Having a mate hadn't changed that at all. Levi admired Sebastian for that, because just having Amaya in his house had his head fucking gone. How his friend concentrated when he was away from his mate was a mystery to him.

"You think it will work?" Bas asked.

"Whether it does nor not isn't the point. I want them out."

"Controlling the Lathams won't be any easier." Sebastian warned him.

Levi conceded his point. "But, they would treat us as equals. If I have to replace every head at that table to get our proper respect, I will. Being punished for some shit that happened with an ancestor hundreds of years ago is fucking ridiculous."

Bas grunted. "On that note, Red say she got some shit to show you."

He turned to his best friend with interest. "Say word."

Bas nodded. Levi gave one final look to the murky water noting how well it fit his mood. He hadn't expected Raven to find anything in his grandmother's old journals. At the most he expected she would maybe find an answer as to why the Collective fought so hard to keep the Bayi from having a representative.

Turning towards their SUV, he started walking. "I'm done for the night then. Let's get home."

"She's at the archive."

Levi paused his step. "Interesting."

Once again, the director of the archive met them at the door. Sophia looked equal parts excited and anxious. Levi frowned as the woman opened the door for them.

"Your highness," she greeted, searching behind them.

"it's just me and Bas tonight," he told her, hiding a smile. "You looking for someone else?"

Bas chuckled next to him. "Leave that lady 'lone. She ain't worried about Lucas. Witches don't do Bayi, right Ms. Sophia?"

She cleared her throat and straightened her posture, ignoring Bas's question. She closed and locked the door behind them which raised Levi's hackles. Are far as he knew, the Archive was opened twenty-four seven. Why would she close it?

"If you'll follow me." Sophia said softly

They followed behind her through the atrium of the Archive, the silence of the building deafening. Sophia led them all the way to the back and up a flight of stairs. Levi could feel the power of the Akachi pulsing around them. He reached his hand in his pocket and fingered the stone, something he'd been doing lately as he was thinking. The stone warmed against his fingers, seeming to pull power from the larger stones below them. Levi stepped into the observatory, impressed with the thick glass wall to his left as well as the skylight above him. It made the room feel like it was floating.

His mate was there with Raven, the two of them standing over a tall table. His great grandmother's journals were scattered across the table top. Amaya's head lifted as they entered and she immediately closed the space between them. Levi opened his arms and his little witch stepped into them, her head resting on his chest.

Ignoring everyone else in the room, he lifted her chin. *"What's wrong, baby doll."*

She sighed and rubbed her hands down his arms. *"This place overwhelms me, but the moment you entered the room, my magic calmed."*

He understood exactly what she meant. Every time he was in her presence, his magic sought her out, peace overtaking his senses.

"How did the meeting go?" She changed the subject.

He kissed her forehead and tightened his arms around her. *"You worry too much, my love. Everything is fine."*

She nodded and stepped back, taking her place at the table with Raven again. Instead of joining them, Levi stepped to the glass and peered down at the sacred garden. According to Bronx, he spent the majority of his time in this space watching Amaya do her work. Levi was blown away by the sacred garden. It was nearly dark, lit only by the stones themselves. They emitted a dim blue glow that disappeared in the dark sand around it.

He understood now that Amaya had set the shielding over his

stone in the same pattern. He was blown away by how powerful his baby was.

Turning back the group, his gaze went straight to Raven. "What did you find, firefly?"

Raven looked at her boss, before spreading his ancestor's journal on the table in front of them. She was wearing gloves.

"I've been going over this, but some of the language is old, and not the Yoruba I've been taught."

He nodded in understanding. There were many tribes that came over and not all of them spoke the same language.

"I brought it to Sophia, she...her magic can decipher any language." She continued shooting him an unsure look.

"It's fine, firefly." He reassured her through their bond that he wasn't upset.

She visibly relaxed. "So, what we've found is actually..." she paused. "I don't even know how to say what we've found. It's the reason we're meeting here and not in Sophia's office. Eavesdropping here is impossible."

He frowned and stepped closer to the table. "What is it?"

"It involves the collective." Sophia spoke up.

Levi forced himself not to look at his second in command. But Bas was present in his head, already knowing what he was thinking.

"What are the odds?" Bas asked him telepathically.

"Indeed." Aloud he said, "Continue."

Raven nodded. "The Collective has told the Chaos Chawis that they would be cursed if they mated with the Bayi. We've found information to say the opposite."

This time he couldn't help his reaction. His growl rattled around the room. "Explain."

"I have to go back to the beginning to explain," she told them, her eyes lighting with excitement. "This journal...Bria Cauly met with the Celestials. There is first hand accounting of that. My hands are shaking even reading her words."

"Red," Bas prodded his mate.

"Right. So, ummm, where was I? Oh yeah. We've all heard the tales about he Bayi vampire that tried to take over the world?"

Everyone nodded.

"Well, it was Bria's father and he wasn't just Bayi. He was a true hybrid, born from a chawi and a Bayi. He held the power of both, which was why he was so hard to stop. According to Bria, she went to the Celestials for help. Which they did. But it cost her. Hell...it cost everyone."

Levi frowned. "In what way?"

"Your great great grandmother was a part of what she calls an Obayifi. It's a mating between a chaos chawi and a bayi vampire. The celestials took out Bria's father, but because his power was the result of the Obayifi, they stripped the supernaturals of it. I'm not explaining that right," Raven looked at Sophia in frustration.

The director took over the story. "The Obayifi is not just a mating. It binds chaos magic with the power of the Bayi, creating a power that raises the magic of the supernatural collectively."

Levi's mind was racing as he tried to process what Raven was telling them. "So, when my grandmother gave up the Obayifi it weakened all of the supernaturals?"

Raven nodded solemnly. "Which helped the Buru overrun the south."

"The fuck," Sebastian said, stepping closer to the table to see.

Raven took a shaky breath and looked at Amaya. "This is why I wanted you in here as well. According to these journals the Chaos Chawi are supposed to mate with the Bayi. Something about their powers balanced the chaos magic within you. The mating kept the witches from going mad. But in mating, you've created the first Obayifi that we've had in centuries."

Levi already knew what she was talking about but every day since he'd mated with Amaya, he'd felt the power of his coven increasing. He assumed it would eventually level out the way it had when Sebastian had mated with Raven. But if what she was saying was correct, the power would keep building, spreading out among all of the supernaturals.

"I can already feel hints of it in my magic, soon, all of us will feel it." Raven echoed his thoughts.

"What does this mean?" Amaya asked.

"It means that we will all get more powerful, but the reason it's most important is that it means, any child born of the two of you, could gain the same power of Levi's ancestor. It increases the chances tenfold. Your ancestor was told that in order to keep that from happening, the chawi and bayi had to be kept separate. She speculated what that would mean for the chaos chawi without the anchor of the Bayi, but what we knew about your grandfather was nothing compared to the atrocities he actually carried out." Sophia told them.

"Wait," Amaya raised her hand. "You're saying that the deaths in my family, in the families of every chaos witch could've been prevented if we were allowed to mate with a Bayi?"

Sophia gave her a sympathetic look. "It was a price they were willing to pay at the time."

"The Collective were already worried that Levi would take them over. What do you think they will do knowing that your mating with Amaya will give you ten times the power you now hold?" Bas gave him a worried glance.

Levi cursed. "They'll do what they can to stop it."

"I think that's the reason for the curse rumor. And I suspect that the reason we haven't had an Obayifi in centuries is because the Collective have been assuring it."

Raven gasped. "You think they were killing couples."

Sophia gave them a grim look. "I don't want to tell you what to do your highness, but if I were in your place, I would double up on security. You've not only mated but you've announced it. They'll be backed into a corner."

Levi nodded taking in her warning. He would be meeting with

his enforcers the moment he got home. He would double Amaya's protection and prepare his coven for a possible war.

CHAPTER
TWENTY-FIVE

The ride back to the compound was quiet as they all sat with their own thoughts. Amaya was both furious and hopeful for her family. There were women in her family who were worried that they would go crazy and die alone in the attic at their chawi compound. Not many women made it past sixty and everyday Amaya had been praying for a miracle for her mother. To know the Collective was sitting on that miracle pissed her off like nothing she'd ever experienced.

They pulled up to the gate and the headlights illuminated a male standing at the gate. He wore a dark tshirt and jeans, with a skull cap pulled down on his head. His beard was short trimmed outlining a strong jaw. The male was brown-skinned, tall and muscular, the only indication of his age the small amounts of gray in his bear illuminated by the headlights of the SUV. His confidence was evident in his casual stance as he awaited them. The guard at the gate was watching the male, but it didn't seem to phase him.

She recognized him immediately.

Amaya gasped. "I know him," she muttered.

"How," Levi asked, an immediate spike of jealousy traveling across their bond.

"He...we rode the bus together," she answered.

Telling Levi that she and her cousin assumed the man was stalking her would probably get the man killed immediately. The truck stopped and Sebastain got out. He approached the man and Amaya was mad she couldn't understand what was being said. Bas came back to the truck and Levi lowered the window.

"What's going on?"

"His name is Richad Fontaine. He wants an audience with you, says you're holding his mate."

Amaya gasped. "I know you fucking lying," she whispered.

Maybe Tracy had been right all this time.

Levi studied her. "You're worried."

"I'm interested to see what he says." She hedged.

Levi communicated something to Bas telepathically and the gates opened. Bas and the security at the gate walked Richard in, and they followed behind him in the truck. When they arrived in the driveway to the house, her mother was standing on the porch.

"Mom!" Amaya slid to the door and grabbed the handle.

Levi held her back. "I wish you would get out of this car before me," he gently chided.

Her surprise tripled when the male vampire roared, being held back by Sebastian and the gate guard. What was going on?

"What in the world?" Raven said next to her.

Levi got out first leaving her and Raven in the SUV. Amaya growled in frustration as she watched them wrestle the male under control. Had he followed her all the way here? How had he found her here? She shook her head already knowing what Tracy would say when she called her cousin to tell her what happened.

"Come, Baby doll," Levi held the door opened for her and Raven to exit the car.

"Thank you so much," she said sarcastically getting out of the truck and rushing to Anita. "Mom, what are you doing outside?"

"He called to me." Anita said and her gaze was clear, her eyes never leaving the male being held back by Bas and the guard. "It's really him," her mother whispered.

Amaya put the pieces together. "The man you feel when we go walking?"

Anita nodded and curiosity propelled Amaya over towards Sebastian and the male.

Levi stepped in front of her. "Maya, I swear I'll tan your ass if you step closer to that male."

Ignoring her mate, she tried to step around him. Levi held her arm in a grip Amaya knew she couldn't escape. She leaned around her mate.

"Why are you trying to glamour my mother?"

The male stopped fighting. "It's all over town that Levi has mated a chawi. I came to claim my mate."

Shock froze her and she looked between the male and her mother.

"I didn't glamour her," he continued, moving closer to Amaya. "I called to her, yes."

"*Step back,*" Levi fussed at Amaya through their bond.

Feeling the anger and distress in her mate she did as he asked. "*I want to know what's going on.*"

"*Then carry your ass in the house. We will talk to this male in the throne room.*"

Sighing, Amaya turned and gathered her mother. She heard the scuffling behind her, but dragged her mom inside. She headed straight for his throne room. She would not be left out of this conversation. Raven was directly behind them as she and Anita headed to the throne room.

Levi shuffled the women behind his throne, shooting a warning glare at his mate. He settled into his throne and eyed the male who was calm, his attention wholly on Anita.

"You were really stalking me to get to my mother?" Amaya broke the weighty silence with her accusation.

The male sighed. "Your mother's thoughts are filled with worry about you. I made sure you reached home safely each night."

"And how would you know her mother's thoughts if you've never taken blood from her?" Levi asked.

The male lowered his head.

"You bastard!" She shouted. "You took blood from my mother without her consent."

"I would never violate my mate like that. I didn't realize that she wasn't in a place to give her consent until it was too late. I...needed a way to keep track of her until I could get settled."

"When?"

Amaya cursed, because it just confirmed to her that her Uncle Paul had been leaving her mother alone more than he'd told her. She would allow Levi to kill her Uncle Paul. That's it that's all. He'd pissed her off for the last time.

"She was lucid a few of the times I'd seen her. It wasn't until after I'd taken her blood that I realized what was happening to her." The male explained.

"You;ve been watching her?" Levi asked.

Richard nodded.

"How long?" Amaya whispered.

"Long enough to know that in her current state I can't claim her."

Amaya put her hand over her thumping heart, hurting for her mother. Levi held his hand out for hers and she clasped it quickly, using his strength as her comfort.

"What has changed?" Sebastian asked.

"I can feel a difference in her. The king has claimed his mate, and even though the city is holding its breath to see what happens, it's the first sign of hope that the Bayi can come out of the shadows and claim the mates the Collective has kept from us. Change is moving through the city with your mating. Even my power has increased."

Levi shared a grim look with Sebastian and Amaya knew the two of them were talking.

"You cannot take her from here." Levi finally said aloud.

Richard growled and her mother whimpered. "She is..."

Levi held up his hand. "I'm not denying your call to your mate. I'm saying to you that my love will not allow her mother from underneath her watchful eye."

Amaya's eyes widened. Levi was allowing this to happen? *"What are you doing?"*

"Securing another powerful vampire to my coven," her mate answered matter of factly.

Aloud, Levi eyed Richard. "I can feel your power, you are clearly the master of another coven and it can't be in my city."

"My coven has set up an hour west of here."

Amaya hid her surprise. An hour! The male had been traveling hours to be in her mother's presence. Mated to Levi, she well understood the compulsion but she would be lying if she denied how hurt she would be if her mother moved out of the city.

"Not if, baby doll. When. I have a feeling this male will not be put off your mother. You will need to eventually loosen your hold over Anita." Levi warned her.

She swallowed the lump in her throat and lowered her head. According to those journals her mother would be healed with the mating. She would never deny Anita that. The chance to have her mother whole, no matter how far away would be better than close and on borrowed time.

"If you swear loyalty to the Cauly Coven, then I will allow you to see Anita." Levi bargained with Richard.

Richard narrowed his eyes. "And if I go through you?"

Levi chuckled. "You're welcome to try, OG."

The last thing Amaya wanted was a bloodbath. *"It's fine, King. I want my mother happy."*

"I'm not opposed to an alliance with you, but I will need to run it by my coven." Richard finally conceded. "But, that ain't got shit to do with me seeing my mate. I'm doing that regardless."

Levi shrugged, knowing the older vampire had called his bluff.

"Fair." The king turned in his chair and lowered his voice. "Ms. Anita, are you okay allowing this male access to you?"

Anita nodded, excitement shining in her eyes. It had been years since Amaya had last seen her mother as excited. She took a shuddering breath knowing that this was outside of her control.

"You are welcome here to see her until we are comfortable that Ms. Anita can consent to leave with you." Levi told Richard, his voice hard and implacable.

"I agree to that," Richard said immediately.

Levi nodded and Anita rushed from around the throne straight to Richard. Tears pooled in Amaya's eyes as she observed the tender way in which the male handled her mother. Richard cupped her cheek, speaking to Anita softly. The two of them left the room and the remaining occupants seemed to exhale at the same time.

"Holy cow," Raven whispered. "That was intense."

Sebastian moved towards them around the throne. "Chances are, he won't be the only Bayi stepping up and claiming their mate."

"Levi wiped a hand down his face. "The Collective finna lose their shit."

"And possibly take it out on you," Raven said solemnly. "What are we going to do?"

"If that's the case, then they'll push more people into Levi's arms," Amaya told them. "If there was a choice between having your mate or not, I know what I would choose."

Levi smiled at her line of thought. "We could always use more allies."

He lifted Amaya's hand in his grip and kissed her knuckles. Her gaze went to the door her mother had just left out of and she sighed. That was a worry for another day.

CHAPTER
TWENTY-SIX

Amaya had been jumpy all day. The archive was protected and a known neutral zone, and yet, she'd jumped at every sound as she went about her work done. She'd never been as happy to reach the end of her work day as she was today. Bronx fell is step with her as she exited the entrance to the sacred garden.

"Long day?" He asked.

She tilted her head. "How can you tell?"

"Energy, ma. Your magic is usually peaceful." He answered.

Amaya sighed. "I don't know what it is. My nerves are bad."

"Let's get you home then." He walked slightly in front her, his eyes scanning the building as they made their way out.

Winter was coming and so the days were shorter. The air outside had cooled and dusk was arriving sooner than it had even a week ago. So, when Amaya and Bronx reached the employee parking lot behind the archive, darkness was quickly falling. That could be the only explanation for why they were caught off guard. Amaya was so in her head that she didn't even realized what was going on until Bronx cursed and shoved her towards their SUV.

He was jumped by three males, but she almost felt sorry for them the way Bronx was laying into them. Before she could even formulate a scream Bronx had one of them on the ground and used one male as a shield as the third one moved to stab him. Amaya felt a tug on her arm and her magic reacted instinctively. A blast of chaos magic had the male trying to grab her screaming on the ground, holding his head. Her heart was racing as she pushed out another burst of power towards the men still trying to attack Bronx. One by one they collapsed on the ground, knocked out. Amaya sucked in a surprised breath. Her magic had never been something offensive she could use, but with her bonding with Levi, she could feel it all under her skin, just waiting on a target.

Bronx rushed towards the car. "Get in, Maya!"

She didn't hesitate to follow his orders, jumping in the passenger seat and locking her door. She didn't know how long her magic would keep them down.

"Baby doll?" Levi reached out, his voice groggy but alert.

He was probably just waking up for the day. His concern swamped their connection as he searched her mind to find the source of the adrenaline coursing through her body.

"We were just attacked outside of the archive," she told him.

His worry spiked. "Are you still there?"

"No. We're headed home now," she assured him as Bronx sped out of the parking lot.

A hale of car horns blasted behind them as he cut in front of traffic.

"Shit," Bronx cursed, his gaze bounced between the side mirrors and the road. His phone rang through the speakers of the truck and Bronx smashed the button to answer. Before the person on the other end could say anything, the wolf was talking. "Two on me."

Sebastian cursed on the other end of the line. "Your back up is still ten from your location. Can you hold them off?"

Bronx shot a quick look at Amaya. "Can you shoot?"

Her eyes widened. "Shoot what?"

"A gun, shawty."

Her stomach plunged. "I've never even touched a gun."

Sebastian sighed. "Hold tight, then, and evade."

The wolf grunted at the instructions and ended the call. "Reach in the glove compartment."

Her hands shook as she did as he said. She reached for the gun and prayed she didn't shoot either of them.

"Pass it here, Maya." He chuckled and grabbed the gun from her, sitting it in his lap.

Just as she was taking an easy breath, Bronx swerved the car and cursed again. Amaya glanced at the mirror on her side and her heart thumped hard. In the car directly behind her, there was a male hanging out the window, a gun pointed in their direction.

"Bronx!"

"I see 'em, shawty. Hold on."

He flung the car to the right, turning down a side street and Amaya gripped the bar over her head and held on tight. She kept her gaze on the car behind them, whimpering when they made the next left turn with their SUV. Bronx mashed down on the gas and the SUV lurched forward. The next right turn they took slammed her into the window and she winced, but kept her thoughts to herself.

She could taste fear on her tongue as Bronx went through his evasion techniques. A wave of soothing energy filled her as Levi tried reassuring her over their bond. It didn't last long though, because two or three shots rang out behind them and hit the back window. Up until that moment, she hadn't even realized they were riding in a bullet proof car.

"*I will always see to your safety.*" Levi assured her.

She would be sure to thank him for that the moment she saw him.

"*I know one way you can thank me.*"

"*Your distractions won't work, King. I'm about to lose my life in a car chase.*" She scolded him.

His chuckled echoed through her mind. "*Bronx got you, baby doll. Breathe.*"

That was easier said than done when another bullet hit the back of the SUV. Bronx swung the car around a corner, dodging the cyclist who had the misfortune of riding their bike along that street. Another left and Amaya just knew she was going on to glory. The street was one way, narrow, and if they made it out, she was going to kiss the ground.

She glanced back and the person had vacated the window, thankfully. At the speeds they were going down these side streets, it was too dangerous. She looked up in time to see them quickly approaching a red light. She smashed her feet into the floor in front of her, but Bronx didn't touch the brakes. Instead, he flew across the interstate and Amaya swallowed a scream. She turned to see if the car behind them would attempt it and they did, but they didn't make it. A black pickup truck slammed into the truck chasing them, sending it spinning in the intersection.

Bronx didn't slow the SUV one whit, continuing to speed through the rest of the city. She held her chest, and forced herself to breathe. The buildings of downtown Black Hollow were distant in the side mirror and from what Amaya could tell, only normal rush hour traffic filled the roads. There were no suspicious vehicles darting in and out of traffic behind them, and Bronx kept a steady path.

"Almost home, love." Levi's presence in her mind reassured her.

Amaya leaned back in the seat and closed her eyes, willing her pulse to slow. The SUV slowed and she opened her eyes, so happy to see the front gates of Levi's estate. She barely waited on Bronx to pull into the driveway and put the car in park before she was jumping out. Levi was waiting for her on the porch. Sprinting towards her mate, she didn't breathe until the king wrapped her in his arms.

She buried her face against his chest, thankful for the rumble of his voice against her cheek. None of the words he said penetrated, but the tone of his voice and his hands slowly stroking her back worked together to calm her. Levi walked them into the house, with her still clutched in his arms. She didn't move until the door closed and locked behind them.

Levi lifted her chin with his fingers. "Go rest, baby doll. I need to take care of this."

She shook her head. "Come with me, please."

His jaw clenched, indecision all over his face. He was torn between taking care of her and handling the situation. Amaya needed him now and she wasn't ashamed about it. Reluctantly, Levi sighed and nodded. He guided her upstairs and into their room. She took a deep shuddering breath and headed towards their closet. Shedding her clothes and dropping them into the hamper, she wanted a shower before anything else.

"Will you stay?"

Levi watched her as she started the water, his touch soft in her mind as he gauged her mood and needs. He tilted his head and nodded after a moment of perusing her mind.

"I just—"

"You don't have to explain, baby doll. I'll just sit here so you can see me."

She exhaled a relieved breath. It was exactly what she needed. If he touched her, she would likely break and she didn't want that. But...she needed eyes on him. He was her touchstone and just his presence close to her made Amaya feel secure. Levi sat on the toilet and watched as she took a quick shower. He held open a towel for her as she stepped from the water, wrapping her in it.

He followed her into the closet, still careful to keep from touching her, his watchful gaze on her as she found a gown and slipped it over her head. Levi was a step behind her as she crawled into the middle of the bed and slipped beneath the sheets. Ever present in her thoughts, he knew the moment she was ready for him. He slid into the bed behind her and gathered her in his arms. The first tear splashed on his chest seconds later, the rest flooding out of her as the adrenaline flowing through her crashed.

Her body shook and Levi held her tight, no words needed between them. She wrapped her legs around him, trying to crawl into his skin as all of her fear and anxiety poured from her through her tears. She didn't know how long he held her, but by the time she was down to shuddering breaths, her mind was clear and all the tension stored in her body was released.

Sensing the storm calmed, Levi kissed the top of her head. "Better?"

She nodded and burrowed into his chest.

His chuckle vibrated through her. "How much closer you trying to get, baby doll?"

"Leave me, 'lone," she muttered, rubbing her cheek against his shirt.

He lifted her head and dropped soft pecks on her lips until she leaned forward and held his head in place to make the kisses longer. His tongue swept into her mouth and Amaya sighed in pleasure. Now that fear was no longer clouding her mind, her need for her mate rose.

"I'm ready for you to put me to sleep now," She whispered against his lips.

Levi growled and slid his hand up her gown, his nails scoring the skin of her thighs. "I want to try something."

She hummed. "Anything."

The smile he gave her showcased his fangs. "I want your permission to roll you."

"What does that mean?"

"Total control, baby doll. I'll let loose my glamor on you."

She nodded, her eyes bright with curiosity. Levi nuzzled against her neck and scraped his teeth across her neck. He pulled back, trailing soft kisses onto her face, forehead, both eyes, her cheeks and chin. He inhaled deeply along her neck but passed it for now to focus solely on her. Slowly and gently, he released his pheromones, amplifying as he kissed his way down her shoulder. He stopped along her clavicle, turning his head to take in her beauty. Amaya lowered her eyes to his, lust, a living breathing monster between them.

Levi tenderly pushed his energy into her as his hands began to touch and draw lines along her body, lulling her. He watched as her eyes lowered to half mast, his power easing the tension from her body. Her world dimmed to him and his will over her. Applying more pressure to his magic, Levi opened the path between them, taking full control of her mind and senses.

His magic flowed into her body and the bond between them boosted it. Amaya's mind stilled, and instead of words, he intensified the sensation of his soft caresses. He filled their connection with his obsession with her, and how beautiful she was to him. His mate whimpered, her hands tracing a lazy path down his back.

"Relax, baby doll, and let your king take care of you," he whispered, expanding his magic. "Can I take care of my baby?"

Amaya undulated beneath him as his power rolled over and through her. Her mouth slack as he built her pleasure in her mind.

"Good, my love?"

Her answering whimper had a smug smile tilting his lips. The very fact that it only took him moments to roll his mate showcased her trust in him. He felt honored by it. Levi directed his power to her thighs, using his magic to part them wider. He repositioned between them, using one hand to grip her hip. His other hand hovered over her sex and he formed a small pearl of power covering her clit with it. Heat and vibration of that magic was his next trick, and his mate responded so beautifully.

Levi stretched her hands above her head, gripping them both with his one hand, using the other to notch his dick at her entrance. They moaned together as he slid himself into her tight sex. He could've easily gotten lost in her and fucked his mate, but he wanted soft, gentle. He'd almost lost her. Something outside of his control. Even though anger still roiled within him, he pushed it aside to care for his baby. His strokes were deep, as he worked to imprint himself on her body.

"I love you, King." Her words were slurred, drunk off his power.

Their bodies moved together. Their powers ebbed and flowed down their bond, stoking the fire between them higher. Her power raised in response to the rising pleasure, sweeping him into the vortex of his own magic. Amaya's legs started trembling around his waist as her climax started to build. Releasing her hands, Levi gripped her waist tight, holding her in place as he plunged deeper.

"Let that nut go, baby doll," he ordered her, his teeth greeted as his own body tightened with an oncoming orgasm.

He hadn't expected his power to backfire on him. Her clenching sex dragged him down with her, his balls tightening. Levi moaned, there was no help for it. Amaya milked his dick and wasn't shit he could do, he was trapped in their joint pleasure. He plunged deeper, delirious from their combined power.

He magnified the magic he had on her clit and she screamed, her nails digging into her back as she came. Her walls clasped down onto his erection and he followed her over the cliff. His teeth scraped his bottom lip as he lost control. He wanted to sink his fangs into her again, but her body went lax beneath him, a languid smile on her face. Levi leaned down and kissed her, their tongues twining lazily.

"Thank you," she whispered, her eyes remaining closed.

"Sleep, my love," he told her softly, nibbling on her bottom lip.

She nodded and he gently extricated his body from hers. Heading to the bathroom, he wet a cloth with warm water and cleaned her, kissing her sex when he was done. She moaned softly, but from her deep breathing his mate was asleep. Levi laid his head on her soft stomach, and breathed deep, indulging in Amaya. Sebastian prodded his mind to let him know that he was ready and Lev kissed her stomach once more and covered her with her gown, waiting just a little longer to make sure she was down for the night.

CHAPTER
TWENTY-SEVEN

Levi was careful as he slipped from beneath her and out of their bed. Amaya made a small whimper of displeasure, but turned over, spreading out across the bed. He let his eyes drift over her beautiful, curvy body a moment longer. He thanked the gods for their bond, every day he felt closer to his baby. Though his body was relaxed with satiation, his mind immediately turned back to the attack on his mate.

"Bas."

"In the basement." His best friend already knew what he wanted.

Wasting no time, Levi took a quick shower and changed into a pair of joggers and a t-shirt. He trusted his men to question the attackers, but he wanted to look them in the eyes and make sure they didn't miss even the smallest piece of information. He put in the code for the basement, smiling as he heard the screaming the moment the door opened. Bas was doing exactly what the fuck he was supposed to be doing.

Sinister glee filled him as he fully entered the space. There were two males shackled to the wall. Levi looked at the blood on the ground and decided then and there that he needed to move this little setup somewhere else. Torturing people in the same place where his mate laid her head didn't seem right. He looked over the males, smirking at the bloodied mess his friend had made of them. They were not Buru which confirmed for him that the Collective really was behind the attempt.

Anger burned through the last of his good mood and he stepped closer to the men. Sebastian stepped back to allow him room. One male eyed him through the eye not swollen shut, though it was well on the way. The other hung useless in his shackles, his breathing labored, on the brink of death. Levi dismissed that one and focused on the male in front of him.

"Who hired you?" He didn't care about any other information the males might have.

The male's body shuddered and he shook his head. "Don't know."

Levi sighed.

The hard way then.

Staring into the male's eyes, Levi delved into his mind, not bothering to be gentle about it. He chuckled as the male's every memory opened up to him. Before Amaya, Levi would have had to take blood to get this type of access to the male, but with their combined power, he easily took over the male's mind. Shuffling through his memories, he saw that the male had been telling the truth. They'd been hired via a website. Levi filed away the address for their safehouse and the others in the crew that had eluded his men.

The male released a relieved breath when Levi retreated from his mind. "See. I'm not lying."

Levi smiled. "I know you don't think that matters. You came after my baby and death is my only response to that." He gripped the male's chin, grunting in pleasure when his jaw cracked. "You'll be lucky if I allow you to die with your sanity intact."

The male whimpered and Levi released him, and stepped back. "Let them rest a while, Bas. Can't let 'em die before we really have fun."

With those parting words, he left the basement. Lucas met him at the top waving an envelop at him. Levi lifted an eyebrow, waiting on his friend to speak.

"Your invitation to the governor's ball came in," Lucas said with a smile.

Levi nodded, no closer to the reason for his friend's smugness. They received the invitation every year. Some years he attended, most he did not. His attendance had always been contingent on his needs that year. While the whole thing was held under the guise of charity, most treated it as the opportunity to make the deals while the city officials were inebriated and feeling generous. Levi was no different.

Lucas waved the envelop again. "I persuaded your favorite governor to hire the same staff the Collective uses for their events."

This time Levi understood the underlying words. Lucas had had a hard time finding the woman who had served him the drink at the Collective's meeting.

"They could've killed her by now." Levi voiced.

"Maybe." Lucas shrugged. "Or maybe they're arrogant enough to think it wouldn't be needed. It's not like we can prove you were poisoned by them."

Levi hummed. "It would be the perfect opportunity to pop out with my mate."

Lucas bowed. "You're welcome."

He could only laugh at his friend. "I applaud your genius," he said dryly.

Lucas laughed and left Levi. With nothing further to do, he wandered towards the dining room. Ms. Anita and Richard were sitting at the table whispering to each other. Amaya's mother had taken a turn for the better as soon as Richard showed up on the scene. As they spent more time together, Anita spent less time in the fugue state her magic had devolved her into. There were still times when she would space out, but they were becoming less frequent.

"Ma," he greeted, bending down to kiss her forehead.

She cupped his cheek. "You're twice my age," she chided.

He chuckled at that truth. "Are you doing okay?"

She nodded. "I want you to talk to Amaya."

Levi held up his hand and sighed. "Ma. You know how your daughter is."

"My home is a fortress, much like yours," Richard spoke up. "I'll be able to keep her safe."

"Your boss at the archive is worried that any of the matings between a Bayi and Chawil will be targeted. You would be safer here."

"With all due respect, Levi," Richard started.

Levi shook his head. He wasn't about to go back and forth with grown ass people. "Amaya was attacked on her way home from work this evening. She'll be resistant to you leaving."

Anita gasped and stood. "Is she alright?"

"She's in our room resting," he told her and she rushed from the dining room.

That left him alone with Richard. The older vampire eyed him. It was clear that while he respected Levi, he wasn't awed by his position. Richard was master vampire of his own coven and that could well be the reason.

"I would feel better with my mate away from here. I believe the Collective will only ramp up their attacks." Richard broke the silence.

Levi nodded. "You could be right, but Amaya and her mom have been a duo for years. Breaking that up won't be easy."

Richard sighed and slid down the chair into a more relaxed position. "I can take her out of the country. Her daughter wouldn't object to a vacation."

"It could work." Levi shrugged. "Are you certain you can keep her safe?"

Richard gave him a droll look. "What will you do about the attacks?"

That was too close to being in his business for Levi's comfort so he said nothing. Richard chuckled and propped his arms on table.

"If you're thinking of taking on the Collective, you'll have more allies than not." The older male, shifted until he was leaning back with his hands behind his head. "Your reputation well precedes your movements. If you were if a mind to unite all of the Bayi under your rule, it could be done."

Levi grunted. He wasn't sure he wanted to King of all the Bayi. But, the Collective wasn't giving him any choice in the manner. He couldn't in good conscious claim his mate and then deny that same right to the other vampires in the south.

"That's a lot of territory." He said non-committedly.

Richard smiled. "All of the south. Not so bad. Uniting the coven masters and leaving them in place will keep you from having to manage the whole of it."

Now that was something to consider. He would talk to Sebastian about it. He didn't move with his best friend and if he were down, then he would take it under advisement.

"And you, master vampire, decades older than me, would willing follow behind me." Levi tested the water.

"As I said, you reputation and that of your enforcers precede you. I would never say no to the vampires under me living a stable, lucrative life."

"And all of that is contingent on my coven taking on the Collective?"

Richard chuckled. "We're just talking in hypotheticals, right? But, without the Collective choking our movements the Bayi would be free."

"And hypothetically the vampires would exchange one rule for another?"

Richard held up his hands. "Just something for you to consider."

Levi nodded. The rest of their conversation was cut off as the dining room started to fill with his men coming down for the evening. He acknowledged Richard with another head bob before he left to go check on his mate. Ms. Anita was coming out of the room as he reached his hallway.

She smiled. "She's fine."

"Of course," he assured her.

Anita touched his shoulder softly as she passed him to head downstairs. He waited until she reached the end of the hallway before he entered his room. His mate was up, her eyes bright with unshed tears.

"Anita tell you she was ready to go with her mate?"

She nodded. "I tried to tell her that it would be safer here."

He chuckled at her smile and joined her in bed. "You have to let your mama live her life, baby doll."

She burrowed into his side and sniffled. "She thinks she's grown."

He laughed full out, pulling her on top of him. "Silly woman," he murmured, kissing her hair.

"You have to go to work, this evening?" She asked.

"You got a better reason for me to stay home?" He lowered his voice, scraping his teeth along her neck.

He'd fed from here not even two hours ago, and the beast within him salivated at the chance to taste her again. Reading his mind, Amaya whined her hips and sighed.

"Tell me something, baby girl," he gripped her waist and position her exactly where he most needed her.

*short sex scene.

CHAPTER
TWENTY-EIGHT

All day, Amaya's thoughts had been consumed with her mother leaving. Levi had let her vent, even while he advocated for Anita. In a way, she understood her mate just a little more. She wanted to hold her mother hostage so that she could never leave the compound. It was the one way she was sure Anita would be safe. But, she and her mother were similar enough for Amaya to know that Anita would only allow it but for so long. Not since she was a teenager and spending weekends with Tracy at their family's compound, had Amaya been separated from her mother.

She was already getting separation anxiety and Anita had just left the house last night.

She sighed and waved off Bronx's concerned look. "I'm fine. Just moping," she told him.

He nodded and led her from the archive. She couldn't wait to get home. She missed her mate. Raven had brought up her working nights and Amaya was giving serious thought to it. Only mated for a few weeks and she already hated being on a different sleeping schedule from Levi.

Amaya frowned when they reached the Atrium. Her cousin was

pacing the space, her face relaxing the moment she spotted Amaya. For a moment deja vu hit her and she feared what kind of news her cousin was bringing to her. It was like Paul all over again. Did her cousin also have bad news?

"Amaya," Tracy breathed out, pulling her into a tight hug.

"What's wrong?"

"Mom wants to see you," was Tracey's answer.

Amaya frowned. "Why didn't she just come with you?"

Tracey gave her a guilty look before looking away. "The elders are calling for you to come to the compound."

She snorted. "The elders can't make me do shit. I haven't been a part of that compound in my life."

Tracey clasped her hands. "Please, Amaya."

Her gaze traced her cousin's face and she saw the concern along with a hint of fear. What had they threatened Tracey with to get her to pass along their message.

"Fine." She sighed. "Bronx, we'll need to stop at my family's compound."

He nodded and pulled out his phone. Amaya knew he was checking in with Sebastian to tell him of the change of plans. She reached out to her mate, wanting him to hear it from her directly.

"King."

He answered her immediately, a warm tide filling her mind. *"Yes, baby doll?"*

"I'm headed to my family's compound. The elders want to see me."

"I'll meet you there."

"I can handle it," she promised him. *"You've had me working on my defensive magic. Trust me, I'll be okay."*

He was silent for a few moments before he conceded. *"Make sure Bronx is with you at all times."*

"I won't play with my safety, baby." That reassured him and he withdrew from her mind. She turned her attention back to her cousin. "Did you drive?"

Tracey shook her head and Amaya nodded. Bronx led them to the

SUV and the ride to the outskirts of town was quiet. Not even the low murmur of the radio could break the tension. By the time the reached the front gates of the compound, Amaya's leg was bouncing in nervousness.

The first thing she saw when the gates opened was the profusion of flowers in various colors in no particular order. There was no path, no rhyme of reason to the garden, just scents and colors scattered across the front and sides of the main house.

Chawi power came in so many different forms, but for her family, channeling chaos was their main magic. It manifested in different ways, the flowers just one aspect of how they released the chaotic power. The car pulled into the circular driveway and her aunt and uncles were waiting for her in the front.

Amaya smiled. She looked back at Tracey and her cousin gave her a guilty look. This was feeling like an intervention and Amaya was getting irritated. She got out of the car and greeted her family.

Tracey's mother hugged her. She looked so much like Anita that Amaya held her tight a moment longer than necessary.

"I'm so happy to see you're safe." Angelica said.

"I told grandfather that I was okay." Amaya said, frowning.

Angelica looked surprised. "Paul has been spinning stories."

Amaya sighed. "What do the elders want?"

"To put eyes on your mostly," her uncle Michael told her giving her an awkward pat on the shoulder.

She nodded and followed them inside. The foyer was massive, the walls wooden like it was stuck in the seventies. She was led into the main family dining room where the elders were seated. It was her grandfather, and his three remaining siblings. Well into their eighties and nineties, these were the oldest in their family, the ones in charge of the way their compounds were run.

The ones mostly responsible for the screaming Amaya could feel in the walls.

Two floors up, in the attic they kept the women who had been betrayed by their own magic locked away. 'For their own safety' they would say. It was her mother's worst nightmare and the reason Anita begged Amaya to never turn to their family for help. She would never allow them to lock away her mother.

"You wanted to see me." She crossed her arms over her chest.

Her grandfather's gaze raked over her neck before coming back to Amaya's eyes. "You've been at the Bayi compound for months."

"And no worse for wear as you can see," Amaya reported dryly.

His eyes hardened at her sarcastic reply. Amaya could never control her mouth, and now that she was mated to Levi, she could swear it was worse.

"A mating between the bayi and chawi are forbidden." Her great aunt intoned.

"That ship has sailed," Amaya announced to them.

Her aunt gasped behind her.

"Amaya," her uncle Michael called.

She ignored them both and kept her gaze on the elders. "I'm mated to King Levi and there is nothing that can be done about it." She challenged them.

"Even as you stand there smug, we've sent men after your mother." The malevolent smile her grandfather leveled at her did nothing but piss her off.

She smiled because they didn't understand the trouble they would invite if they invaded her mate's compound. Sending the information directly to Levi over their link, his answering fury bolstered Amaya.

"You will remain here." Bradford insisted.

"I don't think so." She told them.

Her great aunt slapped her hand against the table. "If you won't exercise self-control, then you will be locked up here where you can no longer put this family in danger."

"There is no danger from my mating. If anything, the danger is right in this house. Should I tell the women in this family that you've been allowing them to go mad instead of letting them find their balance with a Bayi mate?"

"What?" Angelica asked, stepping forward.

Amaya turned to the group that was gathering to see her put down. "Mating with King Levi has balanced my power, and is keeping the chaos from overtaking my mind. My mother, who was unable to form complete thoughts last month has met her mate and just his presence in her life has helped her make almost a full recovery."

"Is this true?" Tracey asked, staring at their grandfather.

Grumblings started throughout the crowd.

"Silence!" Bradford shouted. "That is impossible, Amaya and I will not allow you to spread those types of lies."

"The only ones lying are sitting in chairs, looking down their nose at me. Tell them."

"Take her to the attic," her great aunt ordered.

Bronx drew his gun. "Touch her and see what happens."

"My mate will come for me." Amaya warned them.

Her grandfather smiled. "There are ways in which we can sever the connection between the two of you."

"I would love to see you try." She drew her magic around her, waiting on them to make a move.

Bradford nodded behind her and three chawi men attacked Bronx. He didn't hesitate to fire and the gunshot sent the room into pandemonium. Screams sounded and someone grabbed at Amaya in the chaos. Power surged in her and she funneled to the hands touching her. Using the skills she'd been practicing, she snatched their power and their body dropped to the floor unconscious. Bronx let off another shot and it cleared the space around them.

Since they were still surrounded, Amaya threw up a shield around them both. Her family beat at the shield she'd erected with their power, her grandfather's muffled voice shouting orders. She didn't know how long her shield would hold. It wasn't like the members of her family were powerful in their own right.

One of her cousins got closer to the shield his magic making a dent in it. Amaya dug into her pockets and pulled out the heartstone she carried on herself, directing it at him. Using her connection with Levi, she pulled at his power, and snatched her cousin's power from him, shoving it into her stone. He dropped to his knees.

Bradford held his hand up and the attacks on them ceased. "What did you do to them?"

She held up the heartstone. "If you want their power back, you'll let us leave."

Searching the table where they sat for the easiest target, Amaya reached out again, and snatched the power from her great uncle. He gasped and leaned forward on the table, his face ashen.

Bradford turned to his brother in concern before whipping back to Amaya. "You have betrayed this family."

"It's you who have betrayed the women in this family. Let me go." Unable to maintain the shielding, she let it drop.

No one approached her, the swinging pendulum in her hand stalling their attack. She nudged Bronx toward the door. The crowd parted around them, no one wanting to be next in line to have their power stolen. Little did they know, Amaya had extended all the magic she could at this point. They would be screwed if the family renewed their attack. She didn't breathe easier until they were walking down the stairs of the front entrance. Her hands trembled with the effort to keep the magic she'd stolen contained, so she released it back to its owner.

"Amaya wait!" Tracy called out rushing down the stairs.

Rushing to the SUV, Amaya paused, anxious to see what her cousin would say. Tracy clutched her purse in her hand as she joined her at the vehicle.

"I'm going with you. I swear I didn't know about any of what they were planning. Grandfather asked to talk to you, just talk."

Amaya searched her cousin's eyes and found them shining with the truth. She nodded her head, already formulating how she would ask her mate to take in her cousin. No sooner than she'd opened the door, an explosion rocked the night. Heart stuck in her throat, she searched until she spotted her mate walking through the blown up front gates. His men, clad in balaclavas, followed behind him, their walk unhurried, their guns lifted, pointed towards the main house.

Behind them, black suvs slowed rolled up the driveway. Amaya raced to him, jumping into his arms. Levi lifted her as though she weighed nothing, swinging her away from the eyes that watched them from the front porch.

He cupped her cheek, anger making his eyes red. "Are you okay, my love?"

She nodded. "Mom?"

"Richard confirmed that they were fine and the men they sent to my compound have met their ancestors." His tone was furious.

She buried her face in his neck and released a shuddering breath.

"Do I need to go up there and tear up some more shit?" He questioned, his gaze wandering to their main house.

"I made enough of a mess," she told him. "Let's go home."

He walked her over to the SUV she and Bronx had driven. Setting her down on the driveway, Levi faced her family.

He pointed to Amaya. "That one is mine. Lay another finger on her and I'll wipe all this shit off the map and make sure there ain't nothing left to rebuild on."

Turning his back on them, Levi guided her into the back seat of the SUV. He buckled her in and cupped her cheek.

"You sure you're good?" He asked softly.

She nodded, tracing his face with her hand. Gods, she loved this man. Levi walked around the back of the truck and entered the other side joining her in the back seat. The front doors opened and Sebastian and Bronx got in. He floored it away from the chawi compound and Amaya knew it would be her last time visiting there. Her grandfather would never forgive her and she couldn't find it in her to care.

CHAPTER
TWENTY-NINE

L evi rubbed his tired eyes and adjusted the bow tie at his throat in irritation. It had been a month since Amaya's show down with her family and it seemed the Buru presence in Black Hollow had increased. His men were battling damn near every night to clear the city. His men were tired...hell, he was tired.

He suspected that the Buru were getting through the borders to distract Levi from making his moves against the Collective. He hadn't attended a meeting with them in two months, and until he got an answer about who poisoned him, he would continue to miss them. Tonight, at the governor's ball, he would show his face and let them know despite the pressure they call themselves applying he was still standing.

So far, there had been no further attacks to his mate, but he couldn't rely on that. He needed leverage with the Collective, and his plan tonight was to secure that.

He would step out with his mate to make sure everyone knew that she was his queen and nothing would change that. He'd make them all bend the knee, if necessary, but he would keep his meeting and had no intention of hiding it. As a safety precaution he was rolling with six of his enforcers. He smiled at the spectacle he knew his men would make in their tuxedos and balaclavas.

"Coming down, baby," Amaya slid into his mind, her warm presence halting his fidgeting.

He turned to watch her descent down the stairs, his heart thumping in his chest. Pride swelled within him. His mate was fucking phenomenal and it had nothing to do with the way she filled out the gown she wore. Everything about Amaya from her attitude to the power she wielded made his fall head over heels for her.

The blood red gown she wore sparkled as she walked, the mermaid skirt sweeping the floor as she picked her way carefully down the stairs. Lucas rushed to her side and helped her down. The corset top hugged her breasts and pushed them up in a way that made his mouth water.

"How do I look?" she asked him softly as she reached his side.

"Amazing," he whispered, kissing her ear. "Ain't another bitch touching you."

Her smile was radiant. "Shall we, then."

Levi escorted her outside, and his men bowed their head as she passed. He helped her into the car, and entered behind her. They left the compound, three SUVs deep. Soft R&B filled the truck as they rode and Amaya laid her head on his shoulder, her thumb rubbing along the back of his hand. More than likely, she felt his tension and while her soothing touch helped, his mind was already on the confrontation he was sure to come.

By the time they reached the governor's mansion, he'd quelled any nervousness he had, ready for whatever the night held. He got out of the truck first, helping his mate down. The guard at the front entrance looked like he wanted to say something about the amount of men Levi brought with him.

Bas growled. "Back the fuck up."

The male moved to the side and allowed them entrance. The ballroom was full, the power in the room displayed just as gaudily as the gold and black decorations that dotted the room.

"Fancy," Amaya muttered, grabbing wine from a passing waiter.

"Aht," Levi fussed taking the glass from her. "Don't drink shit out of here."

His mate pouted for a second. "I forgot just that fast. I'm a terrible sidekick."

He chuckled and kissed her lips softly. "Don't talk about my queen like that."

She smiled, and her eyes lowered bashfully. That the woman could still blush from his compliments despite what he'd done with her body amused him. All eyes were on he and his mate as they moved deeper into the room. No one dared approach them, but there were nods of acknowledgment as he passed some of the city's movers and shakers.

"They need a DJ in this place," Lucas muttered next to him.

Amaya snickered and Levi could only shake his head.

"Dance with me, King," his mate demanded.

Telling her no never occurred to him. As far as he was concerned, this woman could get whatever from him. They swayed to the music the quartet played. For a moment, with his mate wrapped in his arms, Levi almost forgot the point of this excursion. Amaya looked at him and smiled, and he tightened his grip on her waist.

"I love you," he told her.

She caressed the back of her head, her eyes going soft and dewy. "I love you, too, King."

He chuckled and kissed her softly before spinning her body. Her giggle as she returned to face him warmed him. If he could have any wish, it would be that he could keep that carefree expression on her face. As though the universe heard him and conspired against him, Levi spotted his prey and his smile dropped.

Amaya looked around. "What's wrong?"

He tugged her gently from the dance floor, his gaze never leaving the female coming out of the side door of what he would assume was a kitchen. He followed her through the door, pleased that it was an empty hallway. Two doors down, the clinking of silverware and soft firm orders let him know that the catering staff was holed up there. Catching up to the woman, he gripped her arm and spun her around. Her eyes widened and fear had her body trembling.

"King Levi," she whispered.

Before he could speak, his mate was pushing past him and in the female's face. "You poisoned my mate."

The woman blanched and her hand started shaking the drinks on the tray trembling.

"Who do you work for?" Amaya asked.

The woman looked around and his mate stepped closer, "ain't nobody coming to save you, girl."

"Who gave you the order to kill my mate?"

"I didn't know it was poisoned."

He opened his mouth, but this time Amaya gripped the woman's throat, squeezing tight.

"Lie again."

Levi smiled and crossed his arms over his chest. Oh, he could get used to this shit. His baby didn't play 'bout him. His dick filled and Levi was ready to take her down right in the middle of all these finely dressed people.

"It was a messenger." The woman hissed out with small amount of air left. "I don't know which contingency he worked for."

"Point him out," Amaya ordered dragging the woman back to the door they'd exited from the ballroom.

His enforcers were posted at the door, keeping anyone from entering the hallway. They blocked the sightline to the door so they were unobserved as the woman's gaze swept the ballroom. After a few tense moments, she lifted a shaky hand, and pointed straight ahead. Levi's eyes followed the path and narrowed on the male standing with some of the Collective members.

"Lucas."

"On it." His friend assured him, separating from the rest of the men.

270

Levi trusted his enforcer to do what was needed. He nodded for his mate to release the woman. Amaya shoved her away.

"Please don't kill me," the female begged. It was directed at Amaya and not him.

That absolutely pleased him. His mate throwing her power around was exactly as it should be. It confirmed her confidence in both herself and her king.

Levi smiled. "My mate would never kill you."

The woman sighed in relief.

"That's what she has me for." Levi captured her eyes and his magic invaded the female's mind. Her mouth went slack, her eyes staring blankly ahead as he exerted his will over her. "Take yourself to my compound and wait for me there."

Her glazed eyes blinked and she turned and walked away straight for the exit. She didn't even both to drop the empty tray in her hand. He turned to his mate and Amaya watched the woman until the door closed. Leaning down, Levi kissed the frown lines on her forehead.

"My lil rider," he murmured.

Amaya scoffed and hit his arm. "I'm queen now. And people gon' feel me behind you."

A happy chuckle was his answer to that. He guided them back into the ballroom and they mingled. Every now and again, his eyes drifted to the male the server had pointed out. Levi wanted to see if he could tell who the male was associated with. Unfortunately, due to the setting, it was impossible to tell. He didn't spend any more time with one person more than the other. He did as everyone else was doing at the event, securing contacts and rubbing shoulders with the city's powerful members.

Amaya's hand skimmed his chest. "How long will we have to be here?"

He checked the watch and realized they'd been here an hour. "You ready to go?"

"I don't like the way these people talk to you." She murmured, her arms going around his waist. "And I'm sick of them staring."

He chuckled and kissed the tip of her nose. "Have you seen yourself in this dress. Of course they're staring."

"King," she said shyly, a smile curling her lips.

"We can go if you're ready." He pulled her into his erection. "I been ready to get you out of this dress."

She giggled softly. "You so mannish."

Levi looked up and nodded at his men. They formed a circle around him and he clasped his hand with Amaya. He passed Lucian on the way to the door.

"You've brought your mate out. Bold," Lucian commented.

Anger clouded his vision for a moment until Amaya gripped his hand, the cool touch of her magic clearing the murderous thoughts from his mind.

"Lucian, I feel like you threatening my mate, and I would rethink that decision." He said after he'd corralled his temper.

Lucian smiled. "The Buru have been overrunning the city. What good are you to the Collective if you can't even do the job assigned to you?"

Levi pulled Amaya behind him and stepped to Lucian. "I don't work for the Collective. Go ahead and say what your scary ass is tap dancing around."

Like the coward Levi knew he was, Lucian backed down. "You've missed the last two meetings. I think at the next one I'll make a motion for you to be expelled."

"That don't mean shit to me." Levi jumped at Lucian and snickered when he flinched. "Bitch ass. I'll be seeing you around," he promised the border mage.

He guided Amaya around the cowering councilman and to their waiting SUV. She clutched his hand tight, not releasing it until he helped her into the back seat. Sebastian slipped off his mask the moment the SUV pulled out and turned to Levi.

"He all but admitted to allowing the Buru past his borders."

Levi nodded. "Yeah, but he won't say that shit out loud."

"Isn't that some type of dereliction of duty?" Amaya asked.

"Only if we can prove it," Levi answered.

He leaned his head back onto the seat, his mind spinning. Proving that Lucian was allowing the Buru into the south would go a long way to getting him replaced on the Collective. But, would that be enough to keep his mate safe from their retaliation?

CHAPTER
THIRTY

Two weeks.

That's how long Levi had been on the edge. The governor's ball had been two weeks ago, and despite Lucian's fake ass bravery, the Collective had made no moves against Levi or Amaya. He'd had her schedule moved to the evenings so that he would be able to get to her faster if something went down. Plus, it settled him to know she would be in his arms safely when he slept.

It was probably the only reason why his nerves weren't completely frazzled.

He was going down to dinner when Lucas touched his mind. He tilted his head and waited on his friend to speak.

"Meet me in the throne room," Lucas said.

There was excitement in his tone and Levi changed directions immediately, curiosity propelling him. He beat Levi there, settling in his chair a few moments before his friend bust through the door dragging a male behind him with one hand and a canvas bag in the other. Lucas dropped him, kicking him in the back of the head. The whimpering male tucked into a ball at his enforcer's feet.

"I caught him meeting with some Buru," Lucas growled. He

threw down the bag he was holding and a head fell out. It was Hale, the young vampire from the other coven. "He was also at that meeting. I been wanting to knock his head off since that meeting."

Shock went through Levi before a smile tilted his lips. Finally! He knew following the male would give them information, but he hadn't expected it to pay off so well.

"I talked to Deonte already, so Hale's death won't cause a war between our covens." Lucas walked over and handed him a few pages of documentation. "This fuck ass mage was giving the Buru information about the borders around the South."

Levi scanned it, fury making his gums ache. There were schedules of border patrols that protected the zones north of Black Hollow. It notated where the guards were heavier and outlined where the Buru could slip through patrol. Treasonous shit.

Questioning the male would not yield the results Levi wanted, instead, he reached out to Sebastian.

"Yeah, boss." His best friend answered immediately.

Through their bond, Levi filled him in on what they had just learned. Bas growled and entered his throne room, his gaze going to the traitor on the floor.

"Who does he work for?" Bas asked.

"Instead of questioning him ourselves, call the Collective together. Here." Levi ordered.

Sebastian smiled and nodded, leaving them to do his bidding. Contacting his other enforcers, Levi instructed them to pick up Amaya. He alerted Bronx that they would be arriving and to pull his mate from work now. He looked down at the joggers and black t-shirt he wore.

"Lucas. Let's get dressed for our company."

His friend smiled and using his power, knocked out their prisoner. He wouldn't be going anywhere. Half an hour later, his mate joined him in their bedroom closet.

"Why did you pull me out of work early? What's going on?" She asked, her eyes heating as she got a look at him "Where you going?"

"We have guests arriving in..." He glanced down at his Patek, "Twenty minutes."

"Guests?" She looked down at the houndstooth slacks she had on, tugging at the maroon tank top she wore with it. "I need to change."

"You're fine, love." He told her, but she rushed to her side of the closet anyway.

He wore a simple black knit top on top of his slacks of the same color. He didn't do too much. His Cuban link and Patek completed his look, the chain of the pocket watch his baby got him, dangling from his belt loop. He slid his gold fangs over his teeth and mugged the mirror. He was ready and a zing of excitement hit him.

Amaya came over to his side. She'd exchanged her tank top for a black button-down shirt. It was unbuttoned to the top of her bra and cinched at her waist. Her wide legged slacks in dark gray conformed to her ample hips. Gods damned his mate was fine as fuck. She'd added the matching chain to his and he smiled, pulling her into his arms.

"You trying to match your man, baby doll?"

"When we step, we step together," she murmured against his lips.

He deepened her kiss, slipping his tongue into her mouth. His mate greedily sucked on his tongue, and Levi wished they had time for him to exchange it for his dick.

She pulled back, her eyes low with lust. "Behave."

"How I'm 'posed to do that when you looking how you look?" he asked spinning her and slapping he on the ass.

Amaya sent him a coy look over her shoulder. "Hype me up, then."

"Let's get out of here before I say fuck our guests."

She chuckled and left the closet in front of him. She waited for him at the door of their bedroom. "Who is our company."

"The Collective."

Her mouth dropped open and Levi closed it with two fingers to her jaw. He smirked at his mate and guided her downstairs. She paused when they entered the throne room and she spotted the male still knocked out on the floor.

"This should be interesting," is all she said to that.

Levi took a seat in throne and pulled his mate into his lap. "I need to get you one of these."

"No thank you," she laughed.

"Boss. Company here," Bas informed him.

"Bring them in." he ordered. He lifted Amaya from his lap and set her on her feet. "Our guests are here."

She stood at the side of his chair, her hand on his shoulder, her head back, looking like the powerful fucking queen she was.

"I'ma fuck you so good when this is over," he promised her.

Her laugh cracked the silence and he joined her. They were both smiling when Sebastian led the first members of the Collective into his throne room. They grumbled as they entered, their faces a mix of anger and curious. Lucas brought up the rear, going to the male he'd left in the middle of the floor. His enforcer woke the male and brought him to the bottom of the raised dais that held Levi's throne. Lucas turned the male to face the gathered crowd and a hush went through the room.

"I thank you all for taking time out of your busy schedules to drop in."

"What is this about?" The witch was the first to speak.

Instead of answering her question, he pointed down to the male Lucas was propping up. "Whose man is this?"

The Collective member looked amongst themselves, but no one spoke. At least until Lucian stepped forward.

"Levi, you've gotten beside yourself. Who are you to summon us?"

"You answered, didn't you?" Levi taunted.

"What is the meaning of this?" The Chawi mage asked.

Again, Levi ignored the question, instead, nodding to Lucas. His friend pulled out a knife and put it to their prisoner's throat. A panicked murmur went through the group.

"We won't sit here and allow you to kill someone in front of us," the witch snapped.

Lucas dug the knife into the prisoner's throat and a line of blood oozed down his skin. Lucian stepped forward quickly.

"Don't."

Levi smiled. "I really thought your bitch ass was gon' hang him out to dry. Are you claiming this male?"

"Why have you taken him prisoner?" Lucian parried back.

"Your answer first," Levi dared him.

Lucas pressed the knife in deeper and the prisoner whimpered, his eyes widening.

"Fine! He works in my cabinet."

Levi hid his triumphant smile. "So, is it on your orders that he exchanges information with the Buru?"

The Collective reared back as a unit, shock covering their faces.

"What?" The chawi mage asked.

Lucian turned to face the rest of his colleagues. "We all agreed that the mating between Levi and the Chawi could not happen."

"But inviting our enemy into our territory? You must be out your mind!" The Mujaji representative bit out.

"None of you had any issues with the way we've ridded the community of these pairings before." Lucian protested.

The hot lash of his mate's anger whipped through their bond. "There have been others before us?" Amaya asked.

Lucian turned his attention to her, a derisive look covering his face. "You are no more special than any of the others who don't obey the laws that hold this society together."

"What your tone when you talking to that one," Levi snapped, sitting forward. He shook his head and rubbed his hands together, fed up with all this shit. "You know what? I tried to be nice I tried to play the game the way y'all had it all set up, but fuck this shit."

He nodded over to Lucas and his enforcer smiled, his fangs

hanging low as he swiped his knife fully over the prisoner's neck, killing him with the silver coated blade. A gasp went up and Sebastian pulled out his gun, pointing it directly at Lucian.

His mate didn't need any prodding from him. Amaya reached down and gripped his wrist, their collective power surging. She pulled the pendulum that held her heartstone from her pocket, holding it high. Before the Collective could react, Amaya's power swelled and, in an instant, her magic sucked the power from every member of the Collective. There was a panicked scream, and someone moaned, the mournful sound marking their loss of control over their magic. His mate dangled her pendulum from her fingers, the taunting motion letting the Collective know that she'd funneled it all into her stone.

Levi chuckled darkly and stood. He looked them all in their eyes. "You were worried about what would happen if another Obayifo rose to power? Well, welcome to your worst nightmare. The Collective answers to me now."

"Levi, we can discuss this," Lucian sputtered out.

Levi leveled a look at the border mage. "It wasn't enough for you that I just wanted the Bayi to have a fair voice in the Collective. You wanted to control and crush my vampires and those in the south that you felt were beneath you. That shit won't fly no fucking more. If I find out that any of you are working against this council or me specifically, my mate taking your powers will be the least of your problem." He sat back on his throne. "Give it back to them baby doll."

Amaya nodded and he felt the surge as she returned their powers. He waited to see if any of them would strike at him. When they didn't, he settled back.

"From now on, we work for the people of the south and if you can't get with that shit, you will be replaced." He smirked at Lucian. "Bas."

Sebastian fired a single shot into the border mage's forehead and the male hit the floor.

"The price for disloyalty is death." Levi announced and shocked silence greeted his statement.

CHAPTER
THIRTY-ONE

Amaya's heart raced as tense silence choked the air from the room. Levi's anger heated their bond and a part of her wanted to soothe him, but the other part enjoyed the dark energy riding through her mate. She waited on someone to break the silence that had desceneded, but none of the Collective members murmured a single sound. Hell, they were stock still, all eyes on the border mage on the floor.

Levi waved his hand and the door to the throne room opened. Three people walked in. Two males and a female between them. Amaya knew they were border mages as they were the only supernaturals that she knew who mated in pairs. All three glowed with power. The woman's step were regal as she sauntered to the front of the room. The two males towered over her, their bodies bulky and strong. They were protective of the woman, their touch gentle as they guided her through the Collective. The male to the right of the woman stepped forward, handsome with his salt and pepper hair in a low hair cut with deep waves.

"Nathanial Latham, you are now the leader of the border mages and will serve as such on the Collective. Do you accept?" Levi announced, his voice uncompromising.

The male lowered his head his mates following suit. "I accept."

Levi relaxed minutely at the male's acceptance. "Now, that's done. Are there any other objections, any other business we have to attend to?"

There wasn't another sound made in the room. Levi smiled, his fangs glinting in the light. A shiver of need went through Amaya. An ache built low in her belly at the way his power crackled around him.

Levi leaned back in his throne, his pose that of a lazy lion. Powerful even in his repose. He grabbed Amaya's hands and brought it up to his mouth, kissing her wrist.

"I thank you all for attending the ascension of the King of the South. I'll see y'all next month." He waved them away and the room cleared, his enforcers leaving with them to make sure they left the compound.

Amaya barely waited until the last body left the room before she straddled her mate's lap, her body overheated. Levi's arrogant words had her clit thumping against the seat of her panties. She wrapped her arms around his neck.

"You had two men killed in front of your mate, King," she whispered against his lips.

He reached down between them and sliced through the seam of her pants. "Is that why you're leaking for me?"

He bit her bottom lip and it fed the hunger building in Amaya. A needy moan was her answer to his question. They weren't making it to their bedroom before she had to have him. She wanted him here, in this place where he had so easily wielded power. It would be a bit of a full circle moment. Here, in this room is where her life had been torn from her control. Who could've predicted that she would be in the arms of the king of the Bayi willingly, and with full abandon.

"Need you," she whispered, fighting to get into his pants.

"And you'll have me, baby doll." He leaned back so she could unzip his pants.

She sighed in pleasure the moment she freed his dick feeling the firmness fill her hand. Her mate's hands gripped her waist and lifted her to give her space to straddle her prize. Sliding her panties to the side, she raised a little more and threw her head back as Levi entered her. She sucked in a breath and instead of moving, she reveled in the feel of the burn as his firm head parted her walls. Soon though, it was not enough, she needed to move. Starting a slow grind, Amaya connected their lips, their hungry kisses elevated the emotions.

Moving her hips in a figure eight motion, she slid up and down on his dick, flexing her walls around his erection. Her hands gripped his shoulder, her stomach tightening as his head hit the back of his throne. Levi fucked her from below, his hips driving upward to drive into her leaking sex as his hands found purchase on her waist. Amaya bit her lips, focused on the sexy faces he made as he lost himself in their pleasure.

It gave her a sense of power that she could control the desire of this influential man. Possessiveness and pride took root in her heart and Amaya didn't balk from it. Instead, indulging in the raging emotions. The King of the Bayi was hers, she would allow nothing or no one to get in the way of that.

Levi pulled from their kiss and nudged her chin to the side. Knowing what her mate wanted, Amaya tilted her head. She slowed their pace, anticipating his bite. A moan slipped from her and her nipples pressed into his chest, rubbing against him with their slow motions. He growled in hunger and gave her no warning before he struck. He bit deep, sucking on her neck with ravenous pulls. The pain quickly morphed into pleasure and her pussy clenched tight. As she neared her peak, her walls spasmed around his dick. Levi tightened his grip on her waist and fucked into her with strong, sure strokes. Amaya was sent reeling into orgasm as he drove into her ewith increasing intensity as he chased his own.

Their arms wrapped around each other tightly, her body locked into place as waves of pleasure had her channel spasming.

Levi came behind her, but still he fed from her, gorging himself.

Amaya held his head to her neck, perfectly content to give her mate everything. His dick twitched inside of her and she rocked her hips as another wave of pleasure filled her. He kept his dick seated deeply as he pulled his teeth from her neck and licked her skin closed. He nuzzled into her neck sighing, breathing in deeply, relishing their connected bodies.

"I love you," was his drunken answer.

She chuckled. "Glutton."

"It's your fault," he murmured against her skin. "I'll never get enough of you."

"I love you, King," she told him, resting her forehead against his.

"When I step, you step?"

"Every time." She promised him. "I'm so proud of you, Levi."

He hummed, and his pleasure filled their bond. They sat in silence, holding each other tight until Amaya remembered something. She couldn't help the laugh that shook her shoulders.

"What are you laughing at?" Was his drowsy question.

"I'm just remembering all the shit you talk to me." She kissed him. "But you were right. I love it over here."

His smile covered his face. "I might tell you a story, but I'll never tell you a lie."

The laugh they shared was cathartic. Amaya realized that with Levi taking over the Collective, they wouldn't have to look over their shoulder any longer. She and her mom were finally safe and she had Levi to thank for that.

"Never thank me for doing what I'm supposed to," he murmured against the skin of her neck.

Her cheeks hurt from smiling. Life was funny. She came to Levi a prisoner to his impulsive whim, and now she was officially Queen of the South.

www.ingramcontent.com/pod-product-compliance
Lightning Source LLC
Chambersburg PA
CBHW020357110726
47899CB00006B/1756